SOMETIMES SHE LETS ME
BEST BUTCH/FEMME EROTICA

Edited by

TRISTAN TAORMINO

CLEIS
PRESS

Published in the United States by Cleis Press Inc., 2246 Sixth St., Berkeley, California 94710.

Cover design: Scott Idleman
Cover photograph: Phyllis Christopher
Text design: Frank Wiedemann
Cleis logo art: Juana Alicia
First Edition.
10 9 8 7 6 5 4 3 2 1

ISBN: 978-1-57344-382-1

CONTENTS

INTRODUCTION

As both separate, distinct identities and identities in dynamic with each other, butch/femme has endured throughout lesbian history in all sorts of manifestations. But it was not that long ago that writers like Cherríe Moraga, Joan Nestle, Patrick Califia, and Amber Hollibaugh were explaining and *defending* butch/femme to some feminists who criticized lesbians and bi women for "mimicking heterosexual roles" and "reproducing patriarchal constructions." Thank god for all the queers who stood up to tell their stories, share their truths, and not be bullied into conforming to one certain model.

In the years since the sex wars of the nineties, butch/femme has blossomed, morphed, and been reenvisioned in myriad ways. As identity categories, butch and femme have expanded and evolved: witness butch bois, femme tops, butch mamas, femme daddies, and genderqueers of all shapes and sizes. Although some people equate genderqueer with people on the masculine end of the spectrum, I've met plenty of genderqueers who queer gender throughout the spectrum. In fact, without the cultural language and theories of butch/femme, our understanding and expansion of gender—erotic and otherwise—would not be where it is today. Although we can see butch/femme as our experienced elder, it doesn't feel old-fashioned since it's constantly being tweaked and twisted.

Butch/femme is a perfect centerpiece for erotica since it is recognizable and meaningful to many people. It's also incredibly multilayered—creating opportunities for characters to play with gender in a sexual context, do unexpected things, challenge conventional wisdom and assumptions, and explore taboo desires.

Butch/femme is erotic iconography.

Butch/femme is sexual electricity.

Butch/femme is power exchange.

Butch/femme is bulging jeans, smeared lipstick, stiletto heels, and sharp haircuts. It's about being read and being seen. Sometimes it's about passing or not passing. It's about individual identity and a collective sense of community. It's personal, political. It's performance and it's not. It's the visceral space between the flesh and the imagination.

Tristan Taormino
New York City

SOMETIMES SHE LETS ME

Alison L. Smith

Last night her back was sore, spasms from the past, a high school injury, and I said that I'd rub it and then we could just go to sleep, and when I finished she asked me to massage her ass and I said yes but I could not do without kissing it, licking that white moon. I ran my teeth along the arc of it, biting, and her ass started to move under me.

Then she rolled over and I pulled off her shirt and she let me touch them. They are secrets she holds separate from me, their roundness flattened against her chest all day. She does not like them, but I do. And sometimes, when she lets me, I fall between them and I breathe in. The tip of my nose measures their softness and the fine, white hair rises and she gets goose bumps.

I took one of them in my mouth last night and the dark snail of her nipple grew under my tongue. Her pelvis moved beneath me, moved up toward mine when she let me. The moon was gone and the river lights outside her window reflected like stars, as if the sky moved beneath us, and she lay on her back for me.

Her hip bones cut the air in thin circles and she tightened under me. She let me unbutton her boxer shorts. She let me take her in my mouth, press my face into her. I cupped her ass in my palms and she got hard for me. She dug her hands into my hair and shivered in the heat-soaked room and I watched her through the keyhole of her thighs.

Sometimes she lets me and when she does she talks to herself. In a low voice, she talks the fear away. Like last night when her ass was cupped in my hands and she was in my mouth and she whispered and her hips circled faster and her voice began to rise.

The dog woke, his pink tongue curling. He yawned. He circled once, twice, spread out beside us again and he watched his master's face change. He watched her call out to the ceiling, watched her back arch, watched her reach over her head, her fisted hands knocking the headboard until her long body tightened and her voice grew hoarse.

Then she begged me. She said *Don't stop don't stop don't stop don't stop* and she trembled under me and her hips pitched and I almost lost her and I pressed my hands into her ass to steady her until she came in my mouth.

Afterward, she pulled the covers up around her. She curled into their soft protection and rolled away from me. She hid. The dog burrowed under the comforter, panting into the darkness. After she let me and she fell asleep on her sore back, the sound of her voice stayed in my ears. I watched her as she kicked the covers off in the night's long heat. First her shoulders appeared, then her breasts, then the damp stain on her boxers where I had put my mouth. And I wanted to put my hands on her again, but I didn't. I just watched. The old radiator cracked and pinged in the corner and light from a streetlamp bled in through the tall window and she slept and I watched and she let me.

SWEET THING

Joy Parks

Watching Petey Ginoa knead bread dough is like watching a thing of beauty.

Watching her do it when she doesn't know anyone is watching her is even better.

First there are her hands, which are large but not too large; peachy pink hands that get washed soft over and over again every day, strong with short square nails and slightly knobby knuckles, the kind you get when you crack them too much. And flour. I don't think I've ever seen those hands when they weren't covered in flour. Strong hands, but not rough at all. Hands that can shape delicate flutes on a tartlet crust or fix a tiny broken motor on the mixer or, I believe, unfasten a button so slow and perfect, sliding a finger down the space between breasts, sliding past a slight mound of belly, sliding down. I take a gulp of Fair Trade fresh-ground something or other to keep me still and watch how she grabs a hunk of sunflower rye or cornbread with organic red pepper slices, or whatever delightful concoction is in her bowl today, and drops it onto the breadboard, her hands dancing it into a perfect round, her fingers disappearing inside, then out, inside again. Kneading. Needing. I watch those fingers turn and poke and stretch the dough. I feel heat welling up between my thighs, try not to squirm. I watch her with my lips parted like I'm waiting for a kiss.

And then she stops. I hold my breath. She pushes up the sleeves of the white shirt she's wearing beneath her apron and begins to knead some more, flexing her perfectly shaped muscles, girl muscles but firm and healthy and strong looking. The kind of arms that make you wonder what it would be like to be inside the circle of her body, to feel those muscles tighten and press against you, what that would be like. That close.

It's warm in here and the windows are sweating from the steam of the kitchen; it's still morning cold outside. I should go. I should get up and walk out of here as best I can and get to work on time for a change; the walk would do me good right now. If I could just stand up.

I could watch those hands for hours.

Yeah, I know I've got it bad. And I don't quite know what to do with it.

Everyone back home told me I was going to hate moving to a small town even if it was the only place I could get a job. In a small town everybody knows everybody's business and I'd have to watch my *P*s and *Q*s, they said. Growing up in the city and having the natural luck to get away with a whole lot of stuff, I hadn't had to work very hard at being discreet. Who was going to know and who was going to care?

So I've been laying low, working at the library as the junior librarian in training, trying to make it look like I'm far more interested in learning how to organize the periodicals and start a community reading circle than I am in running back and forth to Petey's all day to buy coffee. I can't sleep most nights now. I don't know if it's all that caffeine or the fact that when I do sleep I keep dreaming about those hands on my skin and then I have to get up and drink a lot of cold water just to keep from melting in my own heat.

But bless the gossips in town for helping me learn all about Petey. I guess since some of them saw me spending so much time in the bakery, they wanted to warn me so I could be on guard and not fall prey to her seductions. You'd never know from looking at me that I've dealt with plenty of seductions by women like Petey and enjoyed every single one of them. From the very first day I walked into her shop, if she'd ever even looked at me with half a hint that she might be interested, I'd have fallen on my back so fast I might have ended up with whiplash. It's funny being femme. Sometimes you hate the fact that no one knows, and you have to go out of your way to make sure some butch realizes you're available, 'cause you look too straight. But the good ones know. The smart ones. They can look past the heels you wear to work and the lipstick and the girly clothes, and love all that about you, know what you are beneath your clothes, not just any woman, but special. One who would fall on your back for them, let them touch you all over, let them reach inside your body, fuck you hard and tender and whatever it takes to make you both feel so good about what it is that you are.

But since I'm not so obvious to normal people, I got the whole deal on Petey.

Petey Ginoa is a legend in town. Everybody knows she's a lesbian even though nobody's seen her with any woman at any time. She's too smart for that—to get caught. It's a small town and she's got a damn good business and she'd be crazy to take a chance on losing it all. Petey's not her real name; it's Pia, which is the name on the sign above the door. Her father named the shop that back when she was a baby. But everybody calls the place Petey's. They eat Petey's bread and take Petey's cake home for birthdays and baby christenings and stop by Petey's for coffee. Sometimes I think if not for her, the whole damn town would go hungry. Petey suits her more. That's just how it is with some lesbian children; they outgrow the names their mommas gave them, grow into something different, someone different from what anyone could have expected of them. Taking a new name is like being born all over again into who they should have been all along.

Not that Petey's the kind of woman who'd think about it that way. She probably just realized she was becoming someone for whom a delicate name like Pia didn't fit. It made her feel uneasy. So she gave herself a more comfortable handle. I get the feeling she's the kind of woman who would do whatever she needed to do to feel okay about herself and not give a damn about what anyone might think.

I wonder if any of her lovers—who no one's ever seen—call her Pia.

Wouldn't seem right somehow.

I want to be one of those women no one's ever caught her with.

I want those hands needing me.

On a belt under her apron Petey wears a measuring cup that looks like it was made by Black and Decker. She wears clean, crisp, white pants that cup her fine ass just right and a white button-down shirt with the sleeves rolled up to her elbows. She wears a full-length, white apron slung over her neck and tied real loose, and clean white sneakers that don't make a sound. Her dark hair is cut short and loose around her face, which seems a little tanned. Even in winter that hair curls up at the back of her collar when she's moving around the kitchen in the heat. That collar, those curls. I have to keep my hands in my coat pocket or flat, fanned on the counter, when I order my coffee. I look the other way when she slides the little waxed paper bag of cannoli my way; stop myself from reaching across the counter; stop myself from reaching out to touch her neck, smooth those curls. Touch her face real slow. I think her forehead would smell like butter, that her skin would be lightly glazed all over with a fine dusting of sugar, that if you put your mouth to her skin, you would come away tasting sweet.

I'm thinking Valentine's Day will be the time to make my move, 'cause that's when everybody's all crazed over romance and hearts and flowers and wanting to be loved. Petey can't be all that different from anyone else. Can she?

Today is Friday the thirteenth, and not a soul on the street fails to comment on it. I don't feel unlucky, just a little racy knowing I've got just today to figure out how I'm going to pull off the seduction of the town dyke. I wonder if she has a girlfriend now, but only for a minute, because something tells me I'd sense it if she did. At this point I don't think it would matter if she was dating my own best friend—if I'd been in town long enough to have one.

When I hit the doorway of the bakery, I almost swoon. It's the clouds of moist heat that gather inside, rain on the window, plus the scent of something sweet and deep, along with something fresh, like fruit juice, underneath it. And there's Petey. She's behind the counter, smiling at me. It must have been my reaction to the aroma that wrapped around me as I came inside. I wrinkle my nose like I'm sniffing for more and look at her grinning, as if to ask what's making such a delicious smell. Her eyes are actually lit, wide and open, more so than I remember ever seeing them. She motions me over. I've never been that close to her aside from her pouring my coffee or taking my money when I paid for bread or muffins or those slices of all-natural Queen Anne's cake with caramel-covered nut crust swirled with spidery feathers of toasted coconut. Or crème brûlée custard on a toasted almond crust. Or shiny pecan buns, moist and slippery as the flesh of my thigh right now. I'm weak. I don't think she's ever really talked to me. Specifically to me. And she still isn't—talking. I step up to the counter and she's still smiling and motioning me even closer. I move in like I'm in a trance, move in for a kiss, to touch my lips to her cheek, her lips. Desire bubbles up within my belly, there are tiny flutters inside my cunt. Like wings. I wonder if she can see down my blouse, see my breasts nestled in the pink, lacy, silk demicup I bought mail order from Victoria's Secret just in case something like this ever happened. I catch myself when my eyes start to close. She raises a fork to my lips like a present, speared with a tiny piece of something pink and fluffy, like cotton candy covered in chocolate. Oh baby. She directs the fork toward my lips as I open them on command, take the gift inside. Something sweet and deep breaks on my tongue; my mouth wells up with wetness. I think about the pink of it, pink like the tender underside of a breast set free, pink skin of a vulva, all shower fresh and warm; my tongue roaming my mouth to seek out and find every touch of sweetness, the citrusy aftertaste a surprise. I worry about drooling. I swirl it around my mouth, take it in, inhale it. Most of your taste buds come from scent. I taste an orange cream chocolate like from the Whitman's Sampler but warm. I want to tell her it's like sex on a fork, but that's too bold, too early in the dance. She's close still, watching me, silent. I open my eyes wide now, finally able to open my mouth.

Then she speaks real low, her voice deep but clear against the clang of coffee cups and beaters in the kitchen.

"So, you like? It's blood orange cheesecake iced with a bitter-sweet chocolate glaze. Did them special for Valentine's Day this year. It's the blood orange that makes it pink. They're in season right now."

She beams.

Oh the pride in her voice. Hands in her pockets, shoulders dropped back, slight smile drawing tiny lines around her lips like a frame. She makes me want to leap over the counter, pull her head down into the pink silk of my too-far-open shirt, whisper, "You are magical," wrap my legs around the clean white apron over her clean white pants, beg her to take me right there, right on the kneading board covered with flour and dabs of bitter-sweet chocolate glaze.

It takes three more trips to the bakery for me to get up the nerve to do what I have to do. All that coffee and anxiety is making me feel dry-mouthed, and it's now or never. So while she's ringing up the roasted red pepper and cilantro quiche with butter crust that's going to end up being my supper, I finally manage to find my femme courage and make my intentions known. At least to one of us.

"So, what are you doing for Valentine's Day?" I ask her.

She looks down at the floor like I've caught her in a lie.

"Nothing," she says. She kicks imaginary sand with the toe of her clean white shoe.

I'm tempted to look down too, but I keep my eyes right on her, make sure she can feel them.

"How come?"

It hurts almost to keep my voice this even.

More kicking at nothing. I've turned her into a twelve-year-old boy.

"I don't know. I don't go in for that sort of stuff. Romance and stuff. Phony."

Yeah, I think so too. If you do it their way. But I can't say that. Instead, I say, "Me neither. Maybe we ought to hang out and do nothing together."

She stops kicking. Goes still. I wait. There's a buzz rising in my ears. Bubbles flip upside my stomach, more tickle inside. I feel a coffee burp rising, wish it away.

She lifts her head, swings it up slow as if she's trying to get unstuck from something.

I don't think she knows. She doesn't see it. Too long stuck here in town. If she never saw my kind before, how would she know what I looked like?

Sweet thing, I think. *You ain't seen nothing like me yet.*

She finally speaks. "Sure. Why don't you come tomorrow night? I'll be here after we close."

She moves her eyes around the room as if to remind me, or maybe her, where she means.

I say I will. Like it's nothing at all. Like I'm not already thinking about what to wear, what looks best when it's taken off. Like I'm not planning what I'll scent myself with to draw her close, how I want her to remember me when she first sees me naked and vulnerable and writhing beneath her. I smile and turn and take my steps just so, knees bent just so to roll my hips slow, knowing she's watching me walk out the door....

"I'll try to save us one of the cheesecakes—" I hear her call to me.

But I'm already out the door.

I manage to stay away from the bakery all day Saturday until the streets and the lights outside the bakery are dark and the moon is large, ringed with silver bracelets of cold. I can feel the air dry inside my lungs; it almost hurts to breathe. Inside it will be moist as always.

Petey's alone in the bakery when I walk in. She's got an apartment in the back, but it's tiny and it's obvious she prefers being in the shop. The radio is playing low and I keep wondering if she knows why I'm really there. She's a little different now that no one's around. A little more animated. A little more herself, I think. The self she can't be when she's on display. We sit and I talk about nothing at all until there's a Johnny Rivers song on the radio and I start swaying to it without thinking about it. Petey grins at me.

"I bet you like to dance."

"I do." I smile. "Want to dance with me?"

There. I've said it. Turning point. No turning back. Either I'm in her arms or I'm out the door in the next couple of minutes.

"With me?" She acts surprised, but I've been around the block enough to know it's an act. "I'm not much of a dancer."

Wonder how many times it's started out this way.

"Come learn," I say. Stand up. Motion for her to come my way.

While Johnny is crooning on about the poor side of town, I take her hand, which feels as smooth and warm and clean as I knew it would, and put it at my waist. I put my arm around her shoulder, resisting the urge to slide my fingers through the curls that have gathered there. She's sweating. Just a little. I grin and slide my other hand into the one that's dangling by her side.

"You want to dance slow, like this?" she asks. Goes limp. I feel a little like I'm being baited. I nod and try to get us synced up with the music.

All the time she's staring at me like I've grown a second head. And then she starts to laugh.

"You really want to dance that bad?"

I stop moving. That about does it. I'm sick to death of drowning myself in caffeine and eating twice my own weight in pastry to get this sad-ass closet case to realize she's got a willing victim here. And now this. I feel my dignity slipping away like pearls on a broken thread and figure, what the hell. So I reach up and kiss Petey Ginoa square on the lips. I slide my fingers into those dark curls that have been as tempting as chocolate shavings for weeks; they feel like wet silk between my fingers. And I press my breasts into hers and slip my leg around hers, press close so she can't miss the kind of heat I'm giving off. I may not get what I want, but I'm definitely going to give her a taste of what she's missing. And after what feels like about three years, I let go of her and push her back onto her feet and stare at her as if to ask what she plans on doing next.

Petey looks at me sideways, almost glaring, and if I hadn't seen that look in the eyes of plenty of women who remind me of Petey, I'd think she was mad at me. But that look's not about mad. It's about fear.

"You aren't exactly the shy type, are you?" she snarls low.

"You like shy?"

I'm looking at her straight in the eyes.

"No. Not necessarily. Just most people. Most women that I've been with. They aren't full-time like you. Mostly just sad women who want to forget for a little while that they're married to someone they can't stand being touched by. Others that just want a little vacation from their lives, a little adventure, and when it starts to get over their heads or there's a chance of getting caught, they run back to where they started. You're not like that. You're a different kind altogether, aren't you?"

Something about that makes me feel really proud, like I've just won a contest. So I'm her first real lesbian, her first real pure femme.

"And you like it?" I smile all coy. I know she does.

"I could get used to it," she says, noncommittal. But then, before I have time to think about what that means, she is beside me, her arms around me, kissing me, her lips beating a tattoo down my neck, her pelvis pressed into mine, making me strain backward.

"I don't think you should look a gift horse in the mouth," I say.

And she smiles. It's a new one, a little too knowing, but it's a beautiful smile. I'm so heady and fluttering from being so close to the one I adore that I hardly even notice when she pushes me upward onto the breadboard and hoists herself up beside me. I don't know if I am gift or being gifted, treat or being treated, but it doesn't matter. The flour on my back feels dry and the air in the bakery is still warm enough from so many Valentine's cakes that I don't feel a chill at all as she slides off my sweater and pants, runs her fingers over the pearl heart trim of my red lace bra, and kneads the knuckle of her thumb in the crotch of my red lace panties before she slides them over my hips and down to the floor, grinning all proud at the heat and wet inside my cunt, grinning at the way I press against her hand. She whispers, "How long have you wanted this…?" and my head falls back as if it's very heavy all of a sudden and I whisper back, "Forever, since I first saw you, maybe even before that."

And she shudders, that butch shudder of realization at being wanted by a woman. She unbuttons her jeans and slides them off, kicks off her shoes, wraps her arms around me as if I'm something that might slip away, and pushes me gently down on my back.

Petey Ginoa makes love even better than she makes bread and cookies and pies and cakes. She touches me all over slow, achingly slow, and kisses my face and breasts and belly with creamy wet kisses that make me ache and open my legs wide, press hard against any touch of hers I catch just to get some relief. And when she finally slides her fingers between my legs, when my cunt overflows with want of her and opens easy and hot to draw her inside, she cries out my name high and surprised. And Petey Ginoa fucks as sweet as her eight-minute frosting. Her want is hot enough to make me feel the steam rising from her body, her fingers kneading me inside, her mouth hungry on me, her tongue tracing sweet glazed circles, her head rising at times so I see her mouth wet and shiny with me, while I cry out, "Petey!" and tug at those mythical curls at her collar and wrap my legs around as much of her clean, sweet, white-cotton self as I can, try to take all of her inside. I can tell by her eyes and her moans and the way she keeps her lips on me; the way her fingers gather inside me, thrust higher and deeper without asking, simply taking, knowing it's freely mine to give; that Petey Ginoa has never had a woman want her wholly like this, has never had a real love to call her own. I arch my back, strain up against those strong knuckles slipping, twisting, filling me; those dear arm muscles straining to take me as I come screaming, shivering, crying out, grinding my ass hard against the smooth wood.

It's warm here lying beside the oven. Petey lies silently beside me while I come back inside myself, her fingers resting on my hip bone, her cheek against my hair. I snuggle closer; the board is wider than you'd think to see it in the daylight, but I'm not afraid of falling. I'm facing her now, her shirt is open, her T-shirt and plain white underpants still on. I cuddle against her, kiss her neck, then place my hands at the bottom edge of her shirt, slide up slowly, graze her breasts. She catches her breath. Stops my hand. Holds it tight against her heart.

"Aren't you tired?"

It sounds like she's afraid I'm not satisfied.

"Not tired, relaxed," I whisper, "and I want to touch you."

She stiffens slightly beneath my hand. Her heart is beating hard enough for me to hear it; I expect to see it thumping up like a cartoon character's does when he falls in love. Or gets chased by something wild.

"I…usually…don't…"

It hits me. Petey's used to nice straight girls who like to get finger-fucked all night but don't offer to give anything back. No touch back, no tongue back. That might make them gay. And I sigh.

"Do you want this?" I whisper. "Do you want me to love you?"

She turns her face away from me. Mumbles into her arm, into the makeshift pillow the dish towel has become. I lean in to listen and there's only one word I hear.

Never?

Petey the butch goddess is a virgin?

Chaste despite sexually servicing what seems like a third of the married women in town, if you can trust the stories. Forty-something and never been touched. *Jackpot,* I think, but then I panic; I want to get up and—presto change-o—my clothes would be on and I would be gone.

But that doesn't happen.

What happens is…

First I roll my eyes upward and curse and thank the Goddess for making me brave enough to bring Petey out. All the way out.

And I remember everything I know about butches and sex and surrender and what that means, and prepare myself for anything.

Then I slowly slip my hand inside the rib-knit tee she's wearing beneath her open shirt and caress her belly with my open palm. She gurgles something low and deep inside her throat. Her stomach contracts under my touch, new nerve endings coming to life for the first time. I feel terribly powerful and daring. She settles her shoulder closer into me, stretches out her legs; I try not to think of her feet in her white sports socks hanging over the breadboard, but I do and I giggle. She smiles at me as she strokes my hair with her hand. Slowly, oh so slowly, as if her stomach stretched for miles, I take my time and slide my hand further up her shirt, grazing her breasts with my knuckles. She sucks in air, twitches. I can hear my own breathing and hers, imagine it rising up into the moist steamy air that sits inside the bakery. Joined at the breath, I think. I kiss her neck, kiss her shoulders, raise her T-shirt further and bend to trace with my tongue the places my hands have been. Her skin is clean and sweet-tasting, and moist with heat. Glazed. All that sugar, all that goodness. She's moving down, rising up to meet my hand, still palm flat; my mouth, tiny sighs breaking from her mouth. My fingers find her breast; it's small and easy to cup within my hand and her nipple is firm as the dried currants I've watched her stir into dough and almost as dark. She gasps; I find my courage and rise up further on my side so I can move more easily. Gently, I gather her breasts under my hand. She likes a little more pressure than I would have expected, croons out soft little cries of want as I grasp her breasts and release them slowly, knead her gently as I have watched her do so many times. And eventually, when I'm not sure how much more she can take, I smile and kiss her lips and bend my face to her chest, sucking each hard curranty nipple; one, then the other, until her hips start to rise off the board. She's starting to get loud. With my mouth still on her, licking a trail over her breast, I retrace my path down her belly, further, further still, slipping my fingers beneath the waistband of her cotton underwear, moving slowly over a mound of damp curling hair, slowly, so slowly…. She widens her legs to greet me and she is wet and slippery and smooth as pearls underwater, she is open and gasping. In the dark, I imagine shiny deep pink like the filling of the cheesecake she fed me before. And I need the sweetness. She's rising and crashing into my fingers, so hard and so new that I rise up and turn, stretching out, never moving my hand, and use the other to push off what bit of her underwear still clings to her. Spread her open, slip a finger inside, gentle, so gentle, and she yells something I can't hear, as if part of her is far away now. And I move inside her slowly as she wriggles all over the cutting board, and all of a sudden, I need to taste her. I throw my head down between her moving legs, trade my finger for my tongue. She is sweet there too, sweet and fresh and slippery wet as cream. I lap her up, suck her sweetness into my mouth, my tongue fluttering hard and fast, then soft and slow inside her lips. I grasp her thighs on either side so I can hang on, stay with her, buckle in as if she's a wild ride in a small-town midway and she cries out loud, almost a scream, and comes shaking and gushing wetness into my mouth, the insides of her thighs stretching, ass grinding and bucking under my tongue.

And she is done.

For a few moments, she lies in my arms and we ride out her aftershocks with the heel of my hand nestled inside her lips and she sighs over and over, stretches arms out long and languid and pulls me close, and for a split second, I feel all Prince Charming come to curl up and sleep with the princess. Until she kisses me, tongue searching out all taste of her, until she rolls me onto my back, and I feel the wetness spreading out beneath me; I must have come too, when she did. She gathers up the wetness on my thighs and hair and slips her fingers inside me. Oh. One. Two. Yes. Three. More. Petey pushes my knees apart, spreads me wide open, lowers her still trembling body onto mine, grinds her wetness into mine with a fury I never expected, and I wrap my legs around her hips, shelter her as she rides me hard, her hands grasping my shoulders, my body rising up to meet every stroke. She is gasping now, breathing loud and calling out, sweet bits and pieces of words whispered, *fuck sweet wet baby, come, mine, mine, oh fuck, beautiful you, oh.* And I feel the climb and rise of us both as she comes hard and loud into me while I lock my legs around her, grasping, grinding, shivering, up, up and over, screaming and trembling against her as she falls into me, done, head full of dark sweet curls, fine strands of burnt sugar candy, warm and swirled over my breasts.

LESSONS

S. Bear Bergman

She slid her cock out of me slowly, so slowly, then pumped it back in once, hard, to watch me gasp and laugh and grab for it; she knows I can't take that after I've just come but she likes to do it anyhow. It's how she tests to make sure I'm really, thoroughly fucked out, I think. I reached back, grabbed her wrist, and pulled her up and onto my back like so many covers, like I do, snuggling down under her warmth, the weight of her keeping me safe and grounded. She murmured fond and ridiculous things in my ear, calling me *sweet* and *delicious, handsome* and *beautiful,* licking away the sweat on my neck and sliding a hand under my sweaty chest to hug me a bit. We snuggled and rolled with the afterglow, being silly. I sucked gently on the tips of her fingers, lazing along by my cheeks, kissed the palm of her hand, nuzzled and burrowed into it, lapping like a pup. She giggled. I made a noise, a warm one, low in my throat, something between a growl and a groan, and curled myself against her.

Every time we do this, I like it a little better, and I liked it a whole fuck of a lot to begin with. We don't get a lot of chances, living so far apart and not being Rockefellers, either one of us, but between conferences, relatives, and the occasional frequent flyer ticket, we get just enough to never feel too horribly deprived. Still—this particular meeting had been after an especially long hiatus, and I was glad for the three days, glad for the king-sized bed in the anonymous hotel room on the eighth floor, glad for the weight of her on my back and the way that it never seemed like it had been months since we'd seen each other, even though we don't really talk on the phone much.

We email, though. It's the best part about messing around with writers. The email is so, so good.

Recovering slowly, I disengaged myself long enough to dislodge the head of her dick from a tender spot just above my knee, and tugged on it, experimentally, looking to see if she were ready to take it off, to let me touch her, but also ready to let my touch modulate into a jack-off motion at any minute if she wasn't. She has a harder time with it than I do; I was brought up as a butch by sex–positive, radical perverts who thought that any bullshit about butches not liking to get fucked was so much retrograde nonsense, but she grew up someplace outside of Philly and ten years earlier, where the local lesbo culture was strictly a butch top/femme bottom arrangement, where all the butches were presumed stone until proven guilty, and butch-on-butch pairings were as taboo a thing as could be imagined. Good thing that times change.

I cruised her hard when we first met a couple of years ago at a writers' conference. She made several very smart comments during a panel we were on together, and she had a steel-gray brush cut. Sold. I invited her to have dinner with my friends and me, my dear friends who set me up with ample conversational opportunity to both mention my wife at home and discuss being poly, so this hot thing would know the score. That, plus my outrageous flirting, did the trick, and after dessert I was in her room on my knees, being called a delicious assortment of very dirty things while I struggled to get her buttonfly jeans off and a condom on using only my mouth.

I *love* writers' conferences.

Since then, she's let me talk her out of her boxer briefs and into all kinds of hot and nasty fun, and has even developed quite a liking for getting fucked with my biggest dick, one that makes her crack jokes about getting to be a size queen in her old age. But I always have to wait until she's fucked me at least once, first, like she needs to reground herself in the idea whenever we meet again, as if her gentleman butch sense of the rightness and order of the world can't allow her to experience her own desire until everyone else has been squared away first. Not to suggest that fucking me isn't one of her desires. It seems clear to me at this stage that it is. But.... You know what I mean.

I slide my body up until my mouth is right against her ear. I say, "Oh. Oh, you fucking hot thing, so good to me, I want to make you feel so good, man, I want to do you so right...." I brush my lips against her ear, buck my crotch against her hip, start to move next to her. My hands find her nipples and start to rub, gently, just how she likes. She groans, quietly. I go on: "Mmmm. AJ, I want something. I want something from you, so bad."

She picks her head up and looks at me. She loves when I say what I want, she likes it that I trust her, and that I'm so hot for her. She says low, into my ear, "What's that, hm? Tell me. Tell me what you want, greedy."

Pressing myself against her, selling it with my entire body, lacing my fingers through her hair, I let a rush of hot breath out across her ear, and say, "Please. Please, teach me how to make you come."

She draws back, shocked, looks at my face. She travels with a Magic Wand and uses it, buzzing herself off while I fuck her and having noisy good times about it. But I have a secret hunch about her. I think maybe she's like me, that there's some other, nonelectric way to get the job done, something that requires the exact right touch and a lot of work, something she never confesses because she doesn't want to be that much work, or be that exposed, or make someone else work that hard on her behalf, but which is incredibly satisfying in a totally different way. I've seen the signs. I want to know what it is. I want to do her like that, want to make her come for me without her having to do anything at all. I want her to trust me like that.

I slide closer, out of her gaze, heart pounding, positioning my lips next to her ear again. "Please, AJ. Tell me what to do. I promise I'll do a good job for you. I swear I will. Use me to get yourself off. You deserve it, god, you deserve it."

Her big hands close around two fistfuls of hair, and she drags my head away from hers so she can see my face, mouth slack from panting to catch my breath. I hold her gaze and try to make my eyes communicate exactly what I'm thinking, what she wants to see: Yes, I mean it. Yes, I want this.

She drags my head back, my ear against her mouth, and crushes me tight against her in a hug. I wonder whether she's crying. I didn't mean to make her cry, I wanted to make her come, which is wetness at a totally different *end,* and I'm just about to start apologizing all over myself when she says, "You won't want to do it."

The hell I won't. I'd walk barefoot across a mile of burning sand to watch this butch dry dishes on videotape. "Trust me, I will," I say.

After a long, long pause, during which I have the good sense to keep quiet, she says in my ear, so quietly I can barely hear her: "Lick my asshole."

I'm elated. I groan, "Oh, holy shit, yeah," into her ear, start fumbling the harness off, looking for the plastic wrap, so excited I can't remember not to do five things at once. I knock over the lube, right it, find the plastic, get her out of the harness and flat on her back on the bed with a pillow under her hips before she can start waffling or change her mind. I tear off a piece of wrap, put it aside, and start kissing her, laying my body back along the warm, furry, delicious length of hers, kissing her soft and slow with little nips of my teeth, running my hands down the sides of her body, stroking her strong arms and her wide hips, working my way down her body, so slowly, rolling her nipples between my lips for a long time, sucking them so, so gently and making her push her cunt up to me, licking at her tattoos. I keep my knees between her legs so she can't grind. I want her to be hungry when I finally touch her, want her to want it so much. I want this to last. I want to show her what she's worth—all my attention, all my desire.

Finally, I bend my head and start nuzzling against the crack of her ass, kissing and nipping at her asscheeks, reaching surreptitiously for the Saran Wrap while I squeeze her ass between my hands, pulling her cheeks apart, smoothing the plastic into place, and sliding nose first between her cheeks. Her legs are bent at the knee. I can't believe she's so open to me but I am *not* complaining. I dig in.

I trace my tongue up and down her crack, so gently, full of hot breath. I want her to feel the heat even through the barrier, want her to be able to imagine it isn't there. I start to work my tongue in a little deeper, wriggling it against the sensitive spots, taking long, long licks from just below the opening of her cunt over and past her asshole, licking a fraction harder with each swipe of my tongue. She sighs, shifts her hips, presses against me. Encouraged, I keep on, starting to vary the pressure and depth of each lick, sometimes using the broad flat of my tongue and sometimes just the very tip, as hard as I can make it; I trace around the opening of her asshole, crinkled tightly shut, tracing my tongue along each of the tiny sunburst furrows of skin that radiate out from it, trying to get it to trust me. On one of the licks, I miscalculate and start pressing just a bit too soon, pushing the tip of my tongue right against the hole.

She moans. My cunt starts to do a slow boil, and I redouble my efforts. I kiss, lick, and nuzzle against her asshole, pushing my nose against it playfully, working against it with my tongue, feeling it start to open, starting to smell how much she likes it— when I pick up my head to say this to her, I see the small, slow stream of milky come easing its way out of her cunt and down the crack of her ass. Holy Christ. I put my head back down, and get back to work.

How do I describe this? It becomes the Zen of asslicking, the whole world gets reduced to about three inches of warm, wet flesh and every sound she makes. Her hand comes down and locks itself in my hair, she pulls me closer into her asscrack, tongue first, finally opening up enough for me to insinuate it into her hole and wriggle, just a tiny bit, but it makes her make a noise I'd never heard before, and I suddenly don't care how much my neck hurts or how hard it is to get my tongue into her, I just want her to make that noise again. I start fucking her hole with my tongue, slow and steady, the plastic wrap a mess around my face, and she starts grinding back against me, so hard it hurts my nose, but I am on a mission now.

Suddenly she lets loose my hair, and I'm not sure what she wants. I start to pick my head up but she growls, "Don't stop, oh, please, don't, please don't stop," and grabs my hand instead, dragging it up and pulling it hard against her clit, which is harder than I have ever felt it, literally standing straight out of the hood like a tiny cock. I work it differently than I normally would, in a two-fingered jack-off motion I learned for transmen with testosterone-enhanced parts, up and down the sides with occasional swipes across the head, and she loves it, starts panting and gasping while I fuck my face further into her now-open, gripping asshole and work her clit at the same time. I can tell she's going to come soon. I don't change a thing, I keep doing exactly what I'm doing, same speed, same pace, if I'm doing it right I want to keep doing it right, I want to do it right for her, want to make her feel as good as she makes me feel, so I keep my hand steady and blink the sweat out of my eyes and take a deep breath for one more long sally, plunging my tongue back into her ass on the downstroke and pulling it out on the up, letting her buck between the two pleasures, until she yells, "Oh, holy motherfucking god!" and comes with a bellow that even the moderately soundproofed hotel room probably doesn't contain, nearly breaking my neck as she whips her legs together around my face and squeezes them hard, hand clamping down over my hands, writhing on the bed in pleasure and riding what I hope like hell are several strong aftershocks, each one announced with a guttural cry.

Soon, she's still. I tap her on the thigh to remind her that my head is still between her legs and when she opens them, I scramble up, hurrying to cover her naked skin with mine, wrapping her up against me, holding her and whispering, "Thank you. Oh, thank you," into her ear like a mantra, over and over. She looks at me.

"That was...oh. Wow. Em, that was...." She trails off, nuzzles further into the crook of my neck, rubbing her sweaty skin against mine. We breathe together for a minute. I drag the ugly bedspread over us to keep us warm, being careful to hold her tight the whole time, not wanting to break this moment. I can't even believe she trusted me with that. It makes me feel something I can't explain, and while I'm searching for the words, so I can tell her, she picks her head back up, and whispers, so quietly for such a big, confident butch, so shyly, "Did you like it?"

I grin. I take her hand, draw it down to my soaking wet cunt, brushing her fingertips over my hard clit. "What do you think?" I ask, laughing a little into her ear.

She growls hungrily, rolls me over underneath her, and says, "I think you're a little slut, that's what I think."

I nod happily, and spread my legs wider.

ANONYMOUS

Amie M. Evans

She grabs a fistful of my hair before the door closes behind us. She locks the bolt and pulls me over to the bed. "I'll call you Dee and you call me Jimmy. Get on your knees."

As she unzips her pants, the cock I felt on the ride pops out. She pulls my head toward it and hisses, "Suck it, bitch."

It is almost impossible to find anonymous lesbian sex. Maybe in San Francisco or possibly New York City you can find it at an upscale women's club or cutting-edge cruising spots, but not in Boston. Not proper New England Boston. The mixture of Puritan values and lesbian ethics deters casual lesbian anything. But I like a challenge, so I was determined to engage in anonymous lesbian sex in Boston. Anonymous sex with real live lesbians. No exchange of numbers or first-date sex; but rough, hard, no-name sex: the stuff of gay boy novels and urban myths.

It is good to have goals.

I considered personal ads for a while. I read through them, studied them for content and form, and ruled out useless information about beaches, smoking, and cats. Then I wrote my own ad:

> *Hot, femme dyke bottom* (should I hyphenate or not?) *seeks sexy butch top* (again to hyphenate or not?) *for anonymous kinky sexual encounter.*

She would call and leave her name and number and we would set up a time and date and I smelled the U-Haul—parked just around the corner.

The second ad I composed read like this:

> *Hot femme-dyke-bottom seeks sexy butch-top for anonymous kinky sexual encounter.* (At this point I thought hyphens were the way to go. They showed the connection of the identity markers I was using to solicit a sexual partner.) *Meet me at the Duck Statue in the Common Gardens on Saturday at 9P.M. I'll wear a red silk scarf around my neck; you wear a red bandanna on your wrist.*

This ad eliminated the phone calls, the messages, the number exchanges. It created the fantasy of being picked up blindly in the park—something I've envied in gay boys since I was first introduced to their culture. But the problem with this ad was that every horny straight guy with a lesbian fantasy who reads the women-seeking-women classifieds would show up with a hard-on. A male gang-bang was not what I had in mind. Not to mention, what if no one showed up? New England dykes—dykes in general, but especially New England dykes—aren't known for their sexual abandon. How many Saturday nights would I have to spend wearing a red silk scarf and standing by the Make Way for Ducklings Statue waiting for Ms. Butch-Top? The Boston Mounted Police would speculate about what I was doing there. An investigation into possible drug trafficking or prostitution would ensue and countless taxpayer dollars would be wasted before they discovered I was just after a cheap lesbian-sexual thrill. Of course, a whole series of newspaper articles on lesbian sexual habits would appear, and the Boston Pride Committee would have to do more than ban a lesbian float featuring an empty bed to prove to mainstream corporate sponsors and the general public that queers don't really have sex. No, the classifieds, as always, were a bust.

What I really wanted was to cruise lesbians. But as a gay male friend pointed out in the 1980s when I first came out: lesbians don't cruise each other. Then whom do they cruise? I wanted to know. Imagine a place where bunches of lesbians gathered for no other reason than to have sex—anonymous sex. We could have our own system of identifying sexual desires like the boys had with their hankies in the heyday of gay male cruising. Displays on the right for tops and on the left for bottoms carries over into lesbian sex. In fact, a lot of the boys' codes would work for lesbians. Black for leather sex and yellow for golden showers. New colors could be added for lesbian-specific sexual acts. We'd need one for vaginal penetration and one for those who were opposed to penetration. And, of course, a color for the lesbian sexual staple: 69. We could use ribbons instead of those bulky hankies, or colored rope for those in the butchier set.

I'm sure a committee would have to be set up to determine which colors would represent which sex acts. The committee would be charged with making sure the color selections in relation to the sex acts and any social or cultural baggage offended no one. Then they'd want to separate the cruising area by color selections so the antipenetrators didn't have to look at the penetrators while they cruised. Maps of the approved cruising zones divided into plots by activity would be distributed. The zones closest to the bathrooms, center hub, and public transportation would be randomly assigned to the sexual activities the committee members engaged in, and a central, sex-free plot would offer peer counseling for those lesbians experiencing cruising distress. A group of volunteers would patrol to make sure penetrators stayed out of the nonpenetrating plots and that the golden showerers didn't venture into the oral sex–only zones. A statement on diversity and respect would emphasize the needs of sexual assault survivors, but exclude the needs of sexual assault survivors who participate in S/M activities. Before long the committee would make the leatherdykes wear signs announcing that they may cause flashbacks and that lesbian-identified MTFs would be picketing the area. No, this wouldn't work—not for lesbians.

I decided to go to a lesbian bar. There aren't any real lesbian bars in Boston, but there are a number of ever-changing one-night-a-week lesbian clubs. The problem with lesbian bars is the music. For some reason the DJs don't seem to keep up with the new dance music hits. No matter how hip the DJ looks, the music always sucks. But I wasn't going to dance; I was going to find a fuck. The clubs were my only option if I was ever going to have anonymous lesbian sex. I went alone, since taking a femme support group with me would turn the covert sexual mission into a giggle fest, and taking a butch friend would mark us as a couple. Since you can never tell who is sleeping with whom, no matter who I took with me for support, my chances of finding a sex partner would be reduced. Alone was the best choice. If I failed, I could wallow without sharing the details with any of my friends, and if I succeeded I would have one hell of a story to share over brunch.

I slipped into a short, clingy black skirt with thigh-highs and a black garter belt with purple trim. I put on a black lace bra with a long-sleeved fishnet shirt. I finished the outfit with a pair of knee-high, platform, black-leather boots, and a silver dagger necklace that hung just above my cleavage. A little mascara, red lipstick, and a spray of perfume and I was out the door to the club.

The bar was crowded when I arrived at eleven thirty. Bad dance music was blasting, spun by the very punk-looking May, a local lesbian DJ, so wrapped up in herself that she is unable to play requests even if you are the only one dancing. A handful of dykes in groups of twos and threes were on the dance floor. I scanned for potential sex partners. The spectator crowd on the perimeter of the dance floor was a mix of nondescript andro-lesbians in jeans and button-downs over T-shirts, punky Lesbian Avenger–type college students, and sports dykes in athletic tops. I even noticed one or two femmes in skirts. No one caught my eye, but I made a mental note that a few of the women-watchers were kind of cute.

I walked through the table area on my way to the bar and spotted a really sexy blonde punk-dyke, but she was with five other punk-dykes talking and drinking beers. Any one of those hot dykes would have done, and since there were five, there had to be at least one single girl among them. I noted the table location and continued to the bar for a drink.

I bumped into the hottest African American butch I have ever seen. She was wearing black dress pants, a pressed white shirt, and a buttoned vest. Her hair was cut Grace Jones style, and she had a pocket watch in her vest pocket attached to a thin silver chain. Her dark skin was flawless. I smiled and mouthed, "Excuse me." She put her hand on mine and mouthed, "No, excuse me." Hmm. She stepped to the side to allow me to pass, and I saw a royal femme in a red dress move in close behind the butch. The femme placed her hand on the butch's back. So much for that. I smiled at them both and made my way to the bar. It felt good to be in a room full of women.

The bar was lined with an assortment of sitting and standing lesbians. Among them I spotted a dark-haired woman in a pair of blue jeans rolled up at the bottom to expose her biker boots. She had on a bowling shirt with cut-off sleeves and sported a chain wallet. Her dark short hair was slicked back, and she looked like a dyke version of a greaser. I watched her swig her beer from a bottle and light a cigarette as she watched the dance floor from afar. Leaning on the bar, she had one foot hooked on the bottom bar rail. She was tight and lean, though she wasn't my usual type—a bit too much James Dean and not enough Sid Vicious—but she was alone, and James Dean beats early Cris Williamson hands down every time.

Approach was everything, since too much chitchat would ruin the cruising feeling I was trying to create against all odds. There were other factors I had to consider: *I might scare her, since lesbians don't act this way as a rule. Or she might think I'm a straight woman trying to pick up a third since lesbians don't look this way as a rule either. She might get outraged since sexual outrage runs close to the skin of my lesbian sisters.* Even if everything went off and she agreed to do this, she might have been one of those oral-sex-only-please lesbians, or worse yet, a bottom.

I put my faith in the fact that she had her wallet chain on the right and that maybe that tattoo on her arm of the busty Betty Page meant more than that she felt pressured to pick a cool image in the tattoo parlor. Not much to put your faith in, but more than a tale of fish and loaves written by an unknown author. I walked straight up to her and looked into her eyes. She held my gaze, a good sign since lesbians seem unable to make eye contact with each other. I leaned into her, almost touching, and put my mouth close to her ear so that she could hear me over the music.

"Are you alone?" I asked.

"Yes." She slipped her arm around my waist and pulled me closer to her, perhaps to ensure we weren't pulled apart by the motion of the crowd.

"Don't tell me your name. Just listen and a simple yes or no answer will be fine."

"Okay, talk."

I placed my hand on her upper arm near Betty Page and felt the bulge of a well-developed muscle. "I want to have sex with you. Anonymous, rough sex in a sleazy motel room."

She shifted her weight against the bar, and I leaned into her. I thought I felt the bulge of a strap-on, but I was nervous so I didn't pursue the hunch. "No names, no numbers. Are you up to it?"

She pushed me away and looked at me from head to toe, then pulled me back against her. "Are you a dyke?"

"If you are asking me if I fuck boys or if I am a closet case, no to both. I'm a dyke."

"Let's go, then."

I stepped away from her as she took my hand and led me out of the bar. My heart was racing, and I was wet. My head spun since I never thought I would get this far. Outside, the cooler fresh air hit us and we stopped.

"My car's over there," I said.

"Yeah, my bike's right here." She gestured with her chin to a black Triumph with chrome shined for a Saturday night and fire blazing on either side of the gas tank. She really *was* James Dean.

"Your bike it is."

She handed me a helmet and got on. I situated myself behind her and wrapped my arms around her waist. She pulled onto the road, seemingly knowing where she was going. At the first stoplight she reached back and ran her hand up my leg and under my short skirt. "Tell me what you mean by rough sex."

She pulled the bike into traffic before I could answer.

At the next light I said, "I want you to take me, use my body. I want to have my 'no' ignored." I ran my hand down her hip into her crotch, verifying the existence of the dildo I had thought I felt in the bar. I started to think about the implications of this woman alone in a dyke bar packing, but before I got far the bike stopped at another light.

"Do you have panties on and what's your safeword?" Again she pulled out before I could answer.

"No and 'ice cream,'" I said as she parked in front of a rundown wooden building that at one time was painted gray. A neon sign in the window flashed OPEN in red, and a battered metal sign said MOTEL BY THE SEA. A number of small cottages in various states of disrepair all were in need of paint. The landscaping consisted of white rock paths and clumps of weeds. A few bushes growing unattended dotted the muddy area around the Motel by the Sea. The sea was miles from here. This was definitely sleazy.

I waited outside while she went into the office and paid for a cabin. My skin felt cold from the open ride in the night air. Our cabin was number 3—my lucky number—and I felt like a high-school girl as we walked over to it. I was bursting with excitement but maintained a cool, calm exterior like I'd done this a million times. I followed her to the cabin, watching the slight wiggle in her walk. She had a tight little butt, and I could not wait to get my hands on it.

That's how I got here on my knees in front of this butch I don't even know. I take it into my mouth. It isn't the biggest dildo I've ever had, but it's the first I've ever had in my mouth. I take as much of it in as I think I can handle—about half. My mouth slides up and down the shaft that feels bigger than it looked. I moan an "umm" as it eases in and out. This isn't what I had in mind. I release it from my mouth and hold it in my hand, flicking my tongue on the tip and licking the crown. Jimmy D. puts her hands on the back of my head. I look up at her, not raising my head. She intently watches my tongue work on her dildo. The look in her eyes excites me, makes me eager to please her despite the fact that her cock is made of silicone.

I take it back into my mouth, this time relaxing my throat like the drag queens and gay boys I hung out with in college described. I am able to get more of her cock into my mouth, but not all of it. It slides in and out, and she begins to meet my strokes with her hips, her hands clamping into my hair.

After a few moments of deep thrusting, she pulls me off her cock and tosses me next to her on the bed on my stomach.

"Get on your knees, Dee." I get up on my knees and lean on my elbows, my ass in the air.

"No panties. You are a bad girl." I hear her unwrapping a condom. Her hand caresses my bare ass as she gets into position with her knees behind me.

"Such a pretty white ass." Her hand comes down on my cheek in a quick slap, then another. Her strokes are hard and stinging.

"I'm going to put my cock in your cunt and fuck you. Would you like that?"

"Yes," I say and thrust my hips back in anticipation. This is more like it. This is what I had in mind—none of that sucking on silicone; a good fucking is what I want.

She does exactly what she promised, pushing the head of the dildo into my wet cunt and slowly thrusting forward. When the whole cock is inside me she rotates her hips so that the cock bumps against the perimeter of my cunt. She thrusts slow and easy at first, working up my excitement and feeling out my insides. In and out the cock slides, building up speed and strength with each stroke until she is clasping my ass and pounding into me.

It feels good. Really good. She knows how to use that dildo. My body tingles and my cunt feels excited and full. I want her to make me come. She stops buried deep inside me. For one second there is no movement; I can hear her heavy breathing then a popping as she pulls out. She grabs my thighs and flips me onto my back, positioning herself on top of me and reinserting her cock into my pussy. No hip movement as she pulls my shirt and bra up exposing my breasts but not removing my clothes. Her hands grasp my breasts hard. She rubs them, then brings them together.

"Does it feel good to have me fuck you?"

"Yes. I want to come. Make me come." I squirm under her, trying to get her to start fucking me again.

She pinches my nipples tightly, prodding a moan from me. "I won't make you come unless I can hear how good my fucking you makes you feel."

She takes one nipple into her mouth, working it with her tongue, sucking on it, then biting into the flesh. I moan and push against her with my hips. She groans in response and strokes in and out with her cock.

"No one can hear us, Dee, and anyone who can is doing the same thing we are."

I moan again louder and lift my legs so that she can get deeper inside me.

She pins my arms down with her hands and holds her upper body over me. Our eyes lock for a moment as she fucks me harder. I moan and push against her arms, feel her fingers tighten on my wrists. I groan louder as she fucks me harder and faster. Her strokes are even in and out. She is slamming into my cunt.

Her upper body comes down on top of me, and she grabs my shoulders for leverage. I lock my legs at the ankles around her back. She slides in and out, fucking me like a wildcat.

I scream, "Fuck me, Jimmy! It feels so good! Make me come!"

She slips one hand between us and strokes my already swollen clit with two fingers.

"Harder," I gasp.

She strokes my clit in hard tight circles and pounds me with her dildo. I grab her upper arm with one hand and her tiny ass with the other as the shock waves of orgasm rip through me. My hips jerk forward, and my nails sink into her flesh. She stops fucking but stays inside me. Our faces are cheek to cheek, we are covered in sweat, our breathing is rapid. I roll her onto her back. I'm on top now and take a few slow strokes on her cock. She groans low.

"Can I touch you?" I ask, looking into her eyes.

"Yeah," she says, reaching up and pinching my nipple.

I dismount and undo her belt and jeans, pulling them to her ankles. She unbuckles the harness and slips it off. I slide to the floor, and she moves to the edge of the bed as she opens her legs. I spread her outer lips, noticing the soft blonde pubic hair wet with her juices and sweat. I plunge my tongue into her opening then lick straight up from her wet cunt to her clit. Her body involuntarily jerks and she moans. She is so wet. I slip my finger inside her then lightly lick her clit. I move my finger in and out, increasing the speed of my licking and my finger-fucking until she groans and her hand rests on top of my head. Her cunt tastes sweet, and I want to tease her, but I don't stop to pursue that course of action.

She grabs my hair as she comes. Her legs twitch, her hips buck, and her other hand grabs my upper arm. I rest my head on her stomach and push my finger deep inside her as an orgasm rips through her.

Jimmy pulls me onto the bed next to her and kicks off her boots and jeans. We lie there a few minutes before she puts her arm around me and pulls me over to her. I put my head on her shoulder and close my eyes to catch my breath. I am exhausted and content, thrilled with the results of my hunt.

I wake up with a start. The sun shines through the blinds. The clock next to the bed says 9:00 a.m. I am angry for having allowed myself to fall asleep. I had just planned on closing my eyes for a few minutes, then calling a cab to take me back to my car at the club. I wonder if I can sneak out and call a cab from the lobby without waking her. I move slowly, disentangling my limbs from hers, but she stirs and looks at me groggily, then smiles.

"Hi," I say and smile back as I stand up. So much for that plan.

"Morning," she says as she stretches and yawns.

I'm not sure what to do. I am not supposed to be here. I didn't plan this part. We stare at each other for an uncomfortably long time.

"Do this often?" she says, smiling broadly and scratching her head.

"No. You?"

"No." She gets up. She has a really hot lean body with a cute small ass and piercing blue eyes—a little white-blonde hair color would bring out those baby blues. What am I thinking? This is anonymous sex, not a relationship.

"I've been going to that dyke bar for months. I had this fantasy...." She stops short, blushes a little. "Oh, I forgot. You don't want to hear anything about me."

"No, go ahead." I am interested in her fantasy and that she

has been thinking about it and trying to act on it for months.

"Okay," she says, walking into the bathroom and not closing the door. I hear her pee as she talks. "So I wanted to have a girl come on to me for sex—just sex."

I giggle, catch a glimpse of myself in the mirror across from the bed, and stop.

"Last night," she says as she emerges from the bathroom and sits on the bed, "it happened."

"I'd been planning this for a long time but never found the right pickup or the right way to find the right pickup." I smile, "Until last night." We start to get dressed.

"Do you have other fantasies?" she asks as she buckles her belt.

"Yeah, tons of them," I say, feeling unusually flat as I go into the bathroom and close the door. She's not really ruining the fantasy. Last night I knew nothing about her. It's over, and I still know next to nothing about her. What harm is there in sharing our fantasies with each other?

When I come out of the bathroom she is dressed and smoking a cigarette on the bed. I pause for a moment, standing with my hand on my hip, then say, "I want to be paid for sex."

She raises an eyebrow.

"You know: picked up on a street corner dressed like a hooker; negotiate the cost of services; get paid; fucked in the john's car; then dropped off on the corner again."

"Hmm," she says, staring at me, then stands up. "Ready? I'll drive you back to your car."

I nod.

The ride back is uneventful. I am lost in my thoughts and she is quiet. I wonder if I made a mistake telling her my hooker fantasy. I wonder if I'll tell my friends this story or keep it for myself. I wonder about the significance of her packing and if I can go to a restaurant for breakfast on a Sunday morning alone dressed like I am. We pull into the almost empty parking lot of the club, and I point out the blue car as mine. She stops next to it and puts her hand on my inner thigh as I stand between her bike and my car, not knowing what to say.

"What's your name?" she asks.

"Sandy," I say, unusually timid and self-conscious.

"Karen." We both laugh.

"Bye," I say as I walk the two steps to my car and unlock the door.

"Sandy, eight o'clock Saturday night on the corner of Fifth and Washington in Chinatown." She revs her engine.

"What?" I turn toward her, confused.

"Fifth and Washington in Chinatown, Saturday at eight. I have a red '56 Chevy and a dildo twice the size of this." She indicates her crotch with her hand. My mouth drops open at her boldness. "I like my whores in push-up bras and low-cut tops."

She pulls away before I can answer her. My mouth is still hanging open as I get into the car. Cocky butch, what nerve!

I pull the car out of the spot and head for the street. Before I merge into the light Sunday morning traffic I write *5th and Washington, Chinatown* on a scrap of paper. Then under it I write, *Karen, 8:00 p.m., Saturday, push-up bra, red '56 Chevy.*

LIVE: BY REQUEST

Samiya A. Bashir

platform heels so high on these boots i bent down to see you
thru the sky. the brown suede snaked to the tops of my thighs
and grabbed your eyes as soon as i walked in the place. textures
always aroused you.

where did my terra firma brownness end and the smooth
suede begin? my skirt wasn't as short as you like me to wear on
my sluttier days, but it flared and reached heights too dangerous,
for tonight, when i turned. i'd forgotten to think of that.

you sitting at the bar.

i remember it darker than it was perhaps. the beer in your
hand almost empty. the glass the bartender gave you abandoned.
your other hand poised as if just about to check your pocket
for something. i sway over to your end of the bar, try not to
notice all the other butches who try not to watch me sashay my
way down to you. i know that's your job. it's part of our thing
tonight i come to play baby. i bend forward slightly when i reach
you so the ass you grab is just ass. you think it's to show you the

deep valley of barely contained cleavage my tight top presents so you let your tongue linger a moment there after we kiss. you forget to slide your hand up the warm brown suede to the top, forget how bad you wanna know if i wore panties tonight 'cuz i want a drink. now. please, baby.

we get our drinks and the almost relieved kinda jealousy washes over the face of the b-girl bartender who was trying not to cruise you before i got here. i stand behind your stool, my polished hands hide inside your jacket, between your thighs is just you tonight. good. i let you carry my drink saying nothing 'cuz i still can't tell you how that smooth, sure it isn't practiced, voice of yours turns me on, gets me wet. of course i'm not wearing panties tonight—gotta be careful as i swish not to let my backside twirl—i'm glad your hands are full of drinks.

the big back booth i wanted sits empty. you just smile, knowing you worked it out that way before i got here. i'm always late. you wait.

you hold the drinks while i sit down so i won't knock the table. these boots make my knees so high up I gotta work to keep my skirt under my ass. you sit down, take off your jacket. you look so handsome, flash me the most irresistible damn kid-caught-hand-in-cookie-jar grin that i wanna just eat you alive. soon come.

so we talk. i haven't seen you in a week. you missed me. i want you. damn. i wanna talk, catch up, giggle with my drink, cross my legs under this too-short table. but just your voice gets me moist and i ain't got on no panties—tonight is for you. and you don't even know it yet.

it's perfect. you're feelin' yourself tonight in black jeans so tight you give the fag boys a fright when you stroll past. hair oiled just right, new boots, even the tank under your shirt is pressed. i'm impressed. i'll let you play the flirt a little while longer. it's important that this is done right. we gotta get outta here. finish yr beer. please, baby. you're comin' with me tonight.

i ignore the raised eyebrow—a challenge. you ignore the twinge in your cunt—the erotic fear of being known. your eyes linger too long on the butch behind the bar on the way out— you thought neither of us noticed—but that just turns me on tonight.

i feel the cool breeze on the wetness between my legs first, then coming from the cold stares of street strangers as we walk down the avenue. you tighten your arm around my waist and i fold myself more closely into you, stare my adoration into your eyes.

we'd planned dinner, but i can't wait anymore. i've got other plans so we stop off at your place. you get that knowing, arrogant smile on your lips and try to put your hand up my skirt while you get your keys. please, baby. look don't touch tonight. i'll tell you when you can do what you can do.

again with the eyebrows. whatever. this time i walk behind you up the stairs it's all i can do to ask for some water. please, baby.

i'm torn trying to get my nerve up too and restrain my blistering desire to possess you here now. but i know who'd win that internal battle. in the kitchen i walk up behind you at the sink. you look so tough as you wash a glass for me with the tenderest hands i've ever seen. i feel a drop of sweat ride my spine to my ass when i reach around you to run my nails up your stomach, pull your back into my breasts and push my pelvis into your ass, push your pelvis into the countertop like i want you—like you want to need to be when you realize what i've been hiding.

all those nights of erotic imagination didn't prepare you for this stiff reality. you didn't think i had it in me. you open your lips almost as if to protest even as your legs spread wider to meet me, even as your deep soft moan betrays you. my fingers in your mouth become a simple formality.

i gotta move quick before we talk ourselves outta this. i whisper in your ear, say: *you can be mama's queer boy tonight if you like.* my fingers run up the crotch of your jeans, you stifle a scream as my nail grazes your ass.

all butches have a black leather belt somewhere. yours is at hand as i grab it and pull your ass a little higher while you reach between your legs to feel my cock. i'm still rubbing it between your thighs when i see the stubborn relief in your eyes as you realize it's not your dick you're drippin' on. it's mine.

you never knew how much you loved me before you got down on your knees on that dark kitchen floor, lifted up my skirt, and slid my dick down your throat. i showed you mercy, took your hand as i led the well known route to the bed, sat you on it with that dazed, amazed look on your face to watch me strip.

off with my blouse—i left the red velvet bra on for a minute. pulled down my skirt—left the brown suede boots on for a minute. let my locks down and stroked my cock.

i let you take off my bra and play titty games for a while to get you comfortable—make you drip like i dripped all down my girlish thighs. i whispered all the ways i would fuck you tonight. you fought off your fright, felt your throat get tight, wouldn't let emotion overpower desire. you cowered into my breasts. you thought that way i wouldn't make you beg. remember?

i took your shirt off—left you the tank. pulled your pants to your ankles so fast you fell facedown, boxer-clad ass in the air— i'll let you think i practiced that move—tight-ass black jeans locked your legs. i let your black belt fall free—that time.

and yes i rubbed your back and whispered my love in your ear, ran my tongue from the nape of your neck to your rear before i made you say it.

and yes i loved you with every part of my body, every part

of your body, while the last of your time-toughened defenses melted beneath my touch and you knew you were safe.

and when you finally begged—just a whisper—

fuck me

i knew i could tell you to say it louder. i made you beg for it again and again until i heard you cry *if you don't fuck me goddammit, right now, one of us is gonna die!*

all right then. i entered sacred space you opened to me, let you bury your face in the pillow, helped you fight the monsters of old humiliations, new fears that i wouldn't let you keep your swagger, the staggering dread that i wouldn't be able to see the strong, sexy woman you need to be anymore. you let me bite your back and grab your cunt and tits and whisper over and over that you're mine, tell you this time how good your pussy feels from the inside because we know this is the kinda love that reaches thru these barriers.

you scream your release. i do too—after fucking you some more.

we had never known love like this. we lay in bed all night, took turns feeding each other whatever we had delivered. we talked a little and loved a lot more and freed ourselves for our own acceptance. by morning i had put my dick down for a little while, and you got yours up again and it was like never before. 'cuz i knew you, and you were known and still loved anyway. we've had a lot of those nights since then. i always try to surprise you. and when you sit in that bar, when those other b-girls try not to look at you, you can stare straight back and know that—in the next twenty minutes or so—the kinda soft/hard love everyone wants not to speak of gonna storm through that door on five-inch platform boots, worn for your pleasure, and lead you by the hand back home.

COP-OUT

Rosalind Christine Lloyd

Troi was into picking up girls at straight clubs. Tonight, her destination was Butter, a hip-hop club in Tribeca.

An ex-Marine and former college hoop all-star, Troi was now a New York City police detective. Her preoccupation with combat and competition defined a quiet but powerfully aggressive demeanor. She kept her five-ten, 160-pound body buffed to masculine perfection with rigorous daily workouts that involved pumping iron with the muscle queens at a gay gym in Chelsea where she matched their workout regimen to achieve similar macho results. Every inch of her was solid, sinuous, rippling muscle.

Her skin was like dark fudge, as rich and even in tone as a sinfully delicious chocolate cake. When she laughed, a mouth full of perfectly spaced teeth framed by thin, silky lips accentuated a smile that ignited the light in her unusually light brown eyes. Her hands were massive: hands designed to palm basketballs, handle heavy artillery, and apprehend suspects, among other useful things.

Tonight she opted for a pair of soft brown leather pants and a suede camel-colored shirt. She had a knack for choosing loose-fitting clothes that enabled her to neutralize any semblance of femininity. Her breasts were almost always held hostage, bound tightly beneath her clothing. She selected one of her larger dildos, the one she'd named Shaft, along with her new leather travel harness. Shaft was handmade, designed precisely to her specifications to include, among other things, a skin tone that matched her complexion. The startling replica even came equipped with a fake foreskin that made it feel that much more authentic. It served its purpose. It set her back quite a lot of money but she quickly discovered it was worth every cent and more. She finished her outfit with her favorite designer square-toe boots (for men, of course), splashed on a men's designer cologne, and dared to accessorize with a fat ruby in her left ear and a matching pinky ring for that hint of gangsta.

To throw people off her trail, she would often flash her police badge on her way into the clubs she cruised. Besides being allowed admission at no charge, she avoided being carded. This particular evening, it was obvious that Butter was seriously implementing its ID policy because of the excess crowd of underage kids hanging out behind the ropes, trying to get in.

Hip-hop clubs were perfect venues for her obsession because the social element was fiercely dark, wild, uninhibited, and crowded enough for her to move around freely without inciting any suspicion. The carnival feeling reminded Troi of her freaknik college days. Most of the men were typical in their badass attitudes, adhering to the typical negative stereotypes of male posturing, and taking the pessimistic connotations of the music way too seriously. Talk about game—all of this worked in Troi's favor because she offered an *alternative*. Her meticulous, classy, cash-money look attracted the girls' attention every time. The only problem she ever encountered were the down-low, bisexual switch-hitter boys prowling around who correctly detected her on their gaydar, but incorrectly assumed she was a gay man or something even more ambiguous. Troi found these occasions amusing but off-putting. For this reason, using the restrooms, any restroom, was strictly out of the question.

Scanning the club, she easily found her mark: a tall, red bone with the face of an angel dipped in honey, with two long French braids that went down her back tickling a fat, juicy ass squeezed into a cheap, tight, Lycra hoochie dress. The slinky fabric stretched and strained against the milk-fed curves of her breeder hips. Her calves, sprung from svelte, golden thighs, were incredibly sculpted in a pair of chic platform ankle boots that had a sci-fi effect: the entire boot, including the heel, was encased in stretched black leather. Troi liked the way they made her calves look. Long and wispy eyelashes like the fringe on a gypsy's shawl draped huge, sensuous eyes. Wearing too much jewelry, she was definitely into "bling-bling." Her nail tips were long, decorated in startling designs and colors; but her tits, piled into a push-up bra, were voluminously for real. Ms. Thing was ghetto fabulous in all its glory.

Troi watched the girl closely, studied her standing at the bar as if waiting for a bus. At least three men asked Braids to dance, but she declined them all. Braids was waiting for Mr. Right. She was waiting for Troi.

Troi sent her a glass of champagne with a shot of Hennessey poured on top (commonly known as thug's gold) and waited for the young lady's reaction. Initially, Braids hesitated with suspicion, refusing the cocktail. But when the bartender pointed at Troi, Braids stared for a moment with those eyes, assessing her admirer before smiling seductively and mouthing the words *thank you* with lusciously burgundy-coated lips. She then proceeded to sip slowly from her glass as if digesting something very precious. Troi would not allow her much time to think, knowing she would have to crank up the charm to get Braids where she wanted her.

Their eyes locked and remained so while Troi slowly walked to the end of the bar, as if she was a pimp strolling along a catwalk. Unable to read anything from the girl's eyes, Troi relied on her feminine intuition, and she felt the adrenaline surge through her. It was the same feeling she got before taking the winning layup shot or the feeling she had during a stakeout—the feeling of victory in enemy territory. Flexing her muscles, she walked right up to Braids, suddenly feeling the aura of heat emitting from the girl's body. This startled Troi for a moment. As if reading Troi's mind, Braids took another sip of champagne. Taking a deep breath, Troi leaned in toward the girl, telling herself not to inhale her whole.

"I can see you appreciate the finer things in life," Troi whispered in her ear, letting her nose brush against the length of her neck for a trace of her scent.

"Is that your best line? Now I know you can come better than that especially when you sending over champagne and everything. What's your name, Mr. Got-All-the-Right-Moves?" The dark pools turned into magnets, drawing Troi in.

"I'm Troi—and what do they call you, Ms. Got-All-the-Right-Moves?"

"If you're nasty."

"Oh, I'm plenty nasty."

"I bet you are. I'm Staci." She sipped from her glass again, her eyes lowering, her comfort level improving.

The dance floor was a virtual free-for-all. No respect was given and every liberty was taken with the feminine gender. The brothers practically mauled the girls alive and the girls appeared to enjoy the attention, but whether this was really the case was another matter altogether. But this kind of atmosphere played in Troi's favor as she gently removed the glass from Staci's hands and led her onto the crowded dance floor.

It was so hot it seemed like everyone was simulating sex. Staci wrapped her arms around Troi's neck, rubbing herself against Troi's thigh like a puppy in heat. Something was on this girl's mind.

Troi was enamored by the overture and didn't waste any time stroking Staci's back very provocatively and grabbing her ass, positioning Staci so that she was gyrating on the head of Troi's dildo.

"You a big boy, Troi. You could hurt a girl," she purred in Troi's ear.

When Staci stuck her hot, wet tongue into that same ear, Troi wanted to sink her cock right in the ass she held, but she settled for plunging her fingers through Staci's lacy thong and in between her meaty lips.

Staci felt so good riding Troi's dong and fingers, her soft breasts crushed against Troi's bound, puckered nipples. Troi could feel Staci's muscles clench in the palm of her hands. Staci found Troi's lips with her own, forcing them into a kiss so provocative it made Troi's head spin. Sucking tongues, lips, mouths like they were sucking on the world's best-tasting treat, each of them settled into some serious dry-humping, riding the crest of their quivering horniness. Before Troi realized it, the front of Staci's dress was hiked up against her hips and Staci began stroking Shaft through Troi's leather pants: a great big no-no.

Troi reached behind her belt for her handcuffs, and placed them on Staci.

"Am I under arrest, officer?" Staci was unfazed.

"Yeah, I'm taking you into custody." Troi made only a small spectacle leading Staci out of the club in handcuffs. Security and other patrons looked on suspiciously as Troi flashed the badge attached to her belt. Staci loved every minute of the crude public display.

Troi's truck was strategically parked on a secluded side street. Listening to the sounds of their heels clicking against the slick cobblestone street, Troi continued to steer her "assailant" by the cuffs. Her eyes were locked on Staci from behind, while Staci enhanced the view by shifting her ever-ripening ass with every step she took, her calves casting a spell over Troi's mind. They stopped once they reached Troi's jet-black Lincoln Navigator.

"I like your big, black truck," Staci whispered over her shoulder.

"Oh, we'll see just how much you like it," Troi whispered back, gently pressing Staci up against the hood of the truck, the girl's hips and thighs shivering as they met the cold fiberglass.

Staci giggled nervously but obediently spread her legs apart. Troi pushed herself against her; the girl was built like a gazelle, tall and graceful, with limbs so delicate and fine they seemed breakable. If only Troi could feel those long, thin hands wrapped around her Shaft, it would be a sensual nirvana. If only Troi could watch those burgundy lips wrapped tightly around her Shaft, her strong hips pumping into that burgundy mouth like a piston, she knew she could fall in love. Instead, she would have to settle for the ass, which she exposed to the cool November air, her super-tight, lacy, tiger-print thong encasing two fleshy mounds of delight.

"Cool air couldn't cool this ass off." Troi was kneeling now, her eyes taking in the vision before her.

"But I bet *you* can." Staci's tiny voice grew up in a second, morphing into a mature growl.

Troi sank her teeth gently into the flesh of Staci's right cheek, pretending to gnaw while allowing her hand to reach in between Staci's moist bush—to find that her pussy felt like a hot piece of fruit left out in the sun too long, mushy and sticky, oozing sweet nectar along her fingertips. Staci wiggled around, her breathing getting heavier as she whispered, "Come on, baby. Come on. Tear my shit up. I'm ready for you. You better take this pussy now!"

If this girl said anything else to Troi, she knew it was entirely possible that she could come right there, just by the sound of Staci's voice and her scent, sticky on Troi's fingers and thick in the air. Troi reluctantly refrained from any more finger and oral play. Safe sex between two women felt so unnatural to her, but she could not have sex any other way with any woman, straight, gay, or otherwise.

Standing back up, she held Staci down firmly with one hand while the other reached for a condom from her back pocket, ripping the packet open with her teeth.

"What you got for me, Big Daddy?" Staci was writhing now, the handcuffs both restricting and exciting her. As Troi readied herself for the ceremony, steadying them both by shoving a leathered thigh along the slick backside of this hot young thing, Staci began breathing and moaning, as if she had watched one too many porn videos.

Young, "straight" girls really dug Troi's handcuffs. Anything considered freaky and kinky was fashionable. But the handcuffs served a much more important purpose. Troi slid the rubber along the length of Shaft, lubricating the tip with a little of her own saliva before ramming into Staci's hot pussy with a sharp thrust of her hips. Staci went flailing against the hood of the truck while Troi skillfully guided herself deep into Staci's center. They moved together, Troi going in deeper with every forceful thrust, while Staci gyrated against every push, ensuring an easy, slippery fit, full of friction. Her hips swayed and bounced, pushed and pulled, bumped and ground to some mad truncated rhythm in her head and in Troi's pelvis. Troi could have pumped inside of her until the break of dawn, but after the third set of multiple orgasms rocked Troi's body with dizzying episodes of heart-stopping miniseizures, sweat popping from what felt like everywhere, she had to disengage herself from the girl who had resigned herself to Troi in total submission. Troi had to ignore the girl's desperate pleas for more (they *always* wanted more)—a precautionary measure, as she was always in danger of giving too much away.

The drive to Staci's home in Brooklyn was quiet. These were awkward moments for Troi because nothing would ever come from these encounters. This was just how she liked it, just how she planned things. There was always the mystery of whether any of these women knew the real deal. That was part of the allure. Sometimes in the heat of passion, Troi could testify that it didn't really matter, because she knew she had skills, mad skills. She drove the girls insane with her shit.

With Staci, she had half a mind to leave the handcuffs on until they got to Staci's place, because Staci was all over her.

"I can't believe you're still hard!" Staci kept squealing whenever Troi failed to keep the girl's hand out of her lap.

Troi had half a mind to bend her over the back seat and slip her another heavy dose of Shaft, but Staci was too much into it.

In front of her brownstone, Staci wrote her phone number down.

"Can I get yours?" she inquired.

"Nah, that's not a good idea," Troi replied deliberately, not looking at her. It was all part of the routine.

"Why not?"

"It's not important. Maybe I'll see you again at Butter."

"Damn, it's like that?"

"Girl, if you knew, you couldn't handle it."

"Don't be so sure," Staci smirked, crumpling up her phone number and tossing it into Troi's lap before climbing out of the truck. Troi followed those long sculpted legs up the brownstone stairs with her own pretty, seductive, huntress eyes, before pulling away in her beautiful black truck into the cool November night.

NIGHT CRAWLER

Kristen Porter

She's the type who loves her porn, with her biker boots set atop a makeshift coffee table in a living room with mismatched furniture and the smells of stale beer. She likes to watch boys on boys pumping themselves, with mouths filled with throbbing cock. She's particularly fond of the pretty ones all bent over and limp and open, surrendering to their place.

As she looks at me, I can almost see the film frames cloud over her vision. They are of me, and the concrete wall she'd like to take me against and the sounds she thinks will come from my lips. She thinks she knows my kind and imagines that under the pleats of my plaid skirt are thighs covered in stockings built for a rough ride and the sink of her teeth. Her bait is probably dinner; she'll show up in the one suit she owns with hand-picked flowers. Romantic, but beyond dinner she won't part with a buck for her weekend fuck. She's the kind who thinks her humor is witty and, when up against a strong woman, comes up with mathematical equations like "Sorry, honey, two tops don't make a bottom."

I know what she's thinking. I watch as her eyes linger up and down my body. She leans in to speak to me, pausing as she inhales the smell of my still-damp hair. My full lips, perfectly painted the color of a Cape Cod sunset, have probably already got her thinking what it will be like to fuck this pretty little mouth of mine. Tonight, meeting in this bar, will be our first and only date. I picked her from the slew of online personals. Her headline? *Boidyke looking for fine machinery to ride. Hmmm,* I thought. Clearly, someone never taught this boidyke that a woman is not, in fact, machinery custom built for her riding pleasure. Clearly, she needs to be taught some manners. I took it upon myself to instill in her a, shall we say, different perspective of the female persuasion.

In the "interests" section of her personal she noted *schoolgirl skirts*—perhaps the only subject she paid attention to in school? She's probably thinking I wore this short skirt tonight for her visual pleasure, that I gussied myself up real nice in the hope she might find me attractive and grace me with her sexual dynamism. Guess again. I wear short skirts so I have room to pack Big Daddy, whose mission is to put bois like her in their place.

Big Daddy is tucked in under white cotton panties, packed way back with its head smothered tight in the cheeks of my ass. I like the pressure; the way the tip rubs against me when I cross and uncross my thighs. I've even turned it into a bit of a game. I time myself, keeping score of how long I can squeeze my cheeks together to hold it up there while I walk. In the course of one night out I may change bar stools three times, each time moving farther away from the bathroom, just to see if I can improve the number of paces I can strut with my dick wedged way up there. I wear boots up to my knees with room at the top to slide in Granddaddy's fishing knife, ready and willing to gut whatever I might have a taste for that night. I've seldom had chance to use it, but on occasion its handy proximity is without question a revelation.

I'm a product of my environment, you might say. Growing up with the women in my family was like being raised by a pack of wolves. They give new meaning to the words *femme fatale* and *black widow.* Instinctually we hunt, and survival remains our one inspiration. Let's face it, we live in an "eat or be eaten" world and I'm no vegan. I like my flesh right off the bone. The tougher the better. And in my mood tonight, the butcher the sweeter.

In a way, I like this boidyke. Her language is raw and grizzly, but when she laughs, this girlchild giggle comes out and even I admit it's a bit endearing. Her Southern charm is easy to sink into, with her "after you, darlin's" and "yes, ma'am's." But as any good fisherman would tell you, it's the very moment you lose yourself that you sacrifice your catch. I'm on a mission, and I definitely didn't curl these eyelashes for naught, so I use them, like a cat that bats around the mouse before its final kill. I feign the utmost interest in small talk when really she isn't saying much beyond touting her own sexual talents. How, boy, oh, boy can she do me right. Every now and again she points out some young pretty femme and tells me how she *sure* taught her.

"I like a girl who knows her place, if you know what I mean," she says with a wink. "It really just comes down to biology. Girls are built for ridin' and I assure you, pretty lady, you won't find a better driver." I don't bother to tell her that it is anatomy, not biology she is referring to. Her knee brushes up against mine under the wooden bar counter. My lack of yield gives her a moment's pause—but not enough to know what rough waters she's swimming into. She has never come head to head with a woman like me before. In her fantasy she hears me call her Daddy and *ooo* and *aah* over her undisciplined slaps to my ass.

She'll have scenes from porno tapes reeling through her head as my body glides along her torso to suck her off as only a good girl can do. Her dick will chafe the back of my throat as I keep my eyes open wide and look into hers as if this is the best damn lolly I've ever tasted. Then she'll sit up and take my asscheeks into her palms and move me up onto her strapped-on cock. She'll think she's giving me the ride of my life as I grab hold of the back of her head. What I find most amusing is that she thinks at the end of it, I'll feel protected in her well-muscled, butch boi arms. She'll make sure to inadvertently flex a few times with my head resting in the crook of her arm, while she plants kisses on my forehead, thinking *damn*, she did me good.

But her fantasy is just that. I didn't answer her personal because my social calendar had some unexpected openings. I answered because teaching these kind of bois a lesson has become my new vocation. And don't go getting all PC on my heart-shaped behind. I love a great boi. In fact, there's nothing better. But some bois out there are giving the rest of you a bad rap. This one likes those young new-to-the-scene girl-bottoms who, in their aim to please, to fit in, to be liked, snap up her bait—hook, line and sinker. Since I was taught we should aspire to be those things we appreciate in others, I thought I'd help her along.

In *my* fantasy, I lure her into the bathroom of this smoke-filled dive while coyly whispering, "We really shouldn't be doing this," and "What would happen if we got caught?" She latches her mouth onto my sharp hook because in all her bad-boi butchness she's oblivious to the night crawler dangling in front of her. I let her push me up against the wall, but only so I can get a tight grasp on her wrists and lock them behind her back with one hand. I push my pelvis into her and with her newfound awareness of my bulge against her crotch the struggle of forces begins.

"What the fu—" she begins to say as I grab hold of the top of her head and forcefully push her down to her knees. My heart is beating fast as I remember the thrill of fishing, when you first feel your line taut with the thrashing of desperation. She resists until I reach down and pull the shaft from my boot, flicking open its cool silver blade and resting it lightly against the side of her throat.

"Surprise, it's your turn now, *boi*," I say as I release my cramping buttocks and with my free hand pull out my cock. It smells of cunt juice, and her hesitation boils my fire. I think about all the baby girldyke hearts she has busted, all the femmes she has fucked raw, all the women who have succumbed to her guise of chivalry only to find out they were just *her* daily catch. She finishes up her dates with an after-dinner beer at the bar, talking smack about her latest conquest to the buddies. Bois like her have no problem giving it, but...

"Take it. Suck this big daddy down like a good boi now and no one has to get hurt," I say as I slap it against her flushed cheek. She reluctantly takes me into her mouth, my blade resting on her clavicle. "See, there now. With a little practice, you'll have yourself some proper table etiquette." I begin to move my hips back and forth, my ass bumping against the cold bathroom wall tiles. With each thrust, she pulls her head back against my firm hold. I pull the hook out of her mouth, release my hold on the knife, and consider throwing her back in—but I'm not done yet.

I step behind her and drop to the floor. We are both on our knees; with an arm tucked under her stomach, I pull her back onto me. I undo her button fly and shimmy her jeans down to her knees. She whispers something under her breath.

"Now, now, boi, don't you be cussing. You best be saving your breath to ask forgiveness for all your sins," I say, as I part her asscheeks and run the blunt end of the blade lightly across her puckered hole.

"It's about time you learned some manners, don't you agree?"

Her head hangs low, but nods slightly.

"Next time you're fishing for some unsuspecting girl to add another notch to that belt of yours, you'll remember tonight and think twice about it, now won't you?" I tell her as I wiggle the head of my dick against her ass. She's struggling so much I have to get right down to business. I lift her hips back and rest her tight philandering ass on the head of my cock. I rock her back and forth on Big Daddy until her body begins to release and she relaxes limply against the coolness of the concrete floor.

"Get you another?"

The bartender snaps me out of my fantasy. Boidyke's yammering away beside me about how she cleans up real nice. She hasn't even noticed my lack of attention, has yet to realize that if she can't see her reflection in my eyes looking back at her, she simply hasn't earned it. I lean into her and whisper real softly for her to follow me into the bathroom in a few minutes. The glow in her eyes is bright and for a moment I want to sink myself into it, like poor little Carrie Anne running to the light to escape her inner demons. But I know too well what she's thinking. I clench my ass tight and count the strides as I head off to the bathroom.

DOES SHE LOOK LIKE A BOY?

Tara-Michelle Ziniuk

When I ran through the door at work I was glad I had done my hair and makeup on the way. For the past while, my boss had been pestering me to be "as ready as possible as early as possible." She and I both knew that I didn't look quite like this when I wasn't at work, but I'm not sure she understood my untended body hair or my refusing her invitations to tanning salons. I'm a femmey girl, no doubt, but not the type to get all glammed up without occasion to. The other girls at work were the straight girl equivalent to high-femme all the time, mani-cured and face-masked; they also did not understand.

I kissed Darlena on both cheeks then bolted to the walk-in closet, which had been home to much slut-gear as well as my personal dressing room for nearly two years. I breathed in the scent of other people's perfumes and overcompensating chem-ical detergents, all stale and mixed together. Not a minute after I closed the door and stripped down to begin a frantic search for my PVC bra and corset set, Darlena walked in behind me.

"The four o'clock guy called back," she began *(oh please don't tell me he cancelled and I rushed here for nothing),* "and he wanted to know if you looked like a boy."

I laughed. "Did he look at our ad?" I asked.

"Apparently not. I directed him to the website but his Internet service was down. I wasn't sure how to respond so I just joked back with him and said, 'Well no, sir. Did you want her to?' And he said yes."

She was reading me for a reaction. This was not an environment that had fostered any sort of gender-bending positive play in the past, save a few male clients who liked to wear panty hose. My first instinct was that it was a crank call and I was wasting my time, *grrr.*

"So, you think he'll be a no-show?"

"I don't know, he sounded pretty sincere, and you're here now. Do you have a hat?"

I spent the next fifteen minutes scrambling to get out of my makeup and find masculine clothes among the leather and stilettos. I settled on a white dress shirt from an unclaimed bag of uniforms and schoolgirl attire, and found a white tank top to go under it. One of the other women at work had left behind a pair of dark-blue jeans with a wide black belt still in them. I pulled them on and they fit snug against my ass and thighs. I found a black cock in a box of sex toys and rinsed it in the sink before resting it against my already constricted cunt, and allowed myself to feel its stillness, rubbing my middle finger along the shaft. I positioned it so that it would be noticeable but not tacky, and zipped up the now very fitting pants.

When I came out of the washroom Darlena was waiting for me with the only hat she could find, a black cap with some anonymous Celtic symbol on it. It would do. I looked myself over in the full-length mirror. I certainly didn't look macho, I looked faggoty. I hoped that was the idea. The hall clock read five-to-four, the hour I anticipated the caller's arrival.

It was a good scene to have been called in for, more interesting than the bulk of them. I knew only that it was to be a dildo-training session and that this particular client had not seen any of the other girls before. I hoped he wouldn't have any huge unavoidable flaws, specifically that he didn't stink and wasn't eighty years old and waiting for his next heart attack. Though these possibilities occurred to me, I somehow was not as panicked as I had often found myself before. I was quite intrigued by this character who wanted curvy lipstick-lipped me in drag. Why hadn't he booked a call with a male dom? I imagined complicated answers to this question until there was a knock at the door. I poured some water for myself into a crystal wineglass and went into the room to meet my new submissive.

He was definitely more masculine-looking than I had been able to pull off, an interesting element for the scene. He looked young and wide-eyed. He appeared willing and nervous, but not fearful. "Very nice to meet you. You will call me Master," I said, in what I liked to call my best warm/ cool voice. I had impressed myself already by remembering that today I would be "Master" as opposed to "Mistress." I extended a hand and he shook it firmly before kissing it. I hadn't been sure of what to expect, but this pleased me. He was blushing as I motioned for him to have a seat. "We'll just have a little chat and then get things started." He nodded. I was unable to read his anxiety. "We use the code words *yellow* and *red* here, yellow for caution, red to stop the scene. You are familiar with these?" Another nod. "Have you done this before?" I asked genuinely.

"Similar things, but not exactly." He certainly was not talkative.

"But you do have experience with BDSM and you feel confident that you know your limitations?"

"Yes, Master." I could tell by his immediate submission to me that he did. He kept his eyes lowered, but I could see his wanting in them. There was no reason to take up more of our time together. I settled into character easily.

"I am your Master. You will do as I say, when I say to. You will be polite and courteous, and appreciative that I have taken up my valuable time to train you." As I stood he dropped to his knees in front of me.

"Yes, Sir. Thank you in advance for spending your time on me." He offered me a thick black collar with metal rings, and I thanked him by securing it tightly around his neck. He bowed his head and touched his nose to the polished tip of one of the too-large black army boots I was wearing. I rustled his hair before pulling his face up by it.

"Very good. Now why did you come here today?" No answer. "I asked you why you came here today."

"I came here to please you, Master."

"Now go back to what you were doing." He curled by my feet, tracing his nose along the seams of the boots. Then he did the same with his entire face, resting his cheek against my ankle. He slowly licked the stitching around the soles. Before he was quite done with the second one, I interrupted. "Back up on your knees." He was taller than me, and upright on his knees reached higher than my waist. I pushed him back so that he was sitting on the backs of his heels. His eye level was just below my swollen crotch. He seemed to look straight through the tops of my thighs. "You see something you like?" My voice was softer this time.

"Yes, Master. I do."

Again he lowered his head. I felt the rush of excitement that

I was intending for him electrifying my own body. We made eye contact, and though his body looked tough, the steady eyes that met mine looked like they had been hurt. They were focused now on something else. I nodded simply, testing to see if he did as well. A small well-hidden smile appeared as he faced my body. He ran his face along the zipper of my jeans, like he had done with my boots. He was slow and careful already so I didn't have to direct him. He pressed his face harder and harder into me. I could feel myself getting wet as much as I tried not to, as he started kneading my cock with his face. His lips ran over it through the denim, as he looked up for my approval. He looked brave and small. I gave him another nod and he gently started kneading with his teeth. I tried my hardest not to release the gasp in my chest that so desperately wanted to be let out.

I decided to regain control of the situation and, unzipping the jeans, took the dick out inches in front of his face.

I ran my fingers over his mouth and he sucked and lapped at them with his soft tongue. I thrust myself into his mouth. He gave me the sweetest, fiercest blow job I had known, putting everything into it. He let his mouth handle the cock expertly, paying attention to its curves and shape and not leaving out anything. He was in tune to my hips' rhythm and worked with and against it. I allowed myself to breathe heavily to let him know he was doing well, but I restrained myself from making any other sounds. I didn't want to stop him, but I wanted to make sure I took over the scene before I came. I backed out of his soft wet mouth. This time when I looked at him he looked less bashful and more confident, like he had regained some of his pride giving head like that. "Did you like that?" I barked. He did not flinch. He licked his lips and gave me a look I had come to know well through various female lovers. *Did you?* they asked silently.

"Yes, very much. Thank you." He blushed, smiling obviously this time. "Master."

I wanted to see if he was hard but was unable to tell because of the way he sat. I moved along quickly, because he had paid good money for the hour, but also because I was incredibly turned-on and didn't want to ruin the moment.

"You want more?"

"Yes. Please, Master."

"Are you going to behave yourself if I give you more? You are already very lucky to have been allowed to suck your Master's big cock like that. You know that, don't you?"

"Yes, Master. Thank you." He played along, knowing full well what he was entitled to during the session.

"Okay then, you must promise to be on your very best behavior. Bring me a condom, boy." I wanted to continue as much as he did and was pleased that he returned quickly with the basket of condoms and a bottle of lube. I pretended to eye the bottle he had handed me quizzically. "Oh, you were expecting me to go easy on you, were you?" I toyed with him, for both of us. He lowered his head in response, looking like a child about to break out in giggles. I imagined him being a strong butch lover of mine as I snapped on a glove and prepared to ready his waiting ass. I had him face the whipping post on the other side of the room and undress from the waist down. Off came the work pants and a pair of gray-specked boxer briefs. I noticed he kept his body pressed tight against the post. "Are you nervous?"

"No, Master." I didn't push it, as it was ideal positioning for my own fantasy. I instructed him to step back and make sure he kept his forehead touching the post. He complied with my demands easily, and I threw in a threat about the disciplinary actions I would be forced to take if he squirmed out of position.

I entered him at first cautiously, with one finger, then two.

I realized very soon that he had more experience than he had let on. I ran my other hand through what I assumed to be sweat on his inner thigh. He was moving his body accordingly, so I knew he wanted to be fucked. I thought about what he had said when he came in about not having done "exactly" this before, and wondered what specifically he had meant by that. Was he a fag experimenting with women? A "straight man" who frequented cruise parks, having anonymous lovers nightly? Maybe he had played out similar scenes with a woman lover before, who had since left him or become ill. I speculated for a moment too long and then snapped back to reality. Or as close to reality as I chose to make it: he was my handsome boy-dyke slave, a fine butch bottom, helplessly awaiting my hot femme dick to enter and take him over.

Caught up in my own imagination, but not so much that I wasn't paying attention, I spread the soft asscheeks before me and circled the tip of the silicone dick between them. I had, at some point in this fluster of daydream, work, and sweat, remembered to put on the condom. One last time I pushed my lubed fingers in and out firmly, and then pushed myself into him. He let out something between a squeal and a sigh, sounding like a young boy. I liked the power I felt hearing his surprisingly high-pitched sounds and continued to press myself into him and pull back. As this motion quickened and we fell into each other's rhythm, I began to grind my dripping cunt against his ass, playing with his insides. I pretended that the increasing sweat pouring down his legs was sweet girl cum and held the inside of his thigh against the palm of my hand.

I noticed that as he got more turned-on and as the fucking became rougher, he pulled away from me more, and pushed his weight against the post. I brought my arm around to the front of his neck. It was soft and tight. I ran my knuckles against his jaw, finding that his teeth were clenched. I ran my hand along his jawline, also soft and unusually free of stubble. His face was trembling with what seemed like fear.

Leaving one hand on his face, I slowly moved the other hand around to the front of his thigh. It was sticky wet and also trembled to my touch. I tried to stay strong and stern, but was both confused and excited. As I inched my hand upward he jerked away from me. I pulled her close to my body. The hand I had rested on her face came down and pressed against her collarbone. I felt the tiny recognizable ripples of a tensor-bandaged chest.

She heaved the heavy sigh of someone exposing a skeleton.

I moved my hand between her legs, revealing for certain the truth to my fantasy and this boy's well-hidden identity.

I sighed a sigh of relief, of pleasure, of the unknown future. I sat down on the floor, leaning my back against the wooden post. I pulled her down and continued to hold her against me. My hand ran through her sweaty hair. We had not yet made eye contact. When she finally looked at me her eyes were intense and concerned. *Are you mad?* they asked. I flashed her the same sexually charged and wanting smile she had given me after sucking me off.

Are you? my eyes asked back.

TAG!

D. Alexandria

"I hate getting older."

"Who doesn't?"

Keisha turned onto her side and propped herself on her elbow, looking at me. "We used to want to though, remember? I couldn't wait to get to eighteen, twenty-one, twenty-five."

"'Cause those ages mean somethin'. You ain't really legal until you can rent a car without the 'under twenty-five' surcharge." I remained lying on my back, staring up at the night sky. It was Keisha's twenty-ninth birthday and, understandably, she was upset. I had surprised her with a late-night picnic at one of our favorite camping spots, about an hour outside of the city. We were surrounded by dense forest and complete silence, save for crickets and numerous woodland animals going about their business. I'll be completely honest and say that camping really isn't my style. I'm a hundred percent modern butch who likes my TV time, my PlayStation 2, and if I wasn't smoking a blunt right now I'd be seriously missing my tunes. But

Keisha loves the quiet seclusion of camping and getting back to nature, so I deal 'cause I love her and making her happy is my contentment.

She sighed.

I looked over and took in the unbelievably cute pout on her cherubic face and instantly fell in love all over again. Keisha is one beautiful sista, and no one can tell me different. Standing at nearly five feet eleven, with a perfect brick-house body, she is the sexiest female to ever grace my bed. I could spend hours just looking at her whether she's curled up in a chair reading a book or languidly lying in bed after a break-your-back fuckfest. With her supple body, covered in the softest skin known to man, I can only hope I get to spend several blissful lifetimes enjoying this true model of what is Woman.

Out the corner of my eye, I saw her tremble. I immediately put out the blunt and headed for the stack of fallen twigs and branches we had collected to feed the fire.

"You don't care that you're turning thirty in a couple of months?"

I shrugged. "I dunno. I'm not crazy about it, nah, but I don't intend to lose sleep over it either. It's not like I can stop it, know what I mean?"

"I miss being a kid."

Oh, here we go. I rolled my eyes before looking at her. "Now, Keisha Everton, you know damn well you wouldn't want to be a kid again."

She looked at me with slight annoyance. "And what makes you so sure?"

I moved to where she sat, straddling her legs. My voice dipped low as I whispered in her ear, "'Cause if you weren't grown, you wouldn't be able to take my dick deep in that thick pussy of yours, that's why."

I swear I felt her body temperature rise as she took in a sharp breath.

"You're so bad," she whispered, giggling.

I gave her a soft kiss, barely touching her lips, just teasing her. She remained still, eyes closed and face turned upward, allowing me to touch her in any way I pleased. I love that about her. I prefer a woman who just gives in to whatever her lover wants. I'm not saying that Keisha doesn't get hers, 'cause believe me that body holds a very powerful sexual creature, and she can come at you like a pit bull to get what she wants. However, she has this perfect sense of when to just let me do my thing and that makes my head spin with countless ideas of how to make her sing those cums I feel to my core.

When I met Keisha, one of the first things she told me was that she wasn't a fan of kissing. I, for one, feel that kissing is one of the finer points of fucking. Kissing is an intimate act, I ain't about to front on that, but a single kiss, if done right, can make a female part those thighs for you. And right now, Keisha's breaths were becoming shallow as I gently sucked on her lips, letting the tip of my tongue quickly glide across them. I started to lightly nip them, careful not to bite down too hard, and I felt her thighs press together, my signal that she was getting wet and ready.

Despite wanting to just push her down and spread her open, I also wanted to draw this out as long as I could, and just as I was about to settle in for a little torture, she pulled back. "You wanna play tag?"

"Excuse me?" I couldn't have heard right.

"Let's play tag."

I sat back on my heels, needing to look at her face to make sure she was serious. She was. "Keisha, baby, seriously..."

"Angel, c'mon, it'll be fun." She was already wiggling out

from underneath me to get to her feet. "How often can we do silly things like this?"

"Uh, we don't, 'cause we grown," I said.

She made a face, but winked. "C'mon, baby, play with me."

Okay, now she really was losing it. "Keisha, it's almost midnight and we're in the middle of the woods. Who, in their right mind, would play tag right now?"

She reached for her K-Swiss, an old beat-up pair that she wouldn't be caught dead in back in the 'hood, and slipped them on. "Where's your sense of adventure?"

"I was about to show you before you moved."

She smiled. "Please, baby? Just indulge me."

I was already out here complaint free, wasn't I? That, right there, was some serious indulgence. I hadn't answered her and she gave a dramatic sigh, hands on her hips. "Okay, what if I make it interesting for you?"

Hmm. "How?"

She thought for a moment, before a wicked glint came into her eyes. "I'll strip."

I chuckled. "Get the fuck outta here."

"I'm serious." She was now grinning. "I'll strip naked right here and then take off. All you gotta do is catch me. That ain't hard, is it? And if you want, we'll even play back and forth."

"*You* chasin' me?" I smirked.

"What? You afraid I'll be better than you?"

I rolled my eyes. "Whateva."

"Well, what then? Scared? Too dark for ya?"

"Oh, please!" I said sarcastically.

Keisha reached for the hem of her sweater and lifted it slightly, baring her soft stomach. "Don't tell me you're gonna punk out on me, Angel. What would your boys say if I told them you were too afraid to chase *me* in the dark? And naked, at that?"

I stared at her. Well, actually I was staring at the bottom curves of her bare breasts, which she teasingly revealed as she continued to slowly lift her top. I felt my clit twitch at the thought of touching them, getting my hands and mouth on them. Damn, I was aching for her in a serious way.

Her hips swayed provocatively as she pulled the sweater off, dropping it on the blanket. She stood before me, slowly writhing to a melody only she could hear, yet I could see her full hips bumping out the beat in the air. Her large breasts hung freely, moving with her, both nipples tight and hard. I caught myself biting my lip as I watched, and before I knew it I was wondering how long it would take before I could catch her—*if* I gave in, of course. When I said it was dark, I meant it. In fact, if the slightest bit of cloud cover had hit the moon, I wouldn't have been able to see my hand in front of my face. But thankfully, I could probably see about a good ten feet problem free, and even if I gave her a slight head start, I could catch her before we got in too far.

"C'mon, Angel baby." Keisha's hands found her dark nipples and she gently tugged on them. "You *can* catch me, right? I mean, your ass hasn't gotten *that* old yet."

And she knew that shit would work. My pride was too high. I grumbled as I got to my feet, pulling off my jersey. (I'd play along, but I wasn't about to ruin a perfectly good Patriots jersey while up in the mix.)

Keisha's face lit up at my acceptance and she began tugging down her jeans.

"Leave on your panties," I said suddenly, eyeing the pale pink cotton thong hugging her most intimate curves. I wasn't sure why, but I didn't want her completely naked...yet.

She gave me a sly look as she left them alone, pulling the jeans off her long legs and tossing them on top of the sweater. She stood before me in just her panties and sneakers, looking as fine as she wanted to be, and god help me if she didn't look as if she were in her element; her ebony skin glowing from the camp-fire, long limbs ready and taut; even her hair, which was pulled in a tight ponytail earlier, now had strands that had fallen loose, kissing her cheeks. All she needed was some animal skin and a spear and I'd be at her feet in worship.

I silently appreciated my having had the foresight to wear my battered pair of Tims, before I crouched low, feeling my strap press against my left inner thigh, and shuddering in anticipation. "Ten! Nine! Eight!"

Keisha took off. I watched her slip into the darkness, the last sight of her the jiggling of her ass as she ran away. I took a deep breath to calm myself and finished counting, stretching out the last numbers to give her more time.

"Three! Two! One!" I called before I followed. It was dark as hell. I was rushing through the trees, my eyes darting from side to side to catch sight of her as I maneuvered around rocks and brush, batting branches out of the way. I had assumed I'd be able to find her right off the bat, but as I moved, I realized that my first instincts were right and it was going to be a helluva task to see anything. The night air was still, the darkness threatening to envelope me indefinitely. We might as well have been playing hide-and-seek. I was trying to think like Keisha, wondering how she'd try to move, when a branch snapped loudly under my boot. I silently cursed and slowed my pace.

As I moved, taking measured breaths, my heart was pounding and I could hear every pulsing thud in my ears. I was stepping gingerly, trying not to make a sound as I listened out for her, knowing that if she was smart, she would be trying to remain low 'cause of her height. I paused by a slim tree with low-hanging branches and squatted, my eyes now adjusting to the darkness. I was hoping to see the moonlight against her skin, but was having no such luck as I peered all around me. I figured I had been moving for almost ten minutes in one direction, and wondered if I should double back, just in case Keisha was purposely staying close to the campsite.

I was about to turn around when something in the air caught my attention. I stopped and inhaled deeply, my lips spreading in a wide grin as I recognized a scent almost as familiar as my own.

"You're wet, baby girl, I can smell it," I called out, my clit throbbing behind my dick as I surveyed the area. She was close, I knew it; unless she was *so* aroused her scent was just lingering in the air. I took a few steps toward the right and heard rustling to my left. I turned my head in time to see a quick blur of pink rush past a couple of trees.

I chuckled as I quickly followed, barely seeing her move ahead of me, but able to hear her quick, excited breaths. No doubt, she was completely worked up. I was right on her tail and able to smell her arousal even more, knowing at this very moment she wanted it just as much as I did. She suddenly made a right turn, and I did the same, knowing exactly where she was headed. I increased my pace, my breaths short as I pumped my arms, willing myself to pull ahead. In a few minutes I broke through the trees and stepped onto one of the hiking trails we often took, this one leading down to a small pond about a mile away. I stepped back into the trees, and quietly counted until I heard her footsteps.

Just as she was about to pass me, I lunged out, my arms looping around her waist, and pulled her close to me.

"Gotcha!" I roared as she struggled in my arms.

"Dammit!" She gasped heavily before accepting a deep kiss from me. I was feeling drunk on the adrenaline that was coursing through me. Keisha fell into me, her arms lacing around my neck as she hungrily returned my kisses while still trying to catch her breath. I relished the feel of her naked body as my hands glided over her now slightly sweaty skin. I cupped her ass with some force and pulled her tighter against me so she could feel my dick through my jeans.

I pulled my lips away. "You want it?"

"Yes," she hissed, as her lips reached for mine.

I ducked my head, giving her earlobe a soft flick with my tongue. "How bad do you want it, baby girl?"

"Fuck, I want it bad."

"What do you want, Keisha?"

She gave a half groan, half whine. "Angel, I want your dick! Please! Now!"

I gave her ass a tight squeeze with both hands before pulling away. Just as she tried reaching for me again, my hand swung out, connecting with an asscheek, the smack echoing around us.

"You're it!" I smirked before I turned and ran.

"Asshole!" she screamed, but I heard her footsteps behind me.

I stayed on the trail, moving quickly until I was about a quarter of a mile away from camp, before turning left. This part of the woods had trees that grew closer together, and obviously, since there wasn't a defined path, I had to make my own, holding on to tree after tree for balance as I moved. I forced myself to move faster, as the sound of Keisha's footsteps started to fade. When I could still see a glimpse of camp far to the right, I darted to the left and crouched low behind a couple of bushes and waited.

After a few minutes of not seeing her, I began to worry, wondering if maybe the path I had taken wasn't as forgiving to Keisha in her sneakers. But before I could rise to investigate, I heard a branch break to my left. I had to grin. The girl had taken another route, hoping to cut me off as I had done to her earlier. But, of course, she hadn't anticipated my beating her and hiding out. I watched as she stood still, trying to listen out for me as she searched. She looked absolutely gorgeous. Her body glistened with sweat in the moonlight, her hair a complete and captivating mess, and every breath she took forced her breasts to slightly lift. Damn, I needed to have her pussy wrapped around my dick. She caught sight of camp and gave another hopeless look around before taking a step toward the glow of the campfire.

I jumped out and grabbed her, pulling her hard to me as I kissed the back of her neck.

"I guess we know who's best, huh?" I taunted as I held her arms to her side.

She couldn't help but giggle as she squirmed in my grip.

"You cheated," she gasped.

"You *wanted* to fuck up, so I could catch you again, don't front," I pointed out as I took a few steps forward, forcing her to move with me until she stood before a large tree. I placed a hand on her shoulder and forced her down to her knees, facing away from me.

Gasping for breath, Keisha planted both hands on the ground beneath her, her ass high in the air. My movements were quick, and before she knew it, I was behind her, jeans unzipped, dick in hand. I grabbed hold of her panties by the thin strip of fabric in the back, and was about to pull them to the side, when I thought better of it and gave a rough tug, tearing them away from her body. Keisha gave a loud gasp, bucking her hips in anticipation. There was no point in drawing this out, 'cause we were both primed. I pushed into her deeply, my entry the smoothest it's ever been 'cause of how wet she was. She groaned loudly, pushing back against me, her ass warm against my denim-covered thighs.

I sat back on my heels, getting a good grip on her wide hips as I pulled out to the head and then pushed back in, wanting to give her every inch of me. She was so wet that even in the dark I could see her juices glistening on the dick, and she was making guttural noises every time I entered her. My fingers dug into her flesh as I stepped up the pace, just enough to watch her asscheeks shake with every move we made.

"So, you got your ass caught up, huh?" I asked, giving a cheek a playful swat.

"Shiiit," she whispered.

"What was that?" I slapped her ass again, a bit harder.

"Dammit, Angel," she cried out, her ass starting to rotate on my dick.

"What, baby girl?" I asked as I gave her a quick thrust that made her body jump.

"It feels so goooood, fuck." She let her head fall forward as she quickened her hips.

I weighed my options and decided I wanted to enjoy a show. I stopped moving and removed my hands.

Keisha's head snapped up and she looked silently back at me.

"Who told you to stop? Keep going." I gave her ass a hard slap and she whimpered. "Come on, Keisha, move that ass."

Her eyes met mine for a moment, and I saw the lustful twinkle in them before she began moving her hips. I remained still, keeping my hands at my sides as I watched the woman I love fuck herself on my dick. She was working it like only a sista could, her pussy literally pulling my dick into it as she threw herself back and forth. I was mesmerized by every move she made; how her lower half seemed to have a life of its own and how my body was oh so willing to oblige its manipulations. She suddenly lifted her left leg, and I swear on everything that I am, my dick got sucked in deeper, and I quickly grabbed the leg to balance her as her ass started to ricochet off my body. In this position, I had a perfect view of her pussy greedily consuming my dick and her clit swollen and full, standing away from her body. I pulled her leg back, holding it against me, and reached for that clit, massaging it.

"Sweet Jesus..." Keisha wailed and I watched her fingers dig into the earth. I gently pulled on that slippery nub, feeling it pulsate and knowing she was gonna blow at any moment. I started tapping on one side of her clit, as I resumed moving, keeping her locked in her position.

"Yes, Angel, yes!" she cried as I fucked her. I was slamming into her harder and harder, hearing the slapping sounds of her ass connecting with my body, and I could feel the beginnings of my own cum. I was on a mission to fill and stretch that pussy to the hilt, jabbing her like a piston. She was back to whimpering, only louder this time, every lunge I made causing her entire body to convulse.

Just when I was sure she was 'bout to cum, I let go of her leg and quickly pushed a firm finger into her ass and she hollered, her body seizing and then freezing as she came, the song that I practically live for escaping her lips. I was still working her pussy as my finger dug in deeper, forcing every shudder out of her beautiful body. I bit my lip hard as I silently came, unable to take my eyes off her.

Keisha collapsed on the ground, and I knew that once morning came and she saw all the dirt and bits of leaves in her hair she'd freak, but I couldn't care less as I carefully pulled out of both her holes and lay beside her. We were both breathing heavily, and I found myself staring up at the night sky again.

"You were right," she said, still gasping.

"About what?" I turned to look at her and saw that familiar wicked glint in her eyes.

"About not really wanting to be a kid again," she replied. "'Cause only grown folks can play tag like that."

All I could do was laugh.

HOMECOMING QUEEN

Anna Watson

In the park after supper, Jenna leaned against a jungle gym and watched Pierre, her mother's middle-aged Pekinese, totter to and fro, lifting his curly leg. She was home for Thanksgiving, incognito, relaxed. She didn't know anyone in town anymore.

"Mind putting him back on his leash?" The voice was low and raspy, coming from somewhere behind her. Jenna startled, and snapped out of the postbrisket reverie she'd been enjoying. Her mom made killer brisket.

"Sure, yeah, of course. Sorry!" She whistled for Pierre, who obligingly trotted over and let himself be leashed.

"Thanks—it's just that Geordie can get a little too frisky." Jenna looked at the dog, a skinny, cheerful basset hound, then up at the woman, who was wearing a suit and tie, her salt and pepper hair buzzed, her biceps bulging. Jenna came to attention immediately, breasts up and out as if she were modeling the most delectable lingerie instead of her slouch-around-Mom's-house tatty sweats.

"Hey—we were in high school together! You're Maude, right?" It came back to her all at once: the shy, nerdy girl who transferred to Christ the King junior year and became the star of the soccer team. The one who always wore loafers and white button-down shirts; the one Jenna's crowd avoided like the plague; the one, Jenna realized with a feeling like winning the lottery, who was, and always had been, butch, butch, butch.

"That's right." Maude looked her over, grinning and raising an eyebrow. Jenna blushed and put a hand on her arm, about to introduce herself, just as Pierre and Geordie got into a snuffling, yipping scuffle, and had to be separated.

Later that evening, Jenna emerged triumphant from her mother's walk-in closet, a pair of strappy, four-inch heels in one hand, and in the other, a little wisp of a dress, black, low in front and lower in back. Her mother puffed out her cheeks in embarrassment and made a grab, but Jenna held it out of reach.

"Secret life, Mom?" she asked, examining the dress more closely. There was a bust variation between the two of them, but she expected she could squeeze in there, which was good, because the fanciest thing she'd packed was jeans. Who knew she was going to need date wear this vacation?

"Oh, you know." Her mother smoothed the bedspread and straightened a few perfume bottles on the dresser. "Your father likes me to wear that. Not to go out, of course, just, you know, around the house. Now for heaven's sake, I have to go get started on that turkey or we won't have any dinner tomorrow!"

"Huh," Jenna said to her mother's retreating back, adding to herself, "then I bet you have something else I can use in here." Sure enough, after digging through the lingerie drawer, Jenna scored a pair of black fishnets and a lacy, red thong, but the matching bra just wasn't big enough. The dress, though, when she tried it on, was so tight around the chest and provided so much cleavage all on its own, that Jenna didn't need anything more.

After her parents had gone into their bedroom and Jenna could hear her dad snoring over the drone of the ten o'clock news, she got her mother's long down coat—actually, it had been hers for a brief and stylistically unfortunate period in the '80s during high school—and snuck out of the house. She walked to Maude's parents' and settled in to wait in the driveway where Maude had told her to. There was a motion light that came on whenever she shifted position, and she kept expecting Geordie to sense her out there and start barking. It was one of the tract houses near the electrical plant, and over the beating of her heart and the in/out of her breath, Jenna could hear the generator's low hum. She shivered, her feet swelling in the too-tight pumps, her pussy wet and growing wetter as she thought about the quick-but-thorough hug Maude had given her that afternoon.

At last, the lights in what must have been Maude's parents' bedroom clicked off. Almost immediately, the garage door opened, and Maude was beckoning to her. As soon as she got in, Maude wrapped her in another hug, holding her up as Jenna had a bit of a rag doll moment, succumbing to the sensations of Maude's biceps pressing against her ear; Maude's cologne, something with a hint of cedar; Maude's lips in her hair; the feel of Maude's dick pressing against her thigh.

"Come on, now," Maude whispered. "And don't make any noise—they're light sleepers. If my brother finds out you're here, it will be all over school tomorrow, and little Miss Popular won't be so popular anymore."

Jenna muffled a gasp against Maude's shoulder and let herself be led through the dark kitchen and up carpeted stairs to a room at the end of the hall. Maude shut the door quietly.

"It doesn't lock," she said in a low voice. "And my mother

will come check on me if she hears anything—she's been worried about me because my grades are dropping. And you know why? You know why my grades are dropping? Because of you. All I can think about is you." She pushed Jenna against the door and ran her hands up under the coat, her breath deepening and catching in her throat as she felt the dress, the fishnets.

"I've seen you," whispered Jenna, arching her back so her breasts came into Maude's hands. "You sit in the bleachers and watch when we're practicing cheers. The other girls think you're so creepy. I can feel your eyes on me. It makes me nervous, but I like it. I don't know why. You're so strange—everyone says you're a dyke."

Maude pulled Jenna's coat off and let it slide to the floor. The room was dark except for light from a streetlamp shining through the window onto the single bed. "Your boyfriend sits in the bleachers watching you too, doesn't he? He doesn't know you're showing off for me when you do the splits and jump real high, your titties bouncing. He thinks you're doing it for him."

"But I'm showing off for you," sighed Jenna, as Maude's thumbs found her nipples. "When he kisses me, I'm thinking about you, and if he ever found out, he would kill you."

She was pinned to the door, Maude's body heavy against her, Maude's hands on either side of her head. "Don't make any noise, little Cheerleader," Maude hissed, and shoved the side of her hand into Jenna's mouth just in time. Jenna grabbed it with her teeth and moaned. "That's right," breathed Maude, her eyes gleaming. She pulled back her hand and gathered Jenna up, leaving the ridiculous coat crumpled on the floor. Maude laid her down on the bed, propping her head up on a pillow, straightening the dress over her thighs. "Let me look at you, baby. Let me look at Miss Popular, Miss Cheerleader. Let me see you now. Who's got you now, Miss President of the French Club?"

Jenna was panting, her whole body moving with her breath. No one had ever treated her like this, not even her last lover, who had claimed to be such a big bad top, and certainly dressed the part, but had only ever talked about spanking her and never did it.

"You have me!" she said too loudly, and Maude's forearm came down across her mouth, hurting her lips, making it so she could hardly breathe.

"That's right, I do. And you have to be quiet. If you make noise, I stop and you go home."

Jenna nodded, then shook her head, *No, I won't make noise, I promise, no noise.* She put out her tongue to lick the rough material of Maude's suit, then nibbled it. Maude took her arm away and put her lips to the wet spot, looking down at her.

"This is a slutty dress," she whispered, starting to move her hands possessively over Jenna's body. "This is a slutty outfit— look at you, red lipstick, fishnets—you look like a whore in this stuff. I thought you were a wholesome girl, a good girl."

"No," whispered Jenna. "No, I'm not."

"Not a good girl?" Maude came close to her and brushed her lips in a brief kiss. Jenna moaned and arched, and there was the arm over her mouth again. "You aren't a good girl at all," Maude whispered, breath hot in Jenna's ear. "All the time you're walking around school with your pack of popular friends, and inside your Calvin Kleins your pussy is throbbing for this, isn't it?"

She grabbed Jenna's hands and pinioned them over her head, then straddled her face. She pressed her dick against Jenna's mouth, filling her world with its shape and feel. Jenna rubbed her cheek against it, her lips, trying to catch it with her mouth, struggling to get her hands on it.

"You can't wait to get a feel of my cock, can you, Homecoming Queen?" Maude held her hands tighter and all she could do was moan quietly into Maude's zipper.

"No noise," whispered Maude. "No noise, or I stop." She swung her leg over and stood beside Jenna, who closed her eyes in anticipation. She could feel Maude wrapping something around her wrists, tying her to the headboard. She whimpered, opening her eyes, and saw Maude standing over her, inspecting her breasts, her legs. "What a slut," she murmured. "Show me how much you want it, slut," and then she was on top of her, elbows and forearms trapping her head, kissing her hard. Jenna breathed and melted under her weight, letting it push her fully into the bed, opening to the tongue calmly fucking her mouth. She couldn't help herself, a loud moan escaped her, and instantly the delicious weight was gone, Maude had untied her hands and was on the other side of the room picking up her coat and holding it out to her.

"I won't do it again!" Jenna managed in a ragged whisper. "I promise!"

Maude stared at her, eyes narrowed, then nodded and dropped the coat, coming back to stand beside the bed. She placed Jenna's hands on the headboard, but didn't tie them. "Don't let go," she ordered. "Don't make any noise. Wait here."

Jenna closed her eyes, grabbing on to the posts, her body heaving and trembling. Maude left the room and didn't come back for a long time. Jenna could hear the heat in the house going on and off, the dog patrolling the hall, cars on the distant highway, and underneath it all, the steady hum of the power plant, a bass note that went on and on.

At last the door opened and there was Maude, pristine in her suit. Jenna felt rumpled and whorish in her mother's dress, sticky and wanting. Maude gave her a drink of water from a glass with a straw in it, holding up her head, smoothing her hair.

Jenna blinked tears out of her eyes and hoped Maude wouldn't see, but she did.

"Been a long time since you were with someone who knew how to take care of you, baby?" she asked, and Jenna nodded. "Well, I'm going to take care of you, don't you worry. All that time you spend hanging out with those straight rich kids, and they just have no idea, do they, baby? No idea what a slut you are, how much you need to get fucked by the dyke, the one they make fun of, the one you don't say hi to in the hall, but the one you're thinking about when you lie in your bed at night and lift up your nightgown and touch yourself—because you do that, don't you? You're not such a good girl late at night when you're alone in your little Laura Ashley bed, touching yourself, are you?"

Jenna panted, shaking her head. "No, I'm not."

"Not what?"

"Not a good girl. I'm a bad girl."

Maude cocked her head. "What's that?" she whispered. "I can't hear you."

Jenna took a breath, about to say it louder, then stopped herself. It was a trick. Maude was looking at her expectantly and there was that sadistic gleam again.

"I'm a bad girl," breathed Jenna, so quietly that Maude had to lean over to hear her. "Your bad girl." She gripped the bedposts tighter as Maude dropped onto her mouth, kissing her softly, sweetly.

"Hey! What are you doing, slut?" Maude had Jenna's earlobe between her teeth, her hand pressing on Jenna's bucking cunt.

"Please." Jenna pressed her pussy into Maude's hand.

"You want me to do something with this?" Maude asked coolly. "Hmm." She left Jenna's side and knelt on the bed between her legs. She ran her hands up and down Jenna's thighs and calves, the sensation exquisite through the fishnets. Jenna pumped her pussy up and down, past caring about anything but her own pleasure.

"Hmm," said Maude again, slipping her fingers under the waistband of the fishnets and beginning to peel them off. "Let's see." She took the stockings down to ankle level and Jenna hoped she would take off her heels, but she didn't, leaving her hobbled. Maude smiled at the lacy red thong, then slid it down to rest above the stockings.

"Well, well. Do your preppy friends know you shave your pussy, Miss Cheerleader? Does your boyfriend know? Or did you do it just for me? I think you did it just for me, didn't you? And look how wet you are! Just like an animal in rut." She settled into a more comfortable position, her face right above Jenna's pussy, but not too close. "You want to give it to me so bad, then go ahead, baby. Feed it to me."

Jenna grabbed hard on to the bedposts and lifted her ass as high as she could, but she couldn't go quite far enough. She moaned in frustration and Maude smirked. "What are you waiting for? I can smell it, but there's nothing in my mouth. God, you're wet, you whore. All right, I'm going to help you out a little. Stay like that."

She lowered her mouth. Maude hovered there, breathing, then slowly dipped her tongue along the slit, just the slightest pressure, and the warmth of her breath. Jenna trembled, her thighs and belly spasming as Maude brought her hands up under her ass, cupping the cheeks, allowing Jenna to rest there. Maude lifted Jenna's pussy to her mouth and rubbed and licked, sloppy and wet, no pattern, no rhythm, just random pressure, slobbery tongue, spit trickling down the crack of Jenna's ass. If Maude hadn't been holding her up, there was no way Jenna could have kept the position; as it was, her calves and feet were starting to cramp and her hands were falling asleep, although there was no way in hell she was going to let go of the bedposts. Just when she thought she wouldn't be able to stand the rush of conflicting, crazy-making sensations any longer, Maude pulled her face out of Jenna's cunt and growled, "A nasty girl like you can probably come more than once, am I right?" Jenna made a groan of agreement. "So show me," Maude ordered. "Ride me." She lowered her face again, this time her tongue flat and businesslike against Jenna's clit. She pulled Jenna close with one arm and gave her a hand to bite, just in the nick of time, as Jenna was already coming, pistoning herself against Maude's face, screaming as quietly as she could.

"Shh, shh," cautioned Maude, lowering Jenna to the bed and rolling on top of her. "You can let go now. I'll hold you."

Jenna gratefully abandoned her grip on the bedposts and grabbed hard on to Maude who had started rocking against her.

"You liked that, didn't you, baby, you liked feeding me your hungry little pussy, didn't you, Homecoming Queen; you pretender, what would your boyfriend say if he saw you here with me, letting the big dyke eat you out, begging for her dick? Let me hear you, baby. Beg me for it."

Jenna could think of nothing clever to say, only, "Yes, please, I want your dick, fuck me, put it in me, fuck me!"

Maude's eyes were half-closed and her forehead was shiny with sweat. Her breathing quickened as she moved against Jenna, then she rolled off and turned her over, pulling off the pumps and fishnets and thong, and shoving her knees apart. Jenna could hear her unbuckling her belt, unzipping her trousers; then she was covering her, easing her dick in, slowly filling her pussy. Jenna made noise into the pillow, pushing back. Just rocking gently at first, then gaining momentum, hitting her stride, Maude fucked her, reaching underneath to find her tits, squeezing them with both hands, using them for purchase, pinching the nipples hard.

"Such a slut, such a slut," she whispered.

Jenna lifted up onto her hands and knees and pushed back, panting and groaning. Her throat hurt from all the screams she was keeping inside. Maude reached down with one hand and found her clit, and Jenna bucked against the hard fingers, coming with a roar of pleasure that stopped them both cold.

They heard a door open and footsteps in the hall.

"Maudie?" an older woman's voice called. "Maudie, do you have the dog in there with you? Are you all right?"

Maude drew in a breath, trying to stop laughing. The two of them were giggling like fiends, clutching each other, practically falling off the narrow bed.

"Fine, Mom! I'm fine! Nightmare or something!"

"Well, all right." Slowly the footsteps went back down the hall.

"You almost got me busted," Maude hissed, no longer laughing. She had pulled out and was holding Jenna tightly. "I won't forget that. I told you to be quiet, and you weren't quiet. You can't follow the simplest rule. I won't forget that, either, and next time you're going to take your punishment, aren't you, Cheerleader?" She reached for Jenna's ass, roughly shoving aside the dress Jenna had yanked down, squeezing her cheeks, painfully raking them with blunt fingernails. Jenna shuddered.

"Yes," she said so softly she could barely hear herself. "Yes."

Maude pressed her lips together and shook her head, frowning. "Such a slut, such a bad girl. Someone obviously needs to take you in hand. Your boyfriend certainly can't keep you in line, that's clear, and he sure isn't giving you what you need. So next time, we'll go somewhere you can make all the noise you want, little Cheerleader. All the noise your nasty little heart desires. I'll get you alone and you can just go ahead and scream and scream, but your friends won't hear you, no one will hear you, no one will come rescue you. Now come sit on my lap and be good to me until we're sure my mom's gotten back to sleep and I can sneak you out of here. We have school tomorrow. Come here, Homecoming Queen. And remember. Be very, very quiet."

And Jenna was.

ROULETTE

Shannon Cummings

Women got there earlier than the crowds at the nearby South of Market bars. Straight from work, proudly displaying the sweat of a day's work on their clothes. Tidying up would have been a sign of vanity, of femininity. A glob of pomade to grease the hair back was all the evening wear they needed.

There was an unspoken rule that you couldn't park your bike in front of the club if it was smaller than someone's who had already arrived. Think your ride is better than someone else's, you better be prepared to defend it. The only exception was of course if you had a high femme riding bitch.

If you arrived late, you had to park your bike a few blocks away and hope you could get to the club without being roughed up by the neighborhood crew. A few trucks lined the alley out front. No one messed with you if you had a truck. It was assumed it was for work and was therefore off limits. Jobs were scarce, so if you could earn a living without losing your edge you were never ridiculed.

Lou had gone there on many occasions, sometimes returning home via the emergency room after bottles had been broken or blades pulled. Fights often started over motorcycles or the call of a pool shot. Or someone talking about how some stone had cracked.

The worst fight had happened after one girl had underestimated the locker room talk and bravado of both her lovers. While trading tales over whiskey, they realized just how much they had in common and ended up in a brawl. The next day they both called her to say they had defended her honor. But it was their own they were fighting for. One got a cut just above her eye; nearly blinded her, the doctor had said. The other's hand was sliced along the life-line, or was is it the love-line, when she grabbed the blade swinging at her. She lost the use of her thumb and earned three months' disability leave from her machinists union. Women practiced their swaggers and rubbed their imaginary beards during pauses in conversation. It was a club for women with a rule of "no girls allowed." I was dying to go.

For six months, I had been crashing at Lou's place. I had run out on my last lover and showed up on her doorstep. I had taken over closet space and control of the tape deck, had started four kitchen fires, and had run up a long distance phone bill to my sister out east. Lou regularly threatened to kick me out but I would always coo to her until she got into bed so she could get to work on forgiving me. She was a good fuck and I was determined to stay. Sometimes when she was at work I would hustle some money at the pool hall to get by, pay a phone bill, or buy something sexy to wear so she wouldn't notice I had trashed her apartment. And her life. She was the first lover I ever had who knew a compliment should be taken as a request for more. I steadily stroked her ego and she let me stay.

"Dress sexy," Lou tells me. "We are going out."

I dress hurriedly and return for her approval. She looks me over, undoes another button on my blouse, and leans in to trace her tongue over the now exposed lace of my bra. "Tonight I'm taking you to the bar." She grabs her cigarettes, sighs into her nearly empty wallet, and slides both of them into her pockets.

"Who's going to be there?" I ask her, trying not to sound overly curious.

"It will be crowded. Nanc will be there, too. Just be on your best behavior."

Nanc, Lou's best friend and sometimes enemy. We had spoken on the phone a few times.

"Lou there?"

"No."

"She leave you all alone?"

"Yeah, she's out. I'll tell her you're looking for her."

"No, I mean, if you're alone, why don't I just come on over. We can wait for her together."

"I don't think that's the best idea. She'll be home soon."

"She says you're real pretty. Why don't I come over so I can tell her what I think of you."

"Maybe...some other time. I'll tell her you called."

"Ah, come on, she's been talking about how you're a wild one, that you can't ever get enough. You're probably rubbing your clit raw right now. I'll just come over and help you out. Why don't I just come over there and introduce myself to your...."

"Ummm.... I should really go. Bye."

We hadn't met but I had replayed her words in my head enough to recognize her voice anywhere. The best sex is always in your head, and Nanc had a knack for climbing into mine.

Lou parks the truck near the bar's entrance and comes around to open my door and look me over. "Who do you love?" she asks, brushing my hair back.

This well-rehearsed mantra to sooth her fragile ego spills forth: "I love you, Lou, you know that. Only you. You know you are the only one who can keep me happy."

"Is that right?" She smiles a bit and pushes me against the side of the truck to kiss me and then she pulls back, seems to be waiting for more. It is not the cock but the compliment that is the way to a butch's heart.

So I continue. "You know you are my love. You turn me on more than anyone else ever could. How many times have I told you so? I'm not going anywhere. Don't you worry, baby."

Lou looks me square in the eyes and says, "No matter what happens tonight, you just remember that."

With her arm around my waist, we head down the damp back street. I can see the bikes in silhouette and the shape of a crowd of burly women hanging in the doorway of the bar. There is a whistle or two as we approach, then smiles and nods to Lou as she ushers me inside. The room is dim but everywhere I can see the dark huskiness of the most handsome women. There are squeaks of leather as people turn and a hand brushes my leg now and then in an almost accidental way. Now I fully understand why femmes need a chaperone here.

I like my women tough. The rougher edged and bigger, the better. I like to watch them get restless, their tough exteriors trembling under thick denim when they talk to me. I regularly call them *sir* to make them think they are passing. I admire those who don't correct me—it is a compliment. All a good butch really needs is a femme to appreciate her.

I have taken to making myself the most appreciative femme in the city. I can appreciate the fuck out of just about any butch I come across. And it is the fucking that I am really after. The trick is to find the soft spot in the hard women and tickle it until they hike my skirt up to see if my pussy is as sweet as my words.

Their little way of thanking me.

Shy butches on their bar stools want to be told that I can tell they are thinking deep thoughts. One drink later we are in their cars and they are thanking me as deeply as their broad-fingered hands can in such close confines.

A cropped-haired mechanic who has been tinkering on a bike that has been parked, unusable, for months on the lawn wants me to tell her what a fine ride it's going to be. Wants to hear me ask if I can sit on it for a minute, have me hitch my skirt up and place my oops-I-forgot-to-wear-panties-cunt down on the seat, lean forward so my clit slides along the leather to reach the handle bars. "I bet you can make her purr," I say, feigning revving the engine. A minute later, the shop table has been cleared off and she paws me with grease-stained fingernails while her buddies go out for lunch.

Lou had been hard and secretive and didn't fall for any of my usual ploys. Her soft spot was hard to find. Two weeks after moving in with her, I discovered a hidden stash of books. A few worn-out trashy straight novels, an instructional manual called *The Erotic Woman,* and a thoroughly uninteresting not-very-well-illustrated version of the Kama Sutra. To stay with Lou I would need to find a spot I could tease her with that could last months. Ordaining her as the best lover I have ever had was a way to keep my side of the bed vacant and to prevent her from changing the locks. She was good, so it wasn't a matter of faking it with her, as much as playing down every other encounter I had ever had. She knew I played around, but all seemed to be forgiven when I whined about how frustrated I was and how I couldn't wait to come home to be with her. She let the indiscretions go and grew increasingly interested in the fumbling details of lovers I auditioned. Lately we'd been arguing almost every day, and my stories had gone up a notch to counter her complaints. Now, not only was no one even close to her in bed, but no one else could even make me wet. Lou, who had been jamming my things into a duffle bag, stopped what she was doing when I revealed this to her. With almost a sense of pity she seemed to feel obliged to let me stay. I always carried clean panties in my pocket, which I could slip on before I came home to convince her of the lie she so wanted to believe.

We stop to get drinks before heading to the table that Lou's friends have staked out. Nanc speaks to Lou but keeps her eyes on mine, watching me scan the crowd. "Ah, so you finally let her out of the house." They laugh, giving each other a one-shoulder butch hug/pat.

The floor is already sticky with spilled beer. Lou's friends make room for us at the table and I listen to the group discuss work. How the assholes at the plant are reducing overtime, how so-and-so at the cycle shop has some thingy and such part doodad. I can't follow the conversation and don't care. I sip my beer, bouncing my ankle, trying to catch eye contact in a crowd used to avoiding it. Conversations in the room grow louder and women set their beers down so hard in anger or humor that the tables are slick from the sloshing over.

Lou gets up to go fetch more drinks and Nanc slides into her chair. "So, what d'ya think of our little bar?" She moves my hair off my shoulder, giving it a little tug. She leans into me, one hand on my knee. In her familiar voice, she whispers the gossip of those sitting around the table. "Jess—been single for over a year, a pity she can't find a nice femme like Lou obviously has." I lean into her slightly so her mouth grazes my ear as she speaks. "And see Ron there? She passes at work. Takes shots too, when she can get her hands on a dose. Did you know testosterone raises sex drive?" She laughs alcohol-moist breath into my neck, saying she'd bet I already knew that.

Lou interrupts us, shoves Nanc back to her own seat, and pulls me out of mine.

"C'mon, let's go."

"Lou, man, we're just talking. Geez, half the time you want her to find a new man. I was just testing the waters." Nanc punctuates this with a sizzle sound.

"We're just going outside for a smoke. We'll be back."

She leads me out of the bar, squeezing the pinkies on both my hands in her fist as she pushes our way through the crowd.

Lou ignores me when we get outside even when I kiss her throat and try to jam my hands into her pockets. She has rolled us a joint she didn't want to share with her friends and we lean against the wall in silence trying to hang in the shadows. She feeds me drags between her long puffs.

Three women leaving the bar pause as they catch the scent and come over to ask directions to some other bar in an obvious ploy to get offered a hit. Lou vaguely gives them the information they want, and when they linger, she hands them the tight-rolled cig and they chat as they pass it around.

Lou introduces herself. Then she introduces me as the insatiable curse who couldn't be left alone for a minute without trying to make a pass at her best friend. Lou laughs it off and says that even if her friend had taken me into some back corner and tried to rustle up some lust, I would just have come crawling back to her.

Lou tells them that last week I went to the bathroom between pool-shots and convinced someone to feel me up. How after the woman was unsuccessful at using her fingers to arouse anything more in me than a need to pee, I came storming out, saying I'd have to use a pool cue if I wanted to get off. She tells them how she caught me crawling back into her bed with chalky hands and a blue smudge on my nose.

She complains that I am always picking up girls and going home with them, just to end up horny and frustrated and then have to steal cab money or hop a late-night bus back to her place. Like an alley cat who keeps wandering back in the window whenever you shut him out. With this, she lets out a meow-moan and they laugh as if they know what it's like. It is the first time I have heard her retell these tall tales and I can see her eyes sparkle with butch pride. I see how much of herself is tied to this reality I've been weaving for her.

"Baby, tell them how no one can turn you on like I can."

I raise my eyebrows a bit and nod.

"Shit, if you can do it, you can have her," Lou says seriously as she sends the tiny butt around for one last pull from each of them.

The three step back. They look at my boots, the sheer black stockings of my thighs, the skirt that has been inching its way up as I shift from one foot to the other. "I bet I can make the bitch wet," one mumbles to another, meaning for Lou to overhear.

Lou warns them that many women have tried, even a couple of men, with no effect. But if they are willing to give it a shot, they would be doing her a favor. She drops the roach to the ground and grinds it into the sidewalk with the heel of her boot, saying she would be glad to get rid of me so she could get some sleep for a change. She tells them that I've jacked up her phone bill and owe her money. So, for $50 they can have three minutes to get a chance to make me wet. Three minutes of kissing. Lou tells them that she doesn't give a shit, throw in some tit- and ass-grabbing too if they want. She lays out the terms: They can't touch my pussy and I have to keep my hands behind my back. But most importantly, if they make me wet, they have to promise to keep me away from her.

The thought of her handing me over to these women, these

biker chicks with their huge hands and rough talk and their cocky attitudes, has me on the verge of coming already. I am not sure if Lou is setting this up to be rid of me once and for all or if she wants me to prove my devotion to her in some grand Russian roulette gamble based on a lie I've been tickling her with for months. I am still wondering this when the most boisterous one of the group steps up to the bet. She watches Lou as if she is afraid it might end up being a joke worth fighting over and pulls her wallet out of her back pocket. Fifty dollars, surely an entire day's pay if she is one of those lucky enough to have a full-time job. She holds it out, as if daring Lou to take it.

Lou tells her that we need to make sure I am dry, to judge fairly. She reaches up under my skirt and with the sleeve of her shirt wipes my pussy off with a rough stroke. She turns back to the three, takes the money, and announces, "Whenever you're ready."

I can feel Lou's presence behind me. My pussy is already pulsing. I clamp down in an attempt to keep any moisture inside.

Bulldagger number one steps toward me. She chooses the direct route, kissing me confidently, open-mouthed, with her tongue darting deep into my throat. Her hands are on my shoulders, pulling me in, bending my neck back. This eager suitor smells of leather, whiskey, and motorcycle grease—a scent so bewitching I could be Pied Pipered down the street with it. I hold my breath as she strangles me with her mouth. I just let her go at it, barely kissing back, resisting the urge to correct her faulty style with a few quick nips of my teeth to her tongue. I try to force my mind to wander from the situation. I try to think dry thoughts. I will win the bet for Lou and make her proud.

The three minutes are up and I have not so much as sighed. No groan. No pelvis seeking hers. No melting into her.

Lou turns to me. "Anything, honey?" she asks.

I shake my head no and lick the taste of whiskey off my lips.

Lou sighs and says that it's never as easy as it looks.

Number one steps back, tries to laugh it off, saying I am an uptight, frigid bitch, a fucking ice queen. She starts to walk off but her friends stop her.

The second dyke fumbles with her wallet and hands over the cash for her chance at the challenge. She apparently thinks that if the hard teeth-clanking kiss didn't work, perhaps I am a soft femme who needs seduction. She has three minutes. She kneels at my boots, and I avert my gaze to avoid the pull of her green eyes staring up at me. She licks the rim where the leather meets my calves, runs her tongue on the underside of my knee, and slides her hands slowly up my inner thighs. Lou stops her just as her fingers disappear under my skirt. She is stopped just before I make the decision that calloused hands and warm breath are worth bending my knees for, moving myself down to cease the agonizingly slow pace. She is stopped just before I drop my cunt down to meet her palm. Temptation number two moves her hands to softly cup each breast. I stand still, knees braced so as not to lose my balance. My hands search behind me for Lou—she takes both of my pinkies into her fist and gives them an encouraging squeeze. If I can pull this off, I know it will be the best compliment I have ever paid her.

Lou tells her that her time is up. I shrug, act unimpressed.

The two who have tried chide the third into an attempt, telling her it was a good three minutes whether they won me or not. Razz her about how all night she's been lookin' for a femmey girl and here is one standing on the street just waiting.

The third bulldagger wants to know how we are measuring. She wants to see for herself if I am wet, wants proof. Lou reaches under my skirt and runs her fingers under the elastic of my underwear—quick, unceremonious, careful not to rub my clit. Her fingers barely skim the surface, but I gulp a breath of air at the long-awaited touch and they seem sure that she's penetrated me. She takes her hand out from under my skirt, grabs number three's hand, and rubs the definitely dry fingers along her thick wrist.

Lou holds out her hand for the money and bulldagger number three hesitates slightly before lifting her wrist to her nose. Just the faintest scent of pussy assures her that she wasn't tricked. She reaches into her pocket and pulls out some crumpled bills.

Lou resumes her position behind me, taking hold of my pinkies. I take a deep breath, trying to figure number three out so I can prepare myself. She is slow, strong, suspicious. Lou clicks her tongue, worried. We are so close to winning this cruel game that I couldn't bear to lose now. Couldn't bear to disappoint her. I imagine the ways she will thank me for this public gesture of appreciation.

Number three steps forward, trying to read my face for clues as she considers the best approach. She leans heavily into my body, wrapping her arms around me. Pushes her bulk into me. Our legs are interwoven and she pulls my hips into her thigh. She starts in on a brain-fucking whisper. "Oh you smell like sex just like I knew you would. I've been looking for a hot little woman like you. I want you so fuckin' bad right now. I can feel your cunt heat on my leg, burnin' a hole right through my jeans. I can practically feel it swelling. It's making me so fucking horny just thinking about how slick and sweet you're getting for me. I already know how I am gonna fuck you." She hugs me into her and presses me harder down onto her thigh. I struggle to tilt my hips up so as not to catch the fullness of her leg rubbing my cunt. Lou's fist closes down harder around my pinkies, tugging me back enough to relieve the pressure building on my clit.

The bulldagger pulls me hard against her chest, breathing on my neck. "That round sexy ass of yours has been drivin' me crazy since I first saw you. I am getting so worked up I don't think I could stop even if you wanted me too." She clamps a hand down on my asscheek and pulls my cunt up to meet the slow swivel of her hips.

Lou puts her fingertips lightly on my back to steady me and I rest back into her hand. Allow her to ease me back and rescue me from this impending arousal. "When I get you home," she goes on, "I'll give you the fuck you've been looking for. I'm gonna work your hard little clit—just pull it right into my mouth and lick your sweet juices. Then I'll open you up with my fingers, just slide in and out. Swirl my hand into you until you beg me to fuck you harder. Beg me to fuck you deeper until you come."

I think of throwing the bet and wrapping my legs around her, opening my mouth to hers. My cunt is tired from being clamped down for so long and I have lost track of my inhales and exhales, my breath starting to sound like whimpering.

"I know how to satisfy a cat-in-heat femme like you. You won't be stumbling home at night. You'll be flat-out exhausted from all our fucking."

I wonder what Lou would do, wonder what proof would be requested after this test, wonder what I could get away with. My pinkies are locked in Lou's fist and she twists them, bending them back into a stinging stretch, clearing my head.

The three minutes are up and Lou makes sure contestant number three has backed away before she pushes me back up to hold my own weight. I am lightheaded and keep hold of Lou's hand, looking down.

"Sorry," Lou says. "Like I told you, she isn't as easy as she looks." Lou takes my waist and turns to escort me inside, but number three grabs her arm and yanks her back so she can look straight at me. I know this look, the look of having found the soft spot and waiting for the tickle to take hold.

The bulldaggers start throwing insults and accusations at us. Number three in particular thinks she's won. She continues to talk to me, starting in the now-familiar whisper ringing in my ears, but each phrase rising in pitch of anger. "I know I made you wet. I know you're just dying to grind that sweet cunt into me. Let's finish this up and get out of here. Tell them how wet I made you. Didn't I make you wet? Huh, bitch?"

I try to ignore her voice, her words.

Lou tells her to shut up for a minute and we can prove it to her.

In a gesture too quick for me to stop, Lou pushes me back against the brick wall and yanks my skirt up. I take a deep breath and keep my pussy lips clamped together as tightly as I can. Lou pulls my panties down to mid thigh in front of these three bull-daggers whose wallets have just been emptied. Three bulldaggers with wounded machismo can see that I am not glistening.

Lou takes number three's hand and folds it into hers as she would a child's, leaving two fingers out and the rest curled into a fist. Lou guides her hand from one pale thigh, over my pussy lips, to the other. Three bulldaggers who are feeling quite under-appreciated hear her announce it. Dry.

"I don't fuckin' believe it. She must be fuckin' frigid. Whatever. Keep her, man. You deserve the bitch." They saunter off, play-punching each other and grabbing their imaginary cocks.

They round the corner and Lou turns to me, looking me in the eye for the first time in almost a half-hour. She smiles and tells me she is quite proud, tells me she guesses it's okay if I stick around for a while longer.

We go back into the bar and sit down at the table. I excuse

myself and head toward the bathroom. "Nice hip-check," I say as I pass by Nanc at the pinball machine. She follows me, leaving an unplayed ball, and locks the door behind us. After a quick slick finger-fuck that she has been promising me for weeks, Nanc leaves to resume her game and I pull my clean panties out of my pocket, wrapping the damp ones in a paper towel and throwing them in the trash. I return to the table to sit on Lou's lap, whispering to her how I much I love her, that she is the only one who can keep me happy, how she is the only one who knows how to turn me on.

ANGIE'S DADDY

I've never really had one. A Daddy, that is. What I mean is, I've never had a real one, or one that was really mine. But I have had the same dream almost every night. It's about someone else's Daddy. It's about Angie's Daddy.

In the dream, Angie's Daddy gives me what I always want but never get. Angie's Daddy gives me *me*, and makes everything okay just by saying that it is. He perverts and absolves me. He adds to me and subtracts from me. He divides me. And I hate the times in between when I have to wait for him to come, and I have to try to piece it all together myself. I hate those times when I have to stand there, holding on to my perversion like a bag of doggie doo, because no one else knows what to do with it, or how to make it good. And what I really want is to just bring it all into focus, because what I really need is to see the whole picture.

When the dream is over, I feel this sense of renewal that fills me up and bottoms me out because I need him to renew me again and again, and it's never really enough and it's never really over, but it's still good and always worth it. Sometimes I wish the dream was my life and my life was the dream, and then I realize that the only thing that would change is what I believe to be real. And it's hard to figure out what to believe, and it's hard to figure out what's really real. Sometimes my thoughts get lost in the hardness of that.

Angie's Daddy is the kind of Daddy who gets what he wants because he takes it, and because he convinces you that you want to give it. And believe me, you do. Or at least I do, in the dream. But part of why I want to give it is because of Angie. It's because I want to be with her. And because I want to be in this experience with her. And because it's *her* Daddy. Sometimes I wake up with the whisper of her name on my lips, and then I feel the harsh impression of a hand around my face, correcting me, collecting me, like I'm a thousand marbles on the floor.

It's set in different places, the dream. Because what matters is where we're going, and not where we are or where we've been. And where we're going is to another world. Sometimes we take Angie's Daddy's rocket ship to the moon, and the man on the moon is our only spectator. Other times, it happens at the local fair.

This time, we're sitting on the couch in Angie's Daddy's living room. Angie and me are on either side of him. And we're giggly and cuddly, and soft like kittens. The television is on but there is no sound, because it doesn't really matter anyway. And sometimes when we're in the living room, people walk right by us like we're just playing board games, and sometimes we are. But sometimes there are too many games and I'm all played out because every game has rules, and sometimes the rules are red and they're written in blood. And rules aren't made to be broken, you know. You can't bend the rules.

Angie's Daddy is bigger than us, but then again Daddies often are. And there's something comforting about his bulk. I peer at Angie from around his thick chest. Angie is so beautiful. And I love her so, so much. In the dream, my love for her is overwhelming. Sometimes I try to tell her that I love her, but I can only mouth the words and she thinks I'm saying *elephant shoe*. And even in the dream, I sometimes question that it might all be a dream, and I try really hard to stay there, to stay sleeping, to get my beauty sleep, to be Sleeping Beauty, because there are special things for special girls and what I really want is to be kissed by her.

Something about being there feels important. Something about being there feels life changing. And despite the gravity attached to the experience, something about being there feels really comfortable, and really real. It's like coming home and being familiar. But there's this ache that goes with it. The kind of ache you feel when you just can't be with someone you want for whatever reason. And there's that need you have that you know is never going to be met. It's the same ache I feel when I walk around in real life. That terrible ache that I just can't shake because I can't take the dream back. And I'm afraid that if I talk about it out loud, words will fall from my mouth in red letters like rules that can't be changed. I feel that ache every day. And I wish Angie's Daddy could make *that* okay just by saying that it is.

The dream is sometimes like looking at puzzle pieces but never seeing the full picture. And sometimes it's like tunnel vision, and there's no periphery and there's no context. Other times it's like looking through a kaleidoscope of images when I try to remember. And the light behind the images is so bright that I have to close my eyes because they're too bright, and they're shifting too fast. And sometimes the fastness of the shifting makes me feel dizzy, and the details get blurred and hazy, and it's like I'm looking at them through smoke.

But every time I catch Angie's eye, she smiles at me. And I reach my arm way across Angie's Daddy's chest and touch her with an affection I would normally reserve for sick or dying animals. And I have this feeling, this feeling that I need to tattoo her image on my memory because somehow this wonderful thing is going to be ripped away from me. And it's not because we're sick or dying. It's because of something else. So I try really hard to capture the details of her image…her fairy tale–long hair, her chocolate-drop eyes, and those big girlie lashes that sometimes tickle my cheek and neck. Only the details are isolated and abstract, like features cut from a picture that do not add up to a solid whole.

Still, I can't imagine her doing anything other than being right there in the dream. I can't imagine her looking any way other than how she looks when I'm dreaming of her. And I start to wonder how I look to her, but I remind myself that I need to put my energy into remembering. Only I don't know why I need to do that. So I ask the question right out loud in the dream. I ask, *Why do I have to work so hard to remember this?* Only there's no sound, and there's no answer. And I wonder if part of the reason is that they're trying so hard to forget. I wonder if some things are better left unsaid, even in the dream.

I feel Angie's Daddy's hand start to creep up my leg. His fingers are light like a spider at first, and they're tickly like Angie's lashes. I keep looking at her. And I have butterflies in my stomach, fluttering and flapping and determined to escape. If I open my mouth they will fly out in droves, all dotted and speckled and brilliant in color. And despite my apprehension, I feel really good all over. Angie's Daddy makes me feel good, but Angie makes me feel good, too. She's still smiling at me. And I feel my pussy start to get wet, like there's a sea inside of me. I feel a conflict too, but Angie's Daddy murmurs something encouraging in my ear. Something like, *It's okay. It's all happened before.* But it really doesn't matter what he says because what I want is to know that it's him, and not me, doing the encouraging. And I'm not sure why that's important, but I know that it is. It becomes important to me later, during those times in between the dream.

I want him to touch me there where it's wet, and I know that he will because it's all happened before. His fingers get heavier as they reach my thigh and crawl under my dress. He grabs handfuls of my skin and now my panties are wet, too. I'm amazed by how easily it happens and how wonderful it feels, this process of becoming saturated, this process of being taken by him. His hand finds its way around my hip, and it slides under my ass and under the edge of my panties. He easily lifts me with that one mighty hand and places me firmly on his lap, and I'm facing him. His hand is still on my ass and he's gripping me hard, gripping me like I might slip off of his hook and flop away. I lean into his chest and stay still for a moment, play dead for a moment. And in that brief moment of death, I feel that his breasts are bigger than mine. I experience the fullness of his breasts against me, and the firmness of his hand on my ass. I experience the sensation of Angie's fingers twisting and twirling in my hair as it hangs in her face. And I feel like I could fall asleep like this, and then I realize that I am sleeping.

I wait patiently as he moves Angie with the same technique and precision, like it was broken down step by step in some sort of instruction manual, like it's been repeated a thousand times before. Now she and I are side by side, straddling each of his massive legs. We are leaning into him because the angle of his legs forces us slightly forward. I feel Angie's warmth against me. Her warmth makes me feel even closer to her because she fills my senses, and she feels really real, even if it's just a dream. I want her to kiss me on the lips, and Angie's Daddy tells us it's okay to kiss. *It's okay.* And he says it with this authenticity, like it hasn't happened a thousand times before. *Show me,* he urges. And we do. It's like...waking up from a long sleep. It's like waking up and...

And I feel his fingers start to slide around my eager pussy, making me drip. He turns his whole hand to the side and glides it back and forth like he's sawing me in half. His slick fingers separate and reunite, and my compliant lips stretch and form around his changing shape. He grins at me like we're doing something right and like we're doing something wrong, only I sometimes find it hard to tell the difference between right and wrong, and right and left. His fingers push and poke at my tight openings, and swim recklessly around my swollen clit. He feels too big to fit inside of me, but I know that he will because it's all happened before. I let my mouth fall against his ear and my vision relaxes into his dusky hair, and it stays that way for a while. Everything's all out of focus.

I quietly gasp as his middle finger finds its way inside my cunt: partway in, halfway up. I writhe with it and against it, and my pussy opens up like a butterfly spreading its wings. I feel Angie's legs stirring against mine. And I feel the roughness of Angie's Daddy's scratchy face against my cheek and neck. Sometimes I look in the mirror to see if I can notice little scrapes from his stubble, but it turns out to be a fun house mirror and I can't see anything because my image is so distorted and I look so silly, and it's so hard to tell how old you are in one of those things.

I lean back, fighting the gravitational pull. I place one hand behind me on Angie's Daddy's knee, and one hand behind Angie on his other knee. His knees feel like basketballs in my hands.

I hoist myself up and let his long meaty finger fill my cunt, completely. I ride it with a certain kind of deliberateness. I ride it like it's going to save me from a certain kind of elimination. And I let my breath entrust and commit to this experience. I breathe heavy breaths, in and out. And something about all of the breathing makes me feel mature.

I look at Angie's hair. It's draped along her back like a blanket. I carry that image with me as my eyes climb the wall and find a resting spot on the ceiling. I imagine being blanketed by her, hidden in the underworld of her hair. I imagine lots of things as Angie's Daddy gets me off. And I hear him grunt as he drives a second finger inside of me. When I look down, I see my creamy wetness glistening on his knuckles and collecting in his big palm. And it looks like gleaming glossy moondust. His eyes become fixed like he isn't really there, and his cock is hard beneath his pants. I feel a sweat building on my forehead as my pussy gushes and shakes inside his hand. I let myself collapse against his full chest, let myself feel little in the comfort of his bosom. And Angie rises, placing her hand on my shoulder, for balance. I can hear how wet her pussy is in his hand. He's got the whole world there; I can hear it. And I want to feel it, but instead I feel that ache. It's a sinking sort of feeling, a sinking shrinking feeling in the pit of my stomach. *That's right*, he assures, *you feel that?* And I want to look right at her, but there's this undercurrent of pretending that happens in the dream. And I think it's just part of the game we're all playing. I think it's like going to jail without passing go.

Sometimes Angie's Daddy gives one of us a task to do so that he can have private time with the other. These are the times when he undoes his zipper and pulls out his huge cock, first through the hole in his underwear and then through the center of his pants. This time he sends Angie to do something upstairs, only my fingers are entwined in hers and I have to untangle them one by one to let her go, and then she's gone. Angie's Daddy squeezes my face with one giant hand and pulls it close to his. His hot breath blasts me like an automatic dryer in a public bathroom. And my cheeks are hot and scrunched and blushing. I can't close my mouth because of the harshness of his grasp. And a teeny weenie marble spills out from the space between my lips, spills out and bounce-bounce-bounces its way down the hall and out through the keyhole of the front door—a piece of myself that will never come home. He stares me down until I soften and relent, my eyes plunging to the ground like little skydivers without parachutes. I could probably outstare him if I really wanted to, except I feel like I've gotten caught with my hand in the cookie jar and I'm not sure what the penalty is for that. But there aren't any cookies to be had here. There aren't any cookies, just Angie's Daddy's cock.

He spins me around so that I am facing outward and my feet are planted firmly on the floor. Only I don't like standing on the floor because I worry that something under the couch is going to reach out and grab my ankle, and that might make me scream. And my panties are around my knees but I don't know how they got that way. He says, *Special things for special girls*, and maybe that's all I need to know.

He reels me in by the material of my dress like a fisherman reeling in his catch, only he didn't need any bait, and he didn't need any worms. And when I'm close enough he wraps his hands around my waist. His hands reach almost the whole way around my center. He holds me tight, and I am not slippery and I will not flop away. I can feel the round head of his cock bulging and pressing against my needy little fuck-hole. I can feel his desire. And I can feel mine. I bend my knees up onto the surface of the couch, still looking out, and I rest them on both sides of his large thighs. I am spread wide open; my red slit parted in two. I lean forward, placing both hands on the cluttered coffee table, for balance. He tugs on my feet to hurry this process of positioning. Now my panties have completely disappeared and they never do come back.

He secures my hips and guides me toward him. I feel the fat bulb of his cock launching its way inside of me. And I am flooded with images; they roll over me like waves…Angie's tickly lashes, her hand on my shoulder, the kiss, our tangled fingers, and Angie's Daddy's rock-hard cock…his rock-hard cock splitting me open and filling me full. His cock is deep inside of me now, and it feels like real rubber. It feels like a ride at the local fair and I'm going to stand in line to do it again. I catch my image in the television between the commercials when the screen goes black, and I watch my hair bounce back and forth against my shoulders. I watch my tits jiggle underneath the thin fabric of my dress. It's the only clear image I have of myself in the whole dream. And even though Angie's Daddy makes me feel like a little girl, the reflection I see is that of a woman getting fucked. And the proof is on TV just like the proof is in the pudding. Sometimes I see that image when I'm not even dreaming. I see it in those brief seconds when my television screen goes black. And Angie's Daddy's white shirt and big head make him look like a spaceman floating around in the background.

His thrusts become faster and deeper and the coffee table starts to slide forward as he pushes me harder and harder. If he doesn't do something soon, I will fall right on the floor, right between the couch and the coffee table. My arms start stretching out really far so that the tips of my fingers can still reach the edge of the surface. My body starts stretching too, and I feel like that image of myself in the fun house mirror—all drawn out and contorted. The edge slips away from me and I have no choice but to let myself go, to let myself fall. I land with my head right between his feet, and I can see clear under the couch. And what I see among the dust balls are puzzle pieces. Only I couldn't reach them even if I tried. And nothing's reaching out for me, and there's nothing to scream about.

Angie's Daddy shoots his load like the blast of a rifle, right down the center of my ass. The thick lather drips down along my narrow crack, glazing my pussy like a doughnut. He forces my arm behind my back and makes me smear his come all over my skin, hand over hand. And it feels like real lotion.

There's a clunking noise as Angie makes her way back down the stairs. And it sounds like she's wearing high heels, only they're too big for her. I stand on wobbly legs even though I'm not wearing high heels, and Angie's Daddy zips up his pants and clears his throat like there's soot stuck inside. *C'mon girls*, he says with a contrived authority. And the three of us maneuver our way back into our original positions on the couch. I feel that sense of renewal, and I don't want it to bottom out. I revel in the feeling of having a Daddy, even though it's Angie's Daddy. I revel in the feeling of being the apple of his eye, and the apple is clean and pure and there are no worms. I am full with my love for Angie. And it feels really real, even if it's just a dream.

But sometimes, I want to send Angie's Daddy upstairs. Sometimes I want to press a button and make him mute. Press a button and turn him off. And I want for me and Angie to be together without him. I want to play a new game with new rules. And the new game doesn't have any room for silly Daddies, silly rabbits. Sometimes I try to change the dream, but I know that it won't change because it's never happened before. And I wonder if a new game would just be too much for everyone. I wonder if it would make the world explode.

Angie's Daddy lights a cigarette and slowly fills the room with a thick gray haze. And he's there like a big boulder that I can't move, like a big boulder that crashes into me from time to time. I peek around that vast chest of his and look at Angie. I lean into him, stretching my elastic arm across his body to hold her hand. I try to tell her that I love her. *Elephant shoe! Elephant shoe!* And Angie's Daddy gazes vacantly at the hushed images on the screen. I keep looking at Angie. Every few seconds that bright light is flashing against her, affecting and disrupting her appearance. Eventually, the smoke will blur her features entirely, and it will be like looking through a hazy, shifting cloud. *Remember this*, I say to myself. *You have to try really hard to remember.*

VOODOO AND TATTOOS

Lynne Jamneck

It started out so innocuously. Maybe that's why it turned out so fucking hot.

I've had enough of bartending in my life that when Annie asked me to pour drinks at a conference she was in charge of, my immediate instinct was to think—fast—of the first best lie I could offer in order to avoid the prospect.

"I—someone has to feed my cat."

Annie found that excuse pathetic, and gave me a look that said so. "Kyle, that cat died two years ago."

"Fuck, you remember."

"Of course I do. I was at the funeral."

"A little respect, please. Princess Leia was no ordinary feline."

"Sure she wasn't," she said sweetly. Sarcastically. Annie wasn't an animal lover. Curious, then, that she'd refer to her lover as a "tiger" in bed. Makes you think.

"So you'll do it?"

"Is this the fancy-schmancy do you've been planning for the last two months?" Annie was head of conference planning at the Sheraton Belgravia Hotel on Chesham Street in London.

"I'm thrilled. You remembered."

"How could I not—you've been yammering about it nonstop for weeks."

"Oh fuck off, Kyle." Then she went all sweet again. "So then you know how important this is to me, to my *career*." She sidled up next to me, running a long finger along my forearm. "I need the best bartender in London, and you're it."

Annie and I have never slept together. We've come close once or twice in moments when neither of us had been thinking. She was way too driven, and I liked Guns N' Roses. But she knew just how to play me.

"I take it the Sheraton pays well?"

"Oh, *yes*. And I'll get you a uniform... Just do us a favor?"

"I thought I already was."

There was the sweet smile again, laced with sarcasm. "I can see why you manage to fuck any girl you want. Your wit surpasses even my own. No dear, what I meant was the hair."

"The hair?"

"Yes. Yours in particular. Just...try not to look like Ringo Starr on a bad day, okay?" I wouldn't argue with Annie. I'd just lose.

The night of the conference I showed up in my monkey suit at exactly 18:30 as Annie had instructed me. I'd never even asked her what kind of clientele I'd be serving overpriced cocktails and martinis to. It turned out to be some corporate thing. Loads of women in power suits. Blah blah.

When I went in through the service entrance somewhere in the bowels of the hotel, a group of waitresses eyeballed me. A couple of aviation blondes, their black roots starting to show. I smiled favorably and one of them brushed past me just a little too close. A spotty male looked at me like I'd stolen his wallet. Probably the usual bartender. I smirked. Annie could get away with anything. Probably because she was so fucking good at her job.

The conference started at 19:00 sharp. Between then and 21:00 I pretty much did stuff-all except verbally abuse Annie in her absence for making me show up so early. Control freak. Another reason why I would never have sex with her.

At some point, a woman sneaked out from behind the heavy conference room doors. She looked around furtively before making her way over to the bar. I was busy wiping down whisky tumblers, probably for the third time in an hour. When she saw the coast was clear she launched herself across the empty bar area, weaving through the unoccupied tables. and pulled out a bar stool.

She smiled disarmingly. "You'd be out of there too if you had to listen to that tosser."

"I take it the speeches aren't very entertaining."

She looked right at me and smiled widely. "Fucking understatement of the year, lassie."

"You have a great smile." *Stop flirting with the patronage.*

"Thanks." She looked as I dried off the glass. "God, you have really good forearms."

Oh. My.

I'd rolled my sleeves up before washing the few glasses my perfectionist eye hadn't deemed clean enough. If Annie saw me like this she'd have a continental fit. But taking in the present company, I didn't really care.

She was a sort-of redhead. More like copper, flecked with golden brown. Her eyes were dirty emeralds and a crooked trail of freckles were scattered across the bridge of her nose. Her mouth appeared both demure and possibly foul at the same time.

"You got any Jameson back there?" she asked. "Make it quick, before the bastards notice I'm gone. Double, on the rocks."

"So you're Irish," I nodded, pouring the whisky with a steady hand.

"What on earth makes you think that?"

"Trace of the accent. Mild, but there. But in all my time as a bartender, an Irishman wants whisky, he wants Jameson."

"Then you know the Irish were the first to distil whisky."

"That's up for debate."

"Okay. You have something against the Irish?" She swallowed a mouthful of whisky and looked at me. Her eyes held mine for just a moment longer than need be.

"Hardly." An involuntary charge of arousal jolted up my thighs.

"One more. Quickly." She moved her glass closer and watched me pour the amber liquid. "If you don't mind me saying so, you look a little out of place here."

"Thank god for small mercies."

I could see the kinky smile around the edge of her glass. She swallowed the whisky in two, three quick successive tips of her wrist, then said, "Better prepare yourself. There's a lot of bored women about to come out of that conference room in serious need of booze. Hot little thing like yourself..." She slid off the bar stool. "You're going to have your hands full."

"Annie! Annie!"

She didn't see me at first, but how could she? The bar was packed. Women, everywhere. Then finally a gap as I served another Bacardi with a twist of lemon and everyone seemed to have a drink. For now.

Annie walked briskly over to the bar and tapped nonchalantly on the glass top. "Martini, doll."

I scanned the room whilst making her drink. I can prepare martinis in my sleep by now. Then I spotted her. Irish freckles.

I placed the glass on a serviette and slid it across the counter. "Who's that?"

"What? Where? Oh." Annie gave me a smarmy look. "Well, I can't say that I'm surprised; I did expect you to get your leg over. But I'm afraid you're out of luck on that one. That's Jamie Gallagher."

Annie looked at me expectantly. "I get the feeling I'm supposed to know who she is."

"Jesus Christ, Kyle; don't you ever watch the news, read the paper? Jamie Gallagher—as in Gallagher, Sabatini and Larue? The law firm?"

"Can't say I've heard of them. Besides, isn't she a bit young to be a partner in a law firm?"

"Jamie? She's thirty-two. I think. Anyway, like I said Kyle, forget about it. She's got a girlfriend with more piercings than you do. Tattoos up the woo-ha. Bad timing on your part." She took a lascivious sip of her drink. "She likes 'em young."

"Fuck. Double whammy. And to think, I just turned twenty-four last week."

Annie smiled. "Poor dear."

"Her girlfriend's here?"

"Yes. Probably waiting in their hotel room. She's not the type to go round in a business suit."

A woman came to the bar and ordered another vodka tonic. Annie watched, amused, as she blatantly tried to flirt her way into my pants. Sure, I'd be lying if I said I didn't feel flattered. Problem was I couldn't keep my eyes off Jamie. And I found it intriguing that she didn't drink after having come out of the banquet hall for the second time. What made the whole thing even more unbearable was that I noticed the stolen glances she directed my way, too. A quick look over the shoulder of someone she greeted with a hug, or an upward turn of the head when she bent down to say something to a friend or acquaintance sitting at a table...

Now look, I might be young, but I'm not fucking stupid, you know? Sure, I get teased all the time by superior femmes like Annie, and I become brainless at the thought of solving riddles or thinking logically. It's easy for me to let people think I'm a sweet butch who'd rather swing a wrench than fiddle with a pressure cooker. But if there's one thing I know, it's women. I've been learning my entire life.

So I'll tell you this much: every time Jamie looked up and we glanced at one another I could see there was a certain purpose to her. Not just in her eyes, but in the way she brushed the copper from her forehead; the two open buttons of her crisp, starched shirt; and the way her hands touched herself, slightly self-consciously.

She wanted me for something. And I was pretty sure I knew the extent of her motives.

Jamie made the flimsy excuse of ordering a drink from the bar for a friend to come and speak to me again. At the end of the night, when the bar was almost empty, she came up to pay the tab. I told her it wasn't a tab, it was one drink; she insisted.

She paid with a twenty pound note, which was completely over the limit of what she needed to cover. She was gone before I could give her any change. But she'd written her room number on a hotel serviette. It lay open on the counter, daring me.

Maybe Annie'd been wrong. Maybe Jamie was alone. And it's true—I can be morally inept if I choose to be.

So, soon enough, there I was, standing in front of room 27. I lifted my hand and knocked, short and sharp, twice. I waited. Tried to listen for any kind of distinctive sound, but there was none.

The door opened and Jamie stood inside, looking me over. "Hi," I said nonchalantly.

"Nice to see you..."

"Kyle."

"Come in." She closed the door. I was infinitely aware of her presence behind me. I'll admit, I expected her to touch me, but she didn't.

The room was a moderate temperature; comfortable and relaxed. I noticed the big king-sized bed in the far corner had been turned down. With relief I realized there wasn't any music playing in the background.

"Would you like a drink?" Jamie's accent was more prevalent now. Her voice was laced with thick arousal. I heard her move behind me, then she stepped past and headed for the minibar.

"Actually—" I stopped when I saw the other woman step out of the bathroom. She was wearing jeans, heavy black boots and a wifebeater that accentuated her small breasts and flat stomach.

"Hi," she said in a gravelly voice, and smiled. "I'm Nicole."

As if by some form of sexual voodoo, the atmosphere suddenly crisped white-hot with eroticism. I looked over to where Jamie had started undressing by the edge of the bed. She was slowly undoing the buttons of her cotton shirt. I noticed with no small amount of satisfaction that the freckles repeated themselves between the cleft of her breasts. She was wearing a white bra and panties.

Jamie said, "Kiss her," and for a moment I wasn't sure who she'd said it to, or even if I'd heard her correctly. Then I felt

Nicole step up behind me, her masculine presence heavy, and for a moment my body tensed.

I'd never fucked another butch. Maybe because of that, the coil of lust that started in my belly and slithered due south made me groan when I felt her hands, solid and firm from behind, on my hips.

I turned around and looked at her, knowing that Jamie, already naked, was looking at us. Nicole had a silver ring through the right of her bottom lip, and her left eyebrow had been pierced several times. Black, oily tattoos crept out from beneath her vest and veined down her muscular arms. Dangerous, distracting silver decorated all but the thumbs of her two hands.

I placed my hands on Nicole's forearms and felt the coiled tension there. I pulled her closer, just like that, and kissed her, tasting the tang of metallic as the silver ring slid against my tongue.

No matter how tough and rugged she might have looked, Nicole kissed like a woman. Don't get me wrong; she was as hungry as I was. Her tongue stroked mine slowly, probing keenly in a most exquisite way. The air in her mouth was hot. I felt her fingers waver near the waist of my black pants.

She pulled back, both of us breathing hard. All in all, the kiss had been a little demanding, but nothing too violent. As I looked into Nicole's gray-blue eyes I knew that it wouldn't be the two of us ending up in bed together. That wasn't the plan.

She stepped back from me then. We both looked at Jamie, who was lying on the bed, naked, looking back at us. No one said a word. I was ready to fuck her if they asked me.

Nicole tapped a cigarette from an open box on the table and lit it. She drew in deep and expelled a column of smoke. "Don't get undressed," she said to me and pointed at a chair next to the side of the bed. "That's your place. Don't forget it." She winked at me. Some sublime form of butch code passed between us.

As I sat down, one leg resting in a *T* across my knee, Nicole pulled her vest off and tossed it into a corner. Both Jamie and I watched as she unbuttoned the heavy buttons on her black cargos, the cigarette dangling from the corner of her mouth. The sound of the metallic buttons popping was followed by someone exhaling loudly—me, I realized. For an instant I felt as if it was me standing there. I realized my hands were grasping the chair. It took everything I had not to stand up and walk over to the bed.

Nicole stepped closer and held her half-smoked cigarette out to me. I took it, grateful for something to put in my mouth, and watched her strut over to the bed. I glimpsed a broad, black studded belt above the waistline of her pants. *That's a good-looking piece of leather.* Her crotch bulged fetchingly as she climbed onto the bed and crawled over Jamie like a snake. The bed creaked prettily.

Nicole and Jamie kissed, hard, and when I saw Nicole's tongue—which had moments before been in my own mouth—slip past her lover's lips a small sound of satisfaction escaped from Jamie's throat.

My senses began their slow but certain dip into overload. My groin was on fire. I heard the smooth *shhhk* as one of Jamie's legs moved against Nicole's clothed thigh and her heel hooked around the inside of Nicole's knee.

They were making the stimulated sounds of lovers flushed with arousal, and there I was, not four feet away, watching them. Nicole moved her mouth down. When her tongue flicked lewdly before taking Jamie's erect nipple into her mouth, I heard a moan. Involuntarily, I followed with one of my own, short and tight.

Nicole's hand moved down between her legs, and disappeared inside her cargos. When she brought it back out she held at least eight inches of dyke cock in her hand. I grunted at the sight of it; not because I wanted it in me, but because I wished I was Nicole.

Nicole turned her head and looked at me, smiling as Jamie reached down to take the cock in her hand. I was having a hard time taking my eyes off Jamie's hips as they rose eagerly from the mattress. Nicole put one of her big, decorated hands on Jamie's hip and held her down, making the muscles beneath the skin of her taut belly move.

"Fuck her," I snarled, quite unrepentantly, only then realizing how my jaw muscles were clenching. Nicole leaned forward and in one admirably executed move thrust herself into Jamie with a harsh grunt.

I sat and watched, rapt.

At first Nicole was nice and easy. She allowed Jamie to move up to meet her as she kept a fixed tempo. Every so often Jamie would make encouraging sounds, or those of pleasure when Nicole's cock hit the right spot. I watched the tattoos on the butch girl's back as they moved and undulated to the syncopated rhythm of that one weak spot in the mattress. At one point they both looked over to where I was sitting, their movements never faltering, their attention fixed on me. I felt my hand move down to my crotch.

Nicole began to fuck Jamie harder then, no doubt partly due to the fact that I seemed to have found my tongue and was egging her on. She was strong and held Jamie down, fucking her into the mattress while I implored her with rude remarks; ones I realized I'd wanted to say ever since Jamie had the balls to call me "lassie." I wanted to screw Jamie myself...but I knew the magic would end, the spell would be broken if I dared move from that chair an inch. All I could do was grind my teeth and cross my legs while watching the two of them on the bed.

When they were done, Jamie and Nicole fell against one another, kissing like longtime lovers. I wondered at that. Nicole couldn't have been older than myself. Maybe even younger. The idea that they had been in a relationship for some time was perversely thrilling.

I got up weakly to leave when Nicole went into the bathroom. The sound of a tap being opened brought reality back in full swing. Jamie, naked, stopped me when I was halfway to the door. "Thanks for coming," she said and laughed, realizing her pun. She patted and squeezed my ass before disappearing inside the bathroom just as Nicole came out. She walked me to the door.

I reached out to turn the knob but Nicole stopped me. Grabbing my wrist, she shoved my hand inside her cargos. Her clit was hard. I knew what she wanted.

I stroked her, stiff and rough. It was strange but thrilling to hear the low obscenities of another butch in my ear. My coccyx tingled with newfound lust.

It didn't take long for her to come. I didn't know whether Jamie was aware of what we were doing. Nicole pushed me against the door, grinding her hips against mine, and came with a cry of release still stuck inside her throat. I fumbled for the doorknob and fell out into the hallway. The door banged shut loudly behind me. For a moment I just stood there, flushed and getting my bearings back. When I checked my watch I saw that it was almost two in the morning. Too late to catch the Tube. Too late for a bus. Dammit. I should have asked for cab money.

LOOK BUT DON'T TOUCH

Sparky

You look down and see the bottle of whiskey lying in casual spills of come.

You envy the boys for those quick joyous fountains.

It will take you much longer.

The walls are shiny from others before you: a glaze of sperm, sweat, other shoulders in leather jackets, and the strangely mouthwatering smell of cleaning solution.

Your shoulders are narrow. You fit neatly into this dark box.

There is no great mystery, you think, sliding a dollar into the glowing slot. Surrounded by darkness, you think of your mom, comforting you in the locker room: "We're all girls here."

But you smell like cool water for men and pomade, and you wear your most dapper boy clothes, black leather jacket and boots. Your hair is freshly cropped and no one can tell the tinge of lip liner. Your hair is carefully in its borrowed tranny boy flip. You are prepared for a mystery date. Who is behind the glass? That is the mystery.

A bar of light widens. The black window rises.

Five women in red-gold light are surrounded by mirrors. Dancing naked with their own lush bodies, with the mirrors reflecting silver and red flashes, girls upon girls, like the room is packed. One comes over to see you, dances before you. She has small, rounded breasts, rounded hips, catlike black-rimmed eyes, and a ready, naughty smile, stands on tall vinyl stiletto boots. A black bob, a mini-version of Uma Thurman in *Pulp Fiction*.

Your face becomes hot. Your ears burn. Your expression is awe and wonderment. She grins down at you, pleased. Seductive. She shows you her breasts; their skin looks impossibly smooth and clean, with golden-rimmed, small nipples. You see the hollow of her throat, her collarbone, her little belly.

She is the loveliest being on the planet.

She is naked before you and you can do nothing but look and look.

You keep looking at her hips, peek at her pussy, and give long lustful looks to her boots.

"I bet that smile gets them every time," she purrs.

You realize you are grinning like a fool. You shake your head no but cannot stop the grin that is shy, nervous, awed.

She calls the others over. "Look how cute! Look at those dimples!"

Now you could not stop smiling if you tried.

Four of them peep in the window at you, pressing against it. They pretend to poke your dimples. "So cute!" Real smiles from them. You want to duck and you are blushing so hard but there's nowhere to go, the window's open, and your money is in there ticking away relentlessly.

They move to other open windows and you are left with little Uma Thurman. "I like your boots," you say.

You hear the click as she rests one high heel on the window

ledge and bends over so you look up the spike heel and vinyl boot to her incredible round ass. She peeks at you from above her delicate pussy lips and asshole, smiling because, you think to yourself, now she knows. She knows how to get you. You feel tormented with need to be licking those boots.

She turns to face herself in the mirror and lowers herself below your window. She writhes back and forth. You realize with delight that she is fucking your imaginary cock. She's smiling sweet and wicked, as if she knows exactly how hard this gets your clit.

The black square of window lowers. She bends down to grin underneath, waving. You see the shiny toe of her boot, and are left in darkness.

You feel wired and keyed up, you've been here a long time and are likely to stay longer, not willing to jerk off like the others. You told yourself to come here for the experience but you will get yourself turned on until you want to climb the booths, kiss and claw at the glass, so near to those girls. Wanting to please them all.

The next booth smells salty and familiar. You realize it's freshly pumped semen that glitters on the floor. You feel a sense of solidarity. You put twenty into the slot. You are in for the full ride.

The window rises. You lock eyes with a new dancer, across the carpeted, mirrored stage. This one has a cute black bob with little ponytails and bangs. She has little Cupid's-bow pouty lips and huge dark eyes with long lashes. She wears white thigh-high fishnets with bits of lace at the top and high-heeled sandals.

But most of all she has a body that is so lush and curvy, it looks familiar. It could be your own. She has a rounded tummy and her hips and thighs are buttery and luscious. With her black hair and sexy tummy, she reminds you of your first girlfriend. She is innocent and powerfully sexual. It is like the glass is gone.

She looks unimaginably soft and delicious. You want to roll around on top of her and feel her up, lick up and down her luxurious hips and belly.

She comes up and licks her lips, pouting and sexy, thrusting her heavy breasts, writhing her hips against the window. Her lips are trembling. You realize it's an effort for her to keep from cracking up. Soon she cannot stop smiling. Her eyes are half-lidded. She is everything lush and full, and you want to take her around the waist and wrap her legs around you. But she's behind the glass.

You ponder what to say. Poetry? Blank verse? "You are so cute," you say at last.

She smiles for real, her eyes lingering on you. "So are you!"

Her name is Persephone and that is not, she informs you, her real hair. She leans over to pull the wig a little. Her hair is blonde and cropped short, recently shaved.

The window closes and opens again, slowly revealing her white fishnets and finally the lace trim and her ass. She's talking to the other dancers. It's late now, and the catlike Uma Thurman dancer from earlier is stretched out against one wall, naked except for her boots, a lazy smile on her face. You are one of two people still watching. The dancers lounge around naked and hot under the lights, beautiful and untouched. It looks humid. You want to fan them with palm leaves. Suck on ice cubes and breathe mist into their lips. Wear your own outfit of gold sandals, and be their altar boy or temple acolyte....

Persephone does a silly dance, climbs up the pole, and twists her way back down, does handstands for you. She comes back to your window and her eyes focus on you, serious, thinking. She undulates and smiles, showing you her ass, her tits, her shoes, her pussy, right at eye level. You cannot look away, you are enchanted. She is pink and luscious, sparkling, red-gold from the lights. She licks and bites her own nipple and you finally feel your clit so warm and hard the feeling has spread throughout your lower body, the urgency of this is unfuckingbearable. You feel overwhelmed. You do not know what to do. How do guys deal with this? You look at the pools of semen with new understanding, but you're not about to do that here. Instead you feel wild, panicked, worshipful, at a standstill, spending more and more to keep seeing the girls deliciously naked and close enough to touch but you can't, and your breath is steaming up this little stinky booth.

The window lowers. The darkness is comforting after such staring at the light.

You walk outside into the San Francisco night. You turn and the lights of the Golden Gate Bridge stretch across the bay. They are shimmering in the fog. You think of the shimmering girls in their mirrored fishbowl dancing late into the night. The bridge and the girls: glittering, remote, and comforting all at once.

FEE FIE FOE FEMME

Elaine Miller

All night long she wouldn't let me kiss her because—she said—
our lipstick colors clashed.

Checking the address she'd written on a piece of paper, I'd
picked her up at her house earlier. *Rosalie*, the paper said, then
her phone number and address. No last name. Dykes don't need
last names when we have attributes and ex-lovers to be known
by. As a dyke I'm Jez the Goth, or Sharen's-ex Jez, never Jessie
Tate. And Rosalie...could be New-in-Town Rosalie, or Rosalie
the Beautiful. Maybe if I was into U-Haul rental she could be
Jez's Rosalie by the second date.

My heart skipped a beat as she'd appeared in the doorway
dressed like an old-time movie starlet, her loose curls bouncing
around her sparkling brown eyes. She'd taken my hand, and I'd
leaned in for a kiss, which she dodged, laughing impishly. And
explained. I was annoyed that she was right about the lipstick
clashing. I was wearing my usual vampiric matte blood-red, and
hers was something a worker bee would die trying to collect

for her queen. Raspberry pink, glittery under the new-car deep gloss, her lips were startling and perfect jewels against her brown skin.

I took Rosalie the Beautiful to LICK, the only full-time lezzie bar in town. Once there and seated at a table beside the dance floor, we lost no time in flirting. She pretended to lose one of her gold earrings in my cleavage, necessitating that she trail her fingers around my breasts, trolling for it, while I protested that she had to find it, quick, because I wear only silver with black clothing. And of course, I only wear black clothing.

But she still wouldn't kiss me. She would dance so close to me that the lines of her face blurred in our body heat, oh yes. She would let the slick material of her skirt smooth the way as she rode my thigh to the beat of the house music. Later in the evening, she'd let me hold her tight in the dark corners of the bar, one hand cupping her full breast, my thumb strumming across her nipple as she squirmed, my other hand tangled in the hair at the nape of her neck. But every time I tried to kiss her, throughout the evening, she just laughed and twirled away, leaving a cloud of girl-scent, a flare of her skirt, and the teasing word *Lipstick*.

By the end of the night, I was cross-eyed with frustration. When Rosalie the Beautiful whispered a lewd invitation in my ear, I simply answered, "Yeah. Let's go to my house," took her hand, and pulled her out of LICK, past the approving smirks of my friends. And on the way home she wouldn't kiss me. She teasingly said that it was all about preserving her shiny, glossy pink lipstick. Besides, she wouldn't want to distract me from my driving.

We tumbled in my door as one body with eight limbs, panting and pulling at each other's clothes all the way to the bedroom. She didn't seem to want to stop for a tour. We fell across my bed and I unzipped her dress and, with her wholehearted help, peeled off every item of clothing that could get in my way. I left her the pretty white stockings and garters, but threw her pinching high-heeled shoes on the floor. I'm a femme too; I know these things.

I hastily shucked off my own clothes, especially my own damned shoes, and they made little black heaps amidst the white piles of Rosalie's clothes.

She looked…well, you can guess how she looked, smooth-skinned and plump-limbed, all curves and soft lines. But you probably haven't imagined with your other senses yet, so close your eyes and imagine the heat of her skin warming the air around us, and her scent like clean sweat from dancing, and just a hint of her sex.

She lay back against the pillows and smiled at me. She didn't say anything, but I just knew that if I leaned forward now she'd let me kiss her and to hell with the lipstick. I didn't try. Instead I pulled a few coils of rope and some bondage cuffs out from the toy box and onto the bed, knowing that with what she already knew of me she wouldn't be at all surprised. Not in the mood for protracted negotiation, I cocked an eyebrow at her in an inquiring gesture.

"Sure," said Rosalie the Beautiful, her eyes outshining her lipstick. "My safeword is 'Untie me now.'"

I tied her flat on her back, her hips held down by a wide belt of ropes crossing back and forth from two of the many eyebolts on either side of the bed. I clipped her hands to the headboard at full extension over her head, allowing her breasts to poke tempt-ingly at the ceiling.

I buckled cuffs around her ankles, and two bigger cuffs a few inches above each knee. I passed a long, slim white rope through the bolts near her hands, and ran it through the rings on the cuffs around her strong, plump, stocking-clad thighs, and as she squeaked in a surprised way, effortlessly pulled her knees high up toward her chest, exposing her sweet, wet cunt. With a quick knot at the ring of the thigh cuffs, I pulled the ropes down to either side of the bed and ran them through two rings there, parting her thighs farther. As she began to squirm in earnest, I connected the ends of the ropes to her ankle cuffs and pulled her heels tight to the backs of her thighs, hindering her from kicking or moving her legs.

I stepped back to admire her, and paused, conscious of my own wetness and of my clit pulsing with the beat of my heart. I ached to touch her, and I let that ache build as I looked at her. Warily, she watched me watch her, and relaxed when she saw that, in the symbiosis of being desired, her potent femme's power was intact. Held open like a wanton offering, Rosalie's eyes met mine steadily, proudly. She knew her own beauty; pretty, pretty girl.

"Don't just stand there," she said. "I know you want me."

"Oh yeah, I do. I'm dying to have you," I said. "That's why this is gonna hurt me more than it hurts you."

She looked startled.

I sat for a moment on the bed between her thighs, slowly looking at every intimate detail of her body, finally meeting her eyes. She licked her perfect pink lips in an unconsciously catlike gesture of nervousness.

I leaned forward, letting my long black hair brush her thighs, and made myself comfortable on my belly, my face inches from her exposed cunt. Damn, she smelled good.

I exhaled slowly, open-mouthed, warm breath blowing ever so gently across her flesh.

She squirmed.

"Do it," she muttered.

"Do what?" I breathed.

"Go on, taste me."

"Maybe."

She wiggled halfheartedly, but the ropes prevented her from changing position. I moved closer still, my hair swinging once more against her skin, my lips an inch from her clit. I breathed slowly in through my nose, out through my mouth, making the flow of air as warm as possible.

"Fuck," she said, to no one in particular.

"Maybe that's what I'd like to do. Slide my fingers inside you, fuck you," I said, letting each exhaled word play over her clit.

"Yeah, fuck me."

"Maybe," I said.

I noticed the spot I was breathing on seemed to be drying a little from my hot breath, but the very entrance to her cunt was becoming drenched. I lifted up, scooched forward, and dropped a very unladylike wad of spit right at the top of her slit, then added another as I watched the first start to trickle downward.

"Ahh, fuck, what are you...why won't you...? Jez, do something!" she sputtered.

I grinned at her. "Maybe."

I went back to breathing on her, slowly, with all the warmth I could muster. Every so often she tried to shove her cunt in my face, but as she didn't have much slack, it was easy to avoid contact.

I lost myself, as if in meditation, as I pushed each exhale hotly past her clit, thinking nonthoughts about the sweet, musky scent of her cunt and her stifled growling noises. Every so often I added another bit of saliva above her clit, never touching her, but watching her twist and groan at the sudden sensation of wetness.

"There's a puddle under your ass now, not spit but cunt juice," I breathed, whispering to her clit as if it was my secret friend, not mentioning the wetness under my own hips.

"Touch me, you fucker." She started a rhythmic rocking motion, moving as far as the ropes would allow, only an inch or two each way.

I extended my tongue and made it a hard point, letting her make the barest contact between my tongue and her clit.

Immediately I felt her reaching for me with her hips, as far as she was able. But I simply held my place, using the faintest possible pressure as her clit brushed my tongue-tip on the upstroke and the downstroke.

After about a few dozen downstrokes, she suddenly sucked in and held her breath, and I leaned back and away from her, watched her pretty face contort in a snarl and the entrance to her cunt twitch hungrily. Nice.

"Why won't you lick me, you evil bitch-bastard?"

"Because I'm worried about mussing my lipstick," I said.

She started cursing, colorfully. Her cursing would have made a pirate's parrot lose feathers. It would have made a biker blush. It made me laugh, out loud and joyful.

I climbed up her body, nestled my hips between her spread thighs, and snuggled in. She gasped as my pubic hair pressed into her cunt after so long without touch, and I smiled down at her.

"Holy Smoke, you're so wet, I think I might get a steam burn."

"Fuck you."

"Is that your safeword?"

"No!" And then she started cursing again, as I lifted my body from hers and nuzzled into her tits, getting to know them. They were soft and weighty, full and rounded; the left one was slightly larger, a touching imperfection. Her large, dark nipples pointed straight at the ceiling, and went stiff as I watched.

Not every woman considers her nipples an erogenous zone, so I suckled on one for a second, to test. She gasped and bucked toward me, not away.

"Hey—are these candy?" I exclaimed happily, and dove right in.

I happily lost myself in no time again, moving from nipple to nipple whenever I thought the other might be getting lonely, lightly and experimentally sucking, biting, and licking until I thought I had deciphered the language of her curses and wriggles. What she liked best seemed to be a firm, direct suction at the tip of her nipple, with a slight graze of my teeth every so often. She never quite stopped trying to bring her body in contact with mine, but I stayed up on my elbows, with just my soft belly occasionally picking up wet streaks from her cunt. It wasn't just to tease her; I thought I might embarrass myself by coming if I humped her thigh even for a second.

Finally, I left her wet, chewed, lipstick-stained nipples and ran my tongue in a trail down the curves of her belly, across her garter belt, continuing on in a casual fashion along the length of her cunt. She hissed when I contacted her clit on the way, growled when I dipped inside her, and began to rock against me when I slipped my tongue back, making it flat and soft and dragging it so very slowly up between her labia.

"Oh, please," she said when her hard clit just naturally slid into my mouth, my tongue pressing underneath. "Please. That. Do that. Oh...." She sounded sniffly, so I sat up a little to check how she was. Her expression was soft and unfocused, her eyes full of tears. I felt the little spot in my heart grow even warmer with affection for her.

"What do you want, Rosalie the Beautiful?" I asked tenderly, adding my private qualifier to her name for the first time.

She smiled fuzzily at that. "Please touch me, Jez. Lick me. Fuck me. I'm going out of my mind."

"Yeah, I think maybe it's time," I said. And, watching her face, I slid one finger inside her, found she was wet enough, pulled out, and pushed three fingers back in, a little roughly. Her eyes rolled back and her whole body welcomed me in. I slid out and back in again, and her mouth opened soundlessly, her back arched. I did it again, and again, experimenting, trying to learn everything about her in a few short strokes.

I made a guess that she'd like to be fucked hard and fast, in direct contrast to my soft teasing game. Oh, yeah. Then I thought maybe adding direct pressure on her G-spot would feel right, and within a second knew I'd guessed correctly. She held nothing back, her body and face telling eloquent stories about her body's responses.

Time enough later, or tomorrow, for my harness and dick. No time, right now, even to reach for the lube. She seemed close to coming already, and I didn't want to tease her for even one moment more.

I moved and took her clit in my mouth again, soon finding the steady side-to-side rhythm that made her cunt clench around my hand. I closed my eyes and put everything I had into pushing her over the edge, lost in her taste and smell, reaching as far as I could inside her with every stroke of my fingers.

Rosalie went rigid, shaking, and her soft cries grew urgent. Her cunt clamped around my fingers, almost squeezing me out, but I felt I knew what she needed. I pushed harder inside her.

When I felt her muscles flex and heard the ropes attached to the headboard creak, I concentrated on her clit, flicking it hard with my tongue, once, twice, a third time…and she sucked her breath in and then wailed like a cat. She came in intense, shaking waves, her cunt's deep throbbing squeezing my fingers, and I kept going, fucking her more and more gently until the tension slowly melted out of her muscles, and it was time to stop.

I slid up her bound body, released the buckles on her wrist cuffs, and looked fondly at her. Breathing hard, flushed, and tear-streaked, she was more beautiful to me then than any woman I'd ever seen.

Despite everything we'd done in the last hour, her lipstick was still raspberry-glossy and perfect.

So I kissed her.

THE BRIDGE

Isa Coffey

It's dark. We're driving fast. The Coronado Bay Bridge sweeps lights like diamonds overhead. I'm drunk, baby, but not on booze. I'm drunk on you. I don't know your name, but it's good. You're good, and I'm falling, fast. You're hot; your suited self just right, behind the wheel. My wheel. Take over, baby. Drive this car of mine right up to heaven. The ocean's dark, taking off below us, all rocking waves tumbling like crazy. Shit. Throw me overboard; I'm heading there already.

Your fist is tight between my legs; the stars are shooting licks between my earlobes and my naked ribs. You've got me, tied between this bridge and the fucking sea below. I'm full. The moon is too. She's up there, competing with diamonds, competing with stars, competing with you. You've got one hand on the wheel of my black, coal black, cool black, shining black, '69 VW convertible, top way down. The other's opening from fist into hard, fat, dark fingers, figuring me out. Yeah, baby, that's all of me, and I'm gonna slide myself right onto you so you can fill me fast. You do.

Slick, your fingers are your dick. I'm riding, we're riding, the bridge is flying quick. I wanna be on this bridge all night. The wind is blowing out my brain. I gotta pull my tits up to the sky and moan and groan real loud, but—fuck—down's the only way for me. Pull my lever, baby, and there's no way, there's no other way, but down. You're on it, in it, and I'm losing now. Pull this fucking car over to the side, right here, right now, on top, the very tip, of this damn bridge. Fucking pull it fast. You do.

Suddenly balanced between now and then, midnight and dawn, I can't remember who you are, or who I am, but I am falling, fucking, in love with you. You can do your thing to me. Right now. You do. You come down, quick, across the stick, all dark skin, dark suit, dark hair. A huge sex sweep across the lit-up sky. You're heavy on me; you've got me pressed down deep into leather, deep into this fast-moving bridge, deep into you. Push me into the sea, baby. Take my breath. Take it away. Who needs it now?

It's tight; my knees are splayed against metal doors, and rods. My pink silk, soaked panties lost somewhere down there, to lust. And bust.

You got some kinda crazy ass dick burning hard right down my inner thigh. Long and thick and ready to go; you're a breathless femme's idea of heaven.

Your juicy lips are licking, nibbling, my nose, my lobes, my brows, my lashes. Wherever they can get. I'm biting back, real hard. You better eat me fast, baby, or I'll devour you.

Your bound-up chest rests thick on mine. I like the feel. I want some more. My nipples rub up hard against your bind. Pressing tits and nipples up, they're begging, I'm begging, "Suck them off. Suck them the fuck off." We're too crammed up in here for that. You moan, "Baby, you wait. When we've got enough room, I'm gonna suck your nipples off so bad, you're gonna die from cumming."

It's tight, and you're groaning, low, and I'm sweating; getting whatever kinda movement I can get going, going, 'cuz I'm ready to move big against your fucking fingers. You're turning two to four, all wet and fat and kind in me. You're going, baby, right into high gear, pushing it in with your weight, pushing it up with thrusts, suddenly moving faster than those cars speeding by, speeding right over the peak of this sky-scraping bridge. Oh yeah, baby, you've got speed. Run me over. Fuck me with your fingers, then your fist, while I shoot myself, and you, right up into lights, into the goddamn moon.

And yeah, you're curling it up, just right. You know your way around, just right. Rolling your fingers, balling me now, up into where I don't let anyone go. It's deep. You're deep. I'm shooting us into that moon, baby. And I'm falling right off of this bridge.

Falling, whispering, "You're pushing up against my heart, baby."

Falling, whispering, "You've taken my heart, baby."

You murmur back, low and slow, right down into the center of my done-in heart, "I'm all yours, baby; I'm all yours."

I can tell you're gonna cry, but don't. You are one fucking butch.

Then I'm cumming, and I'm cumming, and it's loud, and you're with me.

It's loud, and you're with me. It's loud, and you're with me.

I'm finding that I want you more. I'm fucking crying. For you.

"Hey baby," you say. You hold me real tight. I know you're gonna stay right here, no matter what the fuck you need, no matter how uncomfortable you get, no matter how worried about cops, or cold, or how much you need to pee. You're gonna stay right here, with some femme you hardly know, until I stop crying and say I'm okay; until I'm ready to get dressed and drive off this bridge, for burgers or coffee or my house or yours, because that's what butches do. It's why I started falling for you as soon as we got into my car and I was looking up at the lights and the stars, feeling a little too drunk on you, pulling off my blouse, and bra.

The cop does come, right after my cum. We—we're a we now, that's where my cum's led us, at least while we're still way up high on this bridge—see him first as taillights, heading the other direction, just as we're peeling ourselves up off the seat, back into the land of the bridge and the cars and the rocking ocean waves far down below metal rails by our side. Fuck.

You climb over to your seat, straighten your suit. I gather my bra, my frilly peach blouse, the remains of my panties, stretched out and soaked; then snap, button, draw on in time for the cop, who's turned right around and is coming our way. We knew he would; they always do. They sniff us out. Our scent makes them mad, makes them feral, makes them want to scratch and claw, or shoot and skin.

He pulls up behind us; his head's to our ass. Headlights are blazing, blinkers are pulsing, strobe lights are like a fucking carnival night. He's out of his cop car, strutting our way. Fucking pig. This won't be easy. Not in this town, home to a million studs in uniform. Not with a white cop. Not with a black butch driving a shiny black convertible, owned by the white woman sitting all femme in the passenger seat. Not with two women, any colors, alone in a car on the top of the Coronado Bay Bridge, lit up by cum. Not a chance.

My butch is sweating. Acting tough, for both of us, but scared. It's always harder for butches. I lean over, touch her hand, "You okay?" She says, of course, "Yeah, baby, no problem." I go ahead and ask, now that we're here, close and scared, sitting on top of the chopping dark sea, waiting for harm that's heading our way, "So, baby, what's your name? Tell me quick, before that prick tries to break us with his dick."

"My name's Sun, and baby, I wanna be *your* Sun."

Fucking full Moon on one side of my heart, way up here, way up high, and now Sun's on the other. Damn, what a night. I kiss her lips. Deep down inside I'm thinking, "Yeah, baby, you can sure be my Sun. I'm fucking gonna be your Moon."

The cop doesn't ask for Sun's ID, just tells her to get out of the car. Fuck. He tells her to walk over to his flashing cop car, lean up against the warm metal door, spread her legs, arms up, wide. It's bad. We knew it would be. He can smell dyke dick. Damn if he's gonna let some black butch fuck his white girl. He for sure thinks he owns me, and that he's gonna get me, after he takes Sun out. I'm watching out the window, feeling Sun's fear, knowing she's not going to show it, not to him, not now. Only to me, later, and only after I show her mine.

He starts at the top: bending Sun's arm in toward her head, he holds Sun's fingers, stiff with cum. Looks like he's maybe gonna break them back. Then, one by one, he slides them into his mouth instead, and starts to lick each one. Huh? Placing her hands back on top of his cop car, he pats down the sides of her body, treating that suit like it's worth a million dollars. A cop? He slides his hands, slowly, around to her tight bound breasts, but gently, like there's some kind of respect going on, then draws his body into hers, leaning long against her back, arms still wrapped around her binding. Looks like he's thinking of getting off.

But on a butch? What's happening here? I lean out farther, look more closely. This isn't a man with facial hair. I slide out of my side of the car, make my way slowly up toward them. The cop allows me to; he's clearly gone by now, into his search...for what? Sun wonders too, of course, and turns, to see Cop's eyes, glazed over. Hunting for his hidden world, his secret self, I grab his cop cap, pull it off, and down come waves of copper hair. Well, my. Surprise. A babe.

This he's a She. My she's a He. All up on this crazy ass bridge. Some night.

I push Cop into Sun, real hard. My body's into Cop's, especially down low. Cop seems to come alive, to find that hard-ass copper drive. We're sharing, and it's Sun's turn to get off with that long-ass cock. The three of us are panting now, cars whizzing by. They can't see much beyond the flashing police lights, bridge lights, starlight and that fucking juicy, full-assed moon. Just a little of us, getting off, spreading heat right out, right out, into light.

Cop's hot but acting like she hasn't a clue what to do when faced with the real thing. I reach around, take her hand, slide it down into Sun's pants, tight boxers, and along the full length of that sexy cock. Cop starts to rub, soft, gets the hang and goes on, hard. Turns out this copper's got some style. Sun's breathing is loud grunting; he's gazing heavy in my eyes. He's with me strong. We're in it, deep. We're in it way up to that sky that's dark behind the stringing, singing lights of this vast stretched-out bridge.

While she's on him, I do my own, unbuckle Cop's thick silver belt, let it drop, then slide her zipper down as well. She's sweating now. I want to make her cum; to give her power up to Sun. This doll's one bundle of surprise. She's willing, more than willing, *easy*, to slide in low; her belly breathes me right down deep; her hair is soft, seems sweet. A cop? How did she make it through? But damn is she ready: pearly, slippery, dripping, silky panties glide my hand, easy as can be, right over tiny curls I imagine share the copper of her head. My fingers spread her lips so I can fondle that tender clit, rising and falling as her rhythm decides to join mine. Oh yeah, baby Cop, oh yeah, here we go.

She's busy, too, trying to figure out how to pull Sun's cock out of his pants, and get it inside her. Clearly a virgin dyke. Sun's breathing so hard, he's totally gone, humping that cop's hand like he's gonna explode, not getting that Cop hasn't a clue what to do, except trying to figure out how to handle not falling apart with being about to cum herself, my hand moving that clit so swift now she's breathing like a teenager. Fuck—maybe she is one.

I got it now, I take control, of two way-out-of-it queers stuck in the middle of a great big bridge over a great big sea with a great big moon fucking with everything they got.

I reach around, slap Cop's hands, her fricking hands, out of my way, and shove them down her own, now swollen, chick dick, to keep the rhythm going. I grab Sun's dick—man, that dick's huge—a giant among dicks, out of his pants, pull a rubber from my skirt, rip it with my teeth and pray the bloody thing will fit his thing. It does. I spit some polish onto it, pull the copper's pants down low, the silken panties with them. She's lovely copper underneath, just as I'd supposed. I turn her round and push her back, the first time I've ever shoved a cop. I am into this. I'm turned on, and thrust her onto her warm cop-hood; it's ready for a good hot fuck. Then pull those uniform pants off her kick-ass boots, toss my fingers into her. No way to resist that cop's pussy naked on her machine.

Sun's right here, dick so high, so hard, he's clearly gonna pop if he doesn't get inside that copper's pussy. I wouldn't stand between that urgency, not after what he's given me. I pull out, and in he goes. Slow at first, letting her get used to him, then fuck-ass hard. Cop, wow, she hollers, and just as suddenly, she moans. No doubt it's her first time being butched. Lucky her, to have Sun break her in, and bring her out. Doesn't get much better. And, cool. Right here, with us. We're now a sudden secret sexy team, a sudden secret sexy us. It's cool.

Sun's driving her, Cop on her car; he's pumping it. Up and down and all around. Cop's clearly into it. All she's saying now is "Mmmmm," or "Yeah," or "More, please, more," or "Aaaaaah-hhhhh," or "Oooooohhhhh." She's one damn polite cop fuck.

The cars blaze by. A couple cars, they're in the know; they slow. They watch. Uh-huh. They see. They see, and now they're humping fast in their own cars, whipping out whatever stuff they've got: their toys, their gear, their fists, mouths, sticks and whips. On their way to their own play. Lucky to cross this bridge tonight.

I'm hungry. I want him too. Not Cop. Well, maybe Cop, but I want Sun. I need him now. I got my stuff, right here with me. I reach into my girly skirt, grab another see-through wrap, and some slick-dick lube; stretch my sexy self along his suited side; nibble on his dark, shell ear, and whisper, "Can I rub your butt, slap your ass, slide inside your tender hole? I promise to be true."

Sun's so gone, mesmerized by his thick dick in that soft copper pussy, he isn't thinking much about his butt, or me. He turns his face; he looks at me, remembers me, grabs me with his mouth to suck my face, my lips, my brow, and looks down at my tits. I lift one up, pull back my bra, and press it in his mouth. God, how much I've wanted it inside, ever since we drove onto this smoothly swinging bridge.

Sun sucks. He bites. He licks it light; he licks delight. And all the while pumping copper pussy. This He is Herculean. For the second time this mighty night, I cum, then cum. His eyes light up: a tit-clit dyke. And yeah, he wants me inside that hole of his. My butch.

He turns back to Cop, who's groaning now for Sun to take

her life away, right now. Sun's moving different now, slowing it all down and deep. Cop's cumming; that's sure. Now it's all, "FFFFFFFFFFFUUUUUCCCCCCCKKKKKKKKK!" and "SSSS-SUUUUUUUCCCCCCKKKKKKKKK!" Sweet girl transformed to dyke. Sun surely has just saved her life, in this one night.

I snap my wrap on my fuck finger, bite open my smoothest lube and slip my hand right down his shorts. I feel him whisper to himself, to me. I hear the sound I knew I would. I know it well. Hurt and desire: both. While Sun gentles into Cop's post-cumming melt, right on her hood, I rub my hand just light at first, all over Sun's big butt. He starts to roll, he starts to groan, he starts to have faith in me. He gazes back, and fills my eyes. "You got my heart, baby," he moans, 'cuz I'm right here, real close, about to get closer.

Sun pulls out of Cop, leans over her, unbuttons her uniform shirt. I hear Cop suck in breath as Sun starts to lick, so I lean over to see. Cop's got some fucking big breasts. Her eyes are closed; her breath's coming all strong again, and so is Sun's. He's licking, but he's thinking, he's feeling, he's breathing: ass. Hole. But you're not getting it, baby, not yet, not 'til I'm ready. And I'm not ready. I'm into this big ass of yours. Into it enough to pull down these sharp wool trousers of yours. Into it enough to pull down these black, tight-ass boxers of yours. Pull them down just enough to see your strap, just enough to see your hot double-moon ass, right under the tails of your fine, black-ass jacket.

Rubbing is heading right into slapping, right into licking, right into whacking, and kissing. I'm settling at your butthole, baby, for the gentlest of tender strokes. Looks like you've caught on fire, baby. I'm rubbing; you're groaning; you're pushing back on me. You want me in. No way, baby. No way. Not yet. I know you can handle it with me at the wheel, baby. You drove us already tonight; it's my turn now.

This night was growing long. The bridge was way more empty. Fewer people heading out to the beach to make out. Fewer people heading back into the city to do it in someone's bed. It was starting to feel like it was just us way up here, flying high. Just us and a couple of random cars, too much in their own trip now to get what was going on under our bright, spinning lights.

There was just this one car, some kinda sedan, that had decided to stop, totally stop, and hang: two dykes in their car, checking us out. There they were, poised on the thin inner meridian, close enough to take in what was going on, far enough to do their own fucking in private. I looked up at Car, giving Sun more time to want me moving down and in while I teased that sexy butt of his. I could see a sweet Honey ass in some pretty pink lace panties, big breasts hanging low, falling out of matching pink lace cups, clearly making someone I couldn't catch real happy. Mmmmm. A moment later some high-class wool pants, pulled down far enough to see a black strap tight over a deep Chocolate butt, come up. They'd sure brought the right size car. Was this their second, third or fourth time round tonight?

The two of them, the three of us: clearly Dyke Night now on the Coronado Bay Bridge.

Sun's so ready now he's practically shoving his ass onto my hand, my arm. His groaning is loud enough that Honey and Chocolate have looked up at me: am I fucking with this butch? Sun's taking it out on Cop, as well, and she's liking it, kicking her hips up and down so hard that hood of hers has gotta be denting. I guess those tits of hers are driving her wild. Sounds like she's cumming. Again. Can't keep track, but I'm sure it's a record for her.

Okay, Sun, here we go, baby. I slide right down over your hole, circling like you're my golden crown. And baby do you grow quiet and still. The pause. Like the bridge, the wind, the midnight doves, the shooting stars all decided to inhale and wait, for you. I hold still too, my finger pressing and waiting right at your gate. The shift comes. You open, so far, I slip one finger easily in. Oh man, I forgot. No matter how many asses I've been in, I never remember this moment. You are damn sweet inside, you big tender butch. All soft and smooth and nothing but sugar. But wow do you go, no damn pause anymore. You're pumping on me like heat, like fire, like there's never going to be tomorrow. You need way more than I've given you yet.

I've gotta work fast. No one-finger covers are gonna do this right; you're clearly a full-fisted job. My left hand pulls a purple glove out of my pocket, dangles it from my mouth, while my right finger fucks your butt, your heart, your everything. I grab the lube, squeezing it over those dangling purple fingers, as well as down my clothes. Anything for you. I dip my face down low, to lick your back, while I change gear, then press two, and quickly three, fingers into you. Wow, baby, are you full. And wanting it. You're licking Cop, down to her twat. She's grabbing cock; she needs more now, and so do you. I move from three to four. Your cock's in her, my cock's in you.

I glance back to that Honey-Chocolate car, to see if they approve of what I'm up to. Clearly I'm off the hook, 'cause that car's rocking now. Someone in there's cumming, loud. It's Chocolate's ass that's up and pounding, so Honey's surely ejecting herself right off this planet. And from the sound of it, she's gonna make her way to Mars.

Cop, Sun and me, we're rocking, we're socking, we've got it in sync. You're pumping Cop and I'm pumping you; our rhythm is hot. Our bodies are sweating it out; we're setting it up; we're wanting it now: all Cum.

I'm looking down, right into your butt. And I'm looking up,

right into the stars and the lights and the moon. It's all right together; it's shooting us out: your butt and Cop's heart and my mind and the moon and her cunt and my heart and the stars and your heart and the lights and those strangers just over the lines, that aren't really lines.

Then POW comes the wave and FUCK is it high: a twister, a quaker, a hip-hopping TSUNAMI.

Sun's cumming, Cop's cumming, Chocolate-Honey's cumming, every single fucking star's cumming, every single fucking light on the multi-thousand-foot strands of the bridge's cumming, the moon for sure is cumming, and if I don't cum within the next twenty seconds, I'm going to throw myself off this damn bridge, into the frigid waters of the salt-laden Pacific Ocean, to die.

Of course, Sun gets this, and turns around. Cop and Chocolate-Honey seem to get it too, because Cop sits up, moves off her hood, Chocolate-Honey slide out of their slick sedan and head across the lunar lanes. Suddenly they have rope, lube, gloves, cuffs, belts; everything except blindfolds, because they're gonna let me see the stars, the swaying lights, the moon that never changes course tonight. And them.

They strap me to the bridge, arms spread, legs wide, wind up between my legs, my thighs. They rip off my skirt, my soaked panties beneath, my thin little blouse and my bra just below. I'm naked right here on the Coronado Bay Bridge. It's me and the seagulls, the doves flying by.

The moon that seems bigger, that's filling my heart.

Then these dykes take their turns. They hold and caress me. They sing me love songs. They strap on fresh dildos, don black leather vests, frilly gold panties, with matching gold bras. They start rubbing my titties 'til they're rising, real tight; start licking and sucking, real gentle and tough. 'Til I'm crying and laughing and moaning and groaning. They're caressing my belly, ooh baby, that's nice. They're stroking my hair, all of it, and it's good. They're saying my name, over and over. They're stroking my feet, and sucking my toes.

Songs are coming, and they're going. The stars are sharp; they fill the sky; they fill my eyes. Oh yeah. They're really singing now. My name. My love. Their love for me. It's good. The bridge is holding me. The wind is strong. It's blowing all of us, into each other's arms. Sun's right here, right in my face. He's kissing me, right on my lips, so light, so hard, so everything. Right now, just now, all the slapping I could want, over my entire body, starts. My hands, my feet, my tits, my thighs. And in they go, my holes get filled, and pumped, and I want more. Sun's kissing me, real light. And calling out my name. The singing is so loud by now, up to the stars. It's all I want. I'm filled, I'm fed, I'm held, I'm slapped, I'm loved, I'm high, I'm bright, I'm dark, I'm gone, I'm here, I'm swelled, I'm wet, I'm hot, I am, I'm not.

And I am fucking cumming.

Cumming into everything. Cumming into Sun and Cop, Chocolate-Honey, Moon and Stars, Light and Me. And Not-Me.

Cumming, and cumming. Cumming, and cumming, and cumming.

Now we're all laughing,
and I'm crying.
We're all laughing,
and I'm crying.
We're all laughing,
and I'm crying.
Way up on the bridge.
Way up high on the bridge.
Way fucking up high on the Coronado Bay Bridge.

GRAVITY SUCKS

Skian McGuire

"Oh, shit! Fuck! Goddamn!" I sucked my bleeding knuckle in spite of the grease and shut my smarting eyes against the shower of rust and undercarriage gunk that sprinkled down on my face like fairy dust from hell. Between that and the sixty-watt drop-light frying my ear, I never noticed the garage door closing.

There was no point wiping my eyes. Nothing on me was clean enough. I blinked against the tears and groped for my lost wrench, cursing again. How far could it have gone? I scooted the creeper a little ways out and froze. The radio had come on. Holding my breath, I listened while somebody tuned it to a country station.

For one foolish moment, I imagined I would be invisible if I stayed completely still, like a rabbit. As if half of me wasn't hanging out from under the rattletrap '67 Mustang I called Baby. I forced my voice to work.

"Who's there?" I tried to sound gruff. Big and butch. Yeah, they could see my big threatening butch legs. Right.

No answer. With a shaking hand I switched off the light and squinted into the dark, willing my eyes to adjust. If I could see, I could recognize the intruder's ankles, maybe. If they happened to be in the quarter of the garage available to my sideways, immobile vision.

No such luck. "Fuck," I whispered, barely audible over my jackhammer heart. I dug in my heels and pulled the creeper as hard as I could, right into something solid and warm against my upraised knee.

Someone giggled.

"Natalia?" I breathed, relief flooding in.

The leg that had stopped my creeper pressed against the inside of my thigh, shifted, and then there were two, pressing my legs apart.

"Jeez, Nat," I said in a rush, "you nearly gimme a heart attack. I thought maybe an ax murderer…" I trailed off. What would an ax murderer do, hack off my feet? Still, the thought gave me a shiver. "Natalia?"

The feet stepped back. Awkwardly, I pulled the creeper out and came smack up against the legs again.

Again, the giggle.

Now I was getting pissed. "Come on, Nat. I gotta get this frigging thing off so I can put a new parking brake cable on." I was whining, and I knew it. I tried to sound calmer and more reasonable. "If I don't put a new cable on, the parking brake won't work. If the brake doesn't work, it won't pass inspec—" Cool fingers pushed aside my waffle-knit shirt and grappled with the button of my jeans.

"Whoa!" Startled, I sat up. "Yah!" My head hit the frame. I dropped back, eyes streaming. "Fuck," I whispered and spit a mouthful of rust and gunk bits, hands useless at my sides.

More giggles. The hand worked my zipper down. I lay there,

forehead throbbing. I heard a rustle and a little grunt as she knelt between my feet.

Fingers pushed past my underwear and dove unerringly for my snatch, zinging my clit with what seemed like an electric charge.

"Eeep!" I squeaked. Reflexively, I tried to close my legs. She shifted her weight and shoved them apart even harder. Her forefinger set up a hypnotic rhythm, insistent but not drubbing, teasing but effective. My clit hummed to its tune. My legs fell open, suddenly nerveless.

"Eeeeeeeeeee," I breathed. She laughed out loud. My head didn't hurt at all.

Fingers spread my lips and dipped into the flood of juice I was producing. Wet fingers slithered and danced between clit and hole. My hips bucked. "Ohhhh, jeeez!" I moaned.

The hand yanked out of my pants. "Awww!" I protested, my heels shifting for purchase. I don't know where I thought I was going.

Her hands seized the waistband of my jeans. "Upsy-daisy," a familiar voice said. Familiar, but Natalia? While my fuck-fogged brain tried to puzzle this out, my hips obliged her, all by themselves. Hands tugged my jeans and underwear down past my butt, past my thighs, past my knees, coming to rest at my ankles. I sighed, quivering with anticipation. A cool draft wafted over my thighs as I waited. And waited.

"Natalia?"

Stillness. Silence. "Uh, Nat?" I tried again nervously.

"Whoa!" Hauled by the jeans around my ankles, my legs shot into the air. The creeper trundled backward. Under the car, my arms flailed for something to hang on to. "Whoa, whoa, whoa!" Hands scrabbling on the concrete, I tried to pull my legs down. My bare knees thumped against cold metal.

"Relax," that familiar voice said, "you're bungeed to the door handle."

"Oh," I said, as if that explained it. I craned my neck for a view. All I could see was a denim bell-bottom and the hem of a long crushed-velvet coat. I ransacked my mental inventory of Nat's wardrobe and came up blank.

The air in the garage was more than cool on my naked ass, but I was sweating in my long-john and filthy Carlux hoodie. Before I knew it warm breath had enveloped my pussy, and her mouth touched down like Soyuz docking Mir. "Na'zdorovye!" I shouted, inspired.

Her tongue flicked back and forth and sluiced up and down my labia, darting into my hole like a fish. Her lips closed over my throbbing nub and sucked. Her teeth teased my clit hood and tugged at my short hairs. My legs bounced on their tether as I strained to meet her mouth, the creeper rocking and rolling ever so gently as I moved. I was weightless, trapped in a tin can, floating in space.

My arms stretched out, Christlike, for ballast as I swayed. There was my wrench: the thought drifted through my brain. I panted and licked rust-gunk off my dry lips. Orgasm was inevitable; my lower half was on autopilot. Now that less of me was under the car, maybe I could see my benefactress? No. My own pale goose-pimply thighs blocked the side view. Straight down the middle, tucking my chin hard into my chest and scraping my forehead—"Ouch!"—against the car, only the top of a dark brown head was visible. Carefully, I drew my arms in.

Her tongue moved faster. She stuffed it into my dripping hole, and I clenched and opened, rising to it, trying to draw the slithery coyness of it deeper.

"Oh, yeah," I moaned. In slow motion, my hands met on the silky bobbing top of her head. I twined my fingers in her hair.

Her rather longish hair. Had it gotten that long since I'd seen her last? How long had it been? I'd seen Nat two weeks before. No, wait, it was only....

Under her relentless tongue, the heat and pressure in my groin achieved supernova. Her thumbs dug into the soft flesh of my thighs as I came, bucking, a tiny lightship tossed in the solar wind.

"Cosmic," I breathed.

Her giggles were warm, moist puffs against my engorged clit. I shivered.

"Oh, Natalia," I breathed, the last spasms twitching through my rapidly cooling flesh. "Natalia?" I unwrapped my fingers from her hair—gee, how long was it, anyway?—and groped toward her face like Helen Keller with a load on.

"Ah, ah, ah!" she said, pulling away. Without thinking, I grabbed for her.

"Aaaack!" The creeper teetered sideways. My head hit the car. My shoulders slid toward the floor. My arms, trapped between my pinioned legs, came back too slow to keep my sweaty ass from stuttering off the canted creeper onto icy concrete. My splayed thighs slapped against the car door and bounced maddeningly on the bungee.

"Shit," I muttered. A giggle tinkled out from across the dark garage, somewhere behind me. I didn't dare open my eyes. I spit oily crud and called out, "Natalia? Wait a minute, honey. Help me get out of...."

The garage door opened. And closed.

I snaked a ten-inch breaker bar out from under my left asscheek and scooted sideways. Far and wee, a twangy male voice tunefully exhorted God to bless Texas. I thought of Houston, and Ground Control, and empathized with all those nameless astronauts who came down hard on dry land in dark little capsules and waited, waited, waited, to be set free.

In the end, I toed off my sneakers and tugged numb feet and ankles out of their denim prison, my numb legs flopping uselessly back to earth. I thought about the glory days of Mercury and Apollo while the circulation gradually returned and my cold bare behind absorbed spilled transmission fluid and waste oil from the grimy garage floor. I thought of Natalia—it was Natalia, wasn't it?—and unearthly bliss and my own shocking touch-down on the unforgiving planet.

But what can I do? I am a fool in love, or even in lust, as I suspected it might boil down to. I called Natalia after work the next day. She'd be happy to meet me at Taco Villa for "tapas, or maybe something more?" She breathed into the phone, "I just love eating South-of-the-Border, don't you?"

It took three-quarters of an hour to get the crud out from under my nails. She was waiting at the bar when I finally got there, nursing the last inch of a Corona and bobbing her head to Hank, Jr., on the jukebox.

I stopped dead in my tracks.

"Natalia," I finally managed as she bounced up to give me a hug, "you got a haircut."

"Yes, this afternoon," she whirled and patted her hardly-longer-than-a-crewcut locks. "Do you like it?"

"Ah, sure," I began faintly, until the look on her face told me I was about to make a horrible mistake, "yes, I love it. It's terrific. Absolutely gorgeous."

She took my arm as the waitress led us to a booth in the back. In the dark. My unruly imagination slipped the surly bonds of earth, and I wondered what I would do if she slid down the padded vinyl bench and disappeared beneath the table.

She ordered a Corona for both of us. "Upsy-daisy," I murmured, remembering.

"I beg your pardon?" She cocked her head, smiling the kind of smile no virgin had a right to.

Our drinks arrived at something approaching the speed of light.

"Na'zdorovye!" She tipped her bottle toward me. I sprayed beer across the table.

She graciously helped me mop up the mess and even signaled the waitress for more napkins. Already as mortified as I could be, I forged ahead, boldly going where I fervently hoped no man had gone before.

"Natalia," I began, "did you by any chance stop by my house yesterday? While I was, uh…" I paused, feeling my ears turning hot, "…working on the car?"

"Did I ever tell you, darling," she reached for my hand and gazed deeply, earnestly, into my eyes, only the faintest hint of amusement playing on her lips, "that my father was a member of the KGB?"

"No," I answered weakly, "I didn't know."

"He was assigned to Martina Navratilova. When she defected, so did he. What else could he do?"

"Really." Her fingers were stroking my palm.

"So, you see," she smiled, "secrets run in my family." Her toe nudged my ankle. My heart threatened to achieve escape velocity.

Appearing out of nowhere, the waitress hovered over our table, her pad at the ready.

"We'll have the number five combo, and the number three," Natalia told her, "and the number six as well, hmm?" She looked at me for confirmation. I licked my lips. She took that as a yes. "Unless you'd rather…." She squeezed my hand and cut a look at the exit.

"Could we get that order," I asked the waitress, "to go?"

"Pre-par-ing for takeout..." she enunciated as she wrote.

Time is relative; you don't need a Grand Unified Theory to know that. Several billion years later, we loaded our steaming cartons of enchiladas and chimichangas into the Baby's backseat, where they were swiftly forgotten in our warp speed race across the galaxy to my bedroom. We left a trail of clothing through the house behind us, planetary detritus forming an asteroid field in our wake. I never found out for sure if it was Natalia's mouth I rendezvoused with in the lightless depths of my garage, and I don't know if pistoning fingers and slick thighs actually convert matter into energy. Minutes and seconds can't measure the rate of propulsion of a body rocketing toward orgasm. But this one thing is immutable physical law: when the Big Bang happens, time stops.

Einstein didn't know the half of it.

YOU CAN WRITE A STORY ABOUT IT

Jera Star

1.

I wait to meet you on the porch, your silver rollerblades shining all the way down the street. I finger the chain around my neck as you approach. We are still awkward at first on these casual rendezvous we've been having. You're used to fucking friends. I'm used to fucking strangers. We are neither friends nor strangers. I'm a pink-haired hippie bi chick. You're a crew-cut wannabe-cop boy dyke. Sometimes, we fuck.

"Hey, T," I say.

You've come over after watching that movie you love with the character named Troy in it. Where you got your boy name, the one you just told me about today. I haven't yet called you by it.

"Yo, what's up?" you ask. I ignore your question. I'm distracted because you're wearing a red baseball cap back-ward—my weakness. You sit down beside me on the porch to take off your blades. "Oh, I saw a shooting star on the way here," you tell me, excitement in your voice. You remind me of a little kid and I find it endearing. A nice change from your usual cocky, obnoxious talk. We sit for a while and talk about the stars. Then I bring you inside. You swagger up the stairs to my apartment. Follow me down the hall to the couch in the spare room.

"How was your day?" I ask.

This time you ignore my question. Instead you say, "You have strong hands." I know you are trying to move things along to what we both really want to be doing. But still, it's one of the few compliments you have ever and will ever (I realize later) offer me. I relish it. And take your bait.

"You want a massage?"

You sit on the floor in front of the couch. I start massaging your shoulders through your clothes. After a minute, you bring out a little container of strawberry massage oil from your pocket. I laugh, getting the point. I take off your shirt. Drip the oil onto your back. You say it feels like lube: cold and hot. I massage again, starting at your neck. Mold your skin. Flex my fingers around your muscles. Shoulders, upper arms. Move my hands in front to your pecs. Careful to avoid your breasts. I stretch your arms up and lay them back down against your sides. Touch my fingers to your lower spine, one of your erogenous zones. Stay there for a while, applying pressure. Playing. You cut right to the chase.

"So, Sue, tell me about your first kiss." You want to get at my fantasies. This is what we do for each other. I like the question.

"It felt so good I thought I could go on kissing him for hours. But then later, behind the portable, after school, he said, 'What do you want to do to me?' I didn't want to do anything to him. I wanted him to do things to me. I wanted him to lick my whole body. All the way from mouth to clit."

"What else?" you ask as I work on your shoulder muscles.

"Hmm, I was too shy to tell him what I wanted. So we just kissed some more," I answer, absorbed in my hands pushing into your back. "Eventually I told him I didn't want to be monogamous and he didn't like that." You laugh, not sure about it yourself.

"Tell me, Sue, what you want me to do to you. Who, what, where you want me to be."

I smile.

You try and grab my tits and I love it. You try and tickle me and I don't like it. We laugh as you try to tickle me and I tell you to stop.

"Don't," I say.

"Don't what?" you say, grabbing my tits again, putting your hands in my pants. "Don't, Boy-T? Don't, Daddy? Don't, Troy? Don't touch my tits? Don't touch my clit? Don't make me come? Huh? Don't what?" I squirm. Hot, fucking hot.

"Daddy," I moan, wanting your hand on my clit. "Daddy, please." I squirm more as you fondle me, feel me, make my clit swell. You take your hand away.

I whine, hurt, sad. "Daddy, please. Come on, Daddy. Give me. Give me, please. Daddy, please."

You give in and give me some more. Turn me over on my stomach. I moan and cry with the sensations in my cunt. Your hand still fingers my clit. I want more, you pull your fingers away. I whine.

"Oh, poor baby," you say. "What's wrong? Is there something wrong, baby?"

"Please, Daddy." I'm close to crying. You put your fingers back.

"There you go, baby. Come on. You're a good girl." You move your finger faster on my clit. I moan and say, "Please,

Daddy," again and come madly, sweetly, sadly in your arms.

"Do you love me?" you ask.

"Yes, Daddy, I love you."

I shed some tears. We are both quiet.

Finally I say, "And you, T, what do you want me to do, be for you?"

I straddle you. Take off my shirt. Kiss you. Take off my bra while you watch. Take off your jeans and boxer briefs and spread your legs. Move down your body to your belly. You feel vulnerable with it exposed, I know. I linger there, my eyes on you. My tongue licking around your belly button. I start fingering your clit slowly, gently.

"Do you do this to all the boys?" you ask.

"Just my slave-boys," I say. You make small moans. I stop playing with you. Ask, "Were you a good boy today?"

"I hope so," you answer. You always make me laugh.

"You think you deserve this?" I ask.

"Yes, Mistress," you moan as I push one finger inside your cunt.

"Why do you think you deserve this?" I play with your clit some more.

"Because it feels so good." You start humping my finger. I bend down to kiss you and just when you're ready for it, I pull away. You try to bring my lips to yours again. I don't let you.

"Ah, Boy-T wants to kiss me, does he?" I say to you, holding your arms above your head.

You close your eyes. "Uh-huh," you say, still humping.

"Now why would I want to let him do that?"

"You know you want it," you say, impatient. You shake your hands out of my grasp. Pull me down against you again. I let my tongue brush your lips. Then I grab your hands and put them above your head one more time. You like it.

"Slave-boys don't kiss without asking," I say. "I want Boy-T to learn how to be a gentleman." You smile and grab my boob real quick. Cocky, as usual.

"Ask nicely," I tell you, speeding up my hand on your clit.

"Oh, fuck."

"I said ask nicely." I push two fingers in your cunt. You clutch my arm.

"Kiss me, damn it," you say as I play with your clit and move my fingers in and out of you.

"What was that?" I ask. I start fucking your wet cunt, pushing my fingers deep. My thumb on your clit. You're groaning with each thrust. Keep trying to grab me, pull me to you. I keep pushing you down. Keep thrusting.

"Please," you moan, as your hips rise, try to push my fingers deeper into you with each thrust.

"Please what?"

"Please, please, kiss me, please." You pant between words.

"Ah, that's a good boy," I say. I let go of your arms above your head. You yank me down on top of you, cover my mouth with yours, groan and swear as I fuck you. You come smooth and heavy. Your moans vibrate through me.

2.

It's been a few weeks since our last encounter. Another fight. They keep happening. Our fights remind me of my best friend at ten. How we used to touch tongues in the corner of the school-yard, get mad, and not talk to each other for weeks at a time, then one day start touching tongues again.

You call and ask me to come over. You have something you want to show me. When I hear your obnoxious laughing voice on the phone asking for me, I forget why I was so mad at you.

You come over to show off your new boy clothes. You say you

really feel like a guy in them. Shirt and vest. I tell you that you look hot because I know you want to hear it. You tell me, like it's not a big deal, that I'm the only person you've mentioned all this boy stuff to. I'm surprised. Flattered. I offer to take pictures of you exploring your guy self. You refuse. But I persist and get you. Sitting on the couch, legs spread, taking up space; the rapper look, you call it. Your arm bent, scratching your chin; intellectual. Standing, doing a muscle pose; jock. This is all leading up to one thing, only I don't know it.

You want to go out together to the local straight slutty bar. We've talked about it before. I haven't been since I was in high school. Avoided it since I came out. But I love the idea. I put on lipstick for the first time in ages. Tight jeans and a skinny-strap tank top. For me, this is a performance. Reclaiming sixteen with more power than I ever felt I had then. I know for you, this is it.

We take the bus downtown in silence. Avoid stares. It is our first public appearance as any kind of couple. Your first public appearance as a guy.

Once in the bar we meld into the place. You quickly become my tough-ass boyfriend for the night. Stand on the sidelines, cocky and casual, and watch me dance. I play up to the bio boys until you can't resist and try to feel me up on the dance floor. I pretend to protest, giddy and turned on. You work on one of the straight girls dancing beside us and I pout and act like I'm pissed off. A jealous girlfriend. Until you turn back around to me, push me up against the speaker, and dry hump me, in front of all the bio boys and their straight girlfriends. Your packing cock in your skater pants bulging against the crotch of my pretty-sixteen-year-old-girl jeans. We stay long enough to make a scene. Both of us wet.

"I've decided," you say as we head home to your place, high on the night. "I want you to fuck me with my cock."

I'm shocked. I've brought up the idea of me fucking you before, but you've always refused. Fingers, yes. But never the cock.

"The only way it's gonna happen," you say, not looking at me, "is, you've gotta be a guy."

I am never *boy*. My cunt drips.

"Are you sure?" I ask, anxious about my boy performance abilities.

"Yeah, I'm sure." You pause. We approach your apartment.

"You can write a story about it," you say finally. " 'I fucked this guy once....'"

I smile casually, acting as if I'm not completely nervous and turned on at the thought of being a guy myself, let alone fucking you. You look at me, knowing.

Once we're inside your apartment, I close the door, kick off my shoes, and push you against the living room wall. "Sounds good. But first I want slave-boy to work for his pleasure." You lift up my shirt and start playing with my boobs. "I want you to eat me out. Some good, old-fashioned, cunt licking. And if you're real good," I say slowly, "then maybe...I'll put on your big old cock and fuck you with it." Which makes you smile and move your arms into a surrender position.

"You think you can handle that, slave-boy?" You nod keenly. I push you to the floor. Unbutton my fly. "And you know what I think about good head," I say as I take off my shirt. "It's hard to come by, don't you agree?" You nod again. I unclip my bra. Get rid of my pants and underwear.

"I want it like this," I say, and kneel over you. "With a wall to cling to when I come." I put my arms, my boobs against the cold wall. You slide down onto your back. I bend over your mouth and feel your tongue. My breath catches. "But, as you know, few people can ever really satisfy me."

I bend down lower. You grab my cunt with your whole mouth. I groan. "Do you think you can, slave-boy?"

"Oh, yes, Mistress." I shiver.

"Good. Because I want to come. So you've got to keep it up good. Do you think you can, long enough? Suck my pussy with all its fur until I come? Yeah, that's right, just like that. Oh, fuck, yeah. Do you think you can keep it up, slave-boy? 'Cause I want to come and I want to come good. Long and full and all through me like electricity or something. Can you do it, slave-boy? Come on, keep it up, keep it up. Come on do it keep me coming come on, keep me coming, I'm going to come, no, keep it slow keep it slow, I don't want to come yet. I said, do it slow now, slow now, yeah, that's right. Can you keep it up, boy? Can you? Come on, more tongue, I said more tongue, boy, yeah that's right, faster now, speed it up a bit, tongue and mouth, faster...just like that. Yeah, that's right. Do it like that.... Can you keep it up? 'Cause I want to come so you better keep it up, I said yes, more, faster, faster, fucking fast I said goddamn it. Fuck, keep it coming keep it coming keep me coming there I'm there, I'm there I'm fuck I'm coming goddamn you fucking coming fuck fuck fuck fuck. Commming. Unh unh unh unhhhhhhhhh. Fuck boy, that's it. Hold me now. Just hold me."

I press my cunt into your belly and let your arms go around me. Just long enough to get myself together. Then I sit up and look at you smiling. All proud of yourself.

"So you think you deserve a fuck for that?" I laugh into your neck for a long time.

In the bedroom, you dress me up in your shirt and vest.

"So who am I?" I ask.

"Steve."

"Who's Steve?"

"Just Steve," you say. I laugh.

"And who are you tonight?" I ask, expecting you to say Troy.

"Tammy."

"Your girl name?"

"Yeah, or you can call me slut, bitch, whore."

I'm blown away. You are never girl. Talk about gender fuck. I get even wetter. Wonder if I'll be able to comply. "Those are harsh words," I say. "You know what a good-girl feminist I am."

You smirk. "Just wait, you'll like it. It'll be easier than you think." You get out your big rubber dick and strap it on me. I like it. You are right. I immediately start to feel cocky. Don't know exactly what you mean by "Be a guy," but I like the feeling of the cock between my legs, attached to *my* body for a change.

"I want you to dominate me," you say. "I want it hard. Lots of swearing and shit. I'll protest, but you make me take it. Be aggressive. Be an asshole. Call me a cunt. Yeah, cunt, that's a good one."

I'm unsure of how to begin. I push you down on the bed.

"Oh, please stop," you say. Your voice is suddenly higher pitched. I take it as a sign to start being an asshole.

"Shut up, cunt, Steve's going to do whatever the hell he pleases."

You jump up at me, ferocious. I make you stop. Tell you to lie back and shut the fuck up. And you do it. You moan.

A moan I've heard many times. A pleasure moan. I still don't feel like a guy, just an asshole wearing a guy's shirt and vest. But it's enough. I start to get into my role. I put my hand on my new dick. It's hard. So am I.

"And what I please is to fuck you, bitch."

You moan again like you like it. "Please don't," you say, pulling me toward you at the same time.

"Ah, come on. I know you're a whore. I know you want my big fucking dick pumping your nasty cunt." I shock myself with what I'm saying. You like it.

"Oh, don't make me, don't fuck me," you say. Then cry, "Oh fuck yeah," when I slap the cock against your thigh. That makes me hot.

"Take your goddamn pants off and turn over, slut," I say.

I rub my hand up and down my dick. You stay where you are and watch me. "You heard me. Turn the fuck over, slut! That's right. Now just lie there while I boot up." I put on a condom, drip some lube on your ass. You moan loudly.

"Shut up, bitch," I say and put my cock against your thigh again. You catch your breath.

"Oh, no, please."

"Oh, yes. Lift your ass, girl. I said lift, bitch." You lift.

"Here I come. Oh, yeah, take it like the whore you are."

I slowly move my cock into you.

"Oh, no, please don't." Your voice is still high. You moan a moan I've never heard before. Then grunt, "Fuck yeah." An affirmation.

"Can you feel that?" I ask. I reach my hand around in front and finger your clit. "Can you? You fucking whore." You grunt loudly.

"I said shut up and take it, bitch." I push in farther and start thrusting.

"Yeah," you say, "fuck me hard."

"Oh, I will. That's right. Take it. Fucking take it, bitch. Steve's going to fuck you silly. Fuck you till you can't see. Fuck you till you come all over my cock."

"Fuck. Yeah."

"That's right, Tammy, let Steve fuck you like you deserve. Take it, girl. Fucking take it till you come. You're going to gush, aren't you? All over me. I said you're going to come, aren't you? I said come, goddamnit. Fucking do it."

"Oh yeaaah, fuck me...."

"I said shut up, cunt, and come for your Daddy." And you do. Loud and labored. You soak the sheets. Your cunt throbs long after I stop thrusting. I lie on top of you, exhausted.

"Hold me," you say. You've never asked me to hold you before. Boy. Girl. T. I hold you.

3.

We don't talk for months. Why? Because you're an asshole. Because I'm a bitch. Because you're insensitive. Because I'm too sensitive. Because we walk two completely different worlds. Today, I don't remember why. Just remember wanting you. Today, I walk through this street. *I miss T* goes over and over in my head. When I get home I call you. Ask you to come over. And of course you do. You always do. No questions asked. This is what we do for each other.

I put on lipstick and meet you on the front porch, even though it's freezing out. I don't tell you about my day, even though it was bad. I don't ask about yours. I am so glad to see you. I can tell you're glad to see me too. But we pretend we're not. We stare at each other in the cold. You and I, we sure know how to pretend.

"Well, aren't you going to ask me in?"

"Yeah, yeah, come up."

You follow me to the top of the stairs, through my apartment door. "Look, T," I say, turning around. Your arm is in the air. You drop a snowball on my head.

"Oh, you bastard," I laugh.

"Aw, baby, what's wrong?" Your annoying sarcasm. You laugh, too. Brush the snow off my head, my shoulders. "What's wrong?" You stop laughing. "Baby?"

I don't say anything. Bring you into my bedroom. Pull you down beside me on the bed. Lie with you. You caress me. Move your fingers over my clothes, over my body. My eyes are closed. If this is the only thing we can do for each other, so be it.

"So T, tell me about your first kiss."

You don't say anything right away. Then, "I was nine. He was a man." You say it so calmly. Like it's normal. Then I wonder, what the hell is normal?

"And how was it?"

"It was an all-right kiss," you say.

I'm quiet. You continue to caress me. Slow, sensual. Unusual for us. We stay like that for a long while. Until you move your hands gently under my shirt. My skin gets goose bumps. My cunt gets wet. My body responds with movement. You take my shirt off. Get more aggressive. Kiss my body where your caresses were. Pull at the button of my jeans.

"I want you," you say.

"I want you too. I want your fist."

"You got it."

You move down my body and undo my jeans, pull them off. Slide your hand over my underwear. Apply pressure on my clit. My hips rise and grind. You take off my underwear. Slide your hand along my wetness. Rub a finger against my clit. I open up to your fingers. You push and play with my clit. In no time my cunt gathers around your whole fist. It is always faster and easier with you than with anyone else. I love it more than anything else we do. But I always have to remind you I don't want thrusts. You like getting pumped and don't understand why I don't. But you do what I ask. Just leave your fist there in me. Still.

"It feels so...comfortable," I say.

"I haven't heard that one before," you say. I smile. We're

quiet. You keep it in until I'm ready for you to take it out.

"You're still bleeding." You show me your hand covered with my blood. "Do you have a piece of paper? I'll make a hand-print."

I still feel full. Flayed. Prelingual.

"Well, you've got one inside you already, anyway." You lie down beside me. Lay your hand on my breast. We stay like that for a long time.

"Will you run me a bath?" I ask.

I stay in bed while you go. You clean the tub for me. Then run the water hotter than I'd like. Use shampoo to make bubbles. I know you feel chivalrous. Like this is what a guy does for a girl. Takes care of her.

"I wonder if what we are is anything like being straight," I call from the bed.

"We're still dykes," you say, sounding offended. Sometimes it's true. That's exactly what we are. Sometimes we're not. Sometimes, I guess, it just doesn't matter.

When the bath is ready, you call me. I get in and the water is too hot, like you thought it would be. I turn on the cold and swirl it around. You close the toilet lid and sit on it. Watch me. You've got your boy vest on. I like you watching. I turn off the cold water and lie back. Warm. Smothered. A feeling I rarely enjoy. When I ask you to join me in the tub, you refuse. You don't say why, but I know you well enough to understand what makes you feel vulnerable. You leave the room.

I think about how it feels to do this typical boy-girl thing with you. Sometimes I play girl, and sometimes I am girl. I get confused about which one is which. I think about who you are to me. How, sometimes, you are what I need in the most surprising ways. I hear you in the kitchen.

"Hey T," I call from the bath. You stop moving. You're quiet.

"Yeah?" you finally respond.

"C'mere."

You come back into the bathroom with your swagger. Your casual air. "What?"

"Kneel," I tell you.

"Kneel where?" you ask, pretending to be unsure about wanting to kneel for me.

"Beside the tub," I say, pointing beside me. You just look at me for a second, making like you don't want to. But you do.

"What?" you ask again as you kneel. There's a staccato sound in your voice.

I sit up a bit in the tub and look at you. "Kiss me, Troy."

You hesitate ever so slightly. Then get yourself wet leaning in for the kiss.

GRAND JETÉ

Toni Amato

You ask for a kiss and I refuse. You ask for a kiss and I say no for all the right reasons, and come morning I wait for your sleep-soft face and a chance to say yes, oh god yes please. That evening, the thick smell of paint and a worn mattress in your studio and as your hand leads mine toward your breasts, I become harder than ever before. I become a drowning man as your hand urges mine into a salt-slick sea, and I come harder than ever before.

The first time I dress for you, I am a teenage boy on his first date and I want to be a man for you, I want to be a man who can hold your arm there at the elbow and make you feel safe and cherished and adored. You reach out to straighten my tie and although you don't know all of what you are doing, I am undone.

You reach out to straighten my tie, there, in the hallway, and you have no idea what you have done. And neither, despite my butch-dyke cool, do I. The music is playing softly and you think I am leading as you clap out a rhythm I ache to move my hips to as I watch your woman's hands.

"Can I see it?" you ask, and I am twelve, thirteen, maybe, and suddenly embarrassed and unsure like I have not been in decades. Yes, decades, and for all my boyish ways, for all my teenage charm, I feel as though I may be falling in love again for the very first time, I feel like a baby-faced virgin boy, and I want to disappear as you handle what I have never shown outside my pants, what I have worshipped with and delivered with and sung hallelujahs with, but always from my trousers, always strapped and bound and covered by cotton and darkness.

You sit blindfolded and bound in a plush chair, a woman who has seen more of me than I knew I wanted to show. You sit willing and open for me and I begin the dance that I have mastered, and I watch. I watch the flush and the sheen and the motions of desire. I have become accustomed to knowing that I am wanted, but this time, this time I beg with hands and tongue, and everything I am and yes I pray, I pray to you and what I pray is please, please want this. Oh please want me. And you do. And here begins the dance. A dance interrupted by too many miles and too little time.

I tell myself stories, at night. I tell myself stories, now, to help me get to sleep.

It's hotter than hell here. Can't stand my own skin touching itself, can't stand the weight of even a thin sheet. I'm sweating and twisting and searching for a cool spot on the pillow and there isn't any and the truth is I'm getting restless and cranky and it's too hot even to jerk off.

The truth is, I'm desperate to fuck you. No. That's not the truth, either. The truth is, I need your body. Need your shoulders and your thighs and your belly and your back. Truth is it's very difficult for an animal to talk and what I am right now is a lust-maddened beast and I am trying to make this make sense, to make this something more than guttural noises and deep-throated grunts, trying to be a civilized human being despite the unconscious baring of my teeth. And you think it a lopsided grin, this hungry thing you bring out in me.

I have told you. I have tried to tell you that the veins beneath the skin of your breasts, the blue pulsing of your wrists and neck are a torment to me. But what I can find words to say is only a phantom of what lies down hot and heavy in my own veins and all I can do is show you and there is not space, in this configuration of our lives, there is not time for a complete showing and so the caged animal paces and occasionally growls and so here I am, working words and grinding my teeth and maybe I'll catch it this time.

It's not all sweet romance, it's not all soft and you play with fire when you tell me you remember being dragged into that bathroom.

You play with fire that I want you to swallow, entire and whole, so that I can watch the flush of flame creep across your ribs, along your collarbones. So I can see you burn the way my fingers scorch and sear at the touch of you.

It's not all tender words and longing glances, and the place you have never been to before is a place I have prowled for years but never, not once, has there been a creature like you here. You say you want to have jungle sex with me and oh yes, the jungle, and there I wait, slinking yellow-eyed through vines full of exotic birds and I will hear you coming, yes I will hear you coming again and again.

Nocturnal beast. I am losing sleep over this. Losing sleep and losing rest because when my eyes shut the dreams come and it is difficult to translate dreams into waking words but I will try because you have asked and sometimes, indeed, the hunter gets captured by the prey.

"You have no idea what you do to me," I say, later and from a distance. Wide-eyed wonder across the telephone lines. "What? Tell me what. Go on, give me words."

I am a poor poet deprived of words, a tongue-tied Romeo—I am a woman struck speechless by desire and all the words I know to describe this loosening of muscle, this rhythmic tremolo—all these words are not enough. And these words are all I have.

"Tell me."

All my years of pursuing the one who could take my defiant self and create a safe place for the bended knee I am desperate to offer—all those years of dark and mysterious places, actors so sure of their lines, carefully orchestrated scripts and now, here, this. Your voice. All right. I'll try to tell you.

What would I use to say the unspeakable, to tell you the things that lie heavy on my tongue? The things that I wish had not ever been said before and I want to make a new language, then. A language all ours, a set of sighs and murmurs and exultant shouts. Soft groans of deep surprise and loud, loud earsplitting shrieks of hearts torn wide open. I want a series of clicks and tooth chatters and gusts of breath that will tell you the particulars that are so particular. The peculiar and the personal and I do indeed believe that this can only be said by speaking in tongues. Strange language and insane gesticulation.

In my dreams we have days and nights. Yes, long nights, hot like these I suffer through. In my dreams there are as many hours to the darkness as passion can create, and there is enough of it, of passion and all its attendant desire and hunger and need, enough to make for an eternity.

You lie on a bed of fur, soft and caressing, dark beneath you. You lie on the skin of an animal and this reminds me of what I become for you. More than that—helps me remember what you need from me. Soft despite the hard wanting, the way my muscles tense and flex with needing you. You lie on a bed of fur and look at me, and there are myriad women gazing through eyes I watch go large and dark with the same fierce need that moves me. You are a playful, impetuous child, a young woman discovering what your body can do for you, a temptress who knows quite well what she does to me. That one, the one who taunts and provokes and most certainly dares me. And I am desperate to please them all.

I can smell you from across the room. It's the scent of metal and blood and deep, secret places. Salt of the ocean and tang of pine needles on an ancient forest floor. My teeth ache with it, my mouth waters, and something old behind my eyes drops down. I can smell you and the memory of everything pleasurable lies just beneath that scent. I close my eyes and pull molecules of you deeply into me, the way I long to be pulled into you. Let the capillaries in my chest pass this on to every blood cell and so to the very fibers of my body. This is the first sweet step toward losing track of the boundary between us, toward forgetting where I let off and you begin.

Flooded, saturated, I open my eyes. The arch of your foot. The long curve of calf. The most succulent of all tender places resting beneath a gathering of your own fur. I need to see your belly rise and arch, need to feel your muscles tense and release. Already I can see your pulse lifting the intricacies of your veins closer to that skin, that smooth and supple skin I burn with the heat of, even here across the room.

I need this more than you can possibly imagine. Like a starved thing, too long alone and unfed, and no matter how much you give me, I know this hunger will not be abated.

I need this and I pray for self-control, for the presence of mind to treat you like a precious thing even as I lose my mind in animal ecstasy. Pray for strength and pray in thanksgiving and the words of the prayer fade away into gibberish when I reach you, when I reach down to you, kneel down before you and begin a long night of supplication and speaking in tongues.

Where to begin? A kiss, just one kiss and the fullness of your lips, the taste of your breath are enough to make me shudder. I want to kiss you until your lips bleed, until you come up gasping for air—and even this only once I've had enough. There is danger in this wanting. The continually present danger of the bottomless hungers I suffer in your absence. The hungers that are only sharpened by your physical presence.

A kiss, then. Or more like a thousand kisses in one extreme lingering. I want to feel you move for me. Feel the tip of your tongue and the smooth coolness of your teeth. I want to eat your mouth as though it were a fine, sweet fruit. Crush it and let the juices run down my chin. So easy to slip from mouth to cheek and follow that first downy caress to your ear. To that place which brings from you the shy turning of your head, the quick intake of breath.

And once my lips have made that journey, once I have mouthed a trail of desire across the delicate bones and bitten more gently than is imaginable, then I exhale. Allow the deepest of sighs to escape my lips and enter the echo chamber of your ear. Imagine the hot, wet wind before a storm, imagine the force of murmured words—"Jesus god I want you"—able to course the distance to a place I long to be but will not go for a long, long while.

Instead, I caress the delicate contours with my tongue, the ridges and folds and the astounding contradiction of soft skin over cartilage. Between my teeth a fragile thing. Instead I burrow into a small indentation, an almost secret tender place, and drink deeply.

There is a shift, then. The last vestiges of control shatter, and my hands are creatures unto themselves. My hands that knew their way across your body from the very beginning. I want to cup the weight of your head in my palm, push my fingers through the fineness of your hair. Want to place the full grip of my desire on either of your strong and freckled shoulders, pushing into you all my want and need. Here I can feel the first soft surrendering, the first relaxation of your muscles. The giving in and letting go. If I close my eyes, I see you naked in the cool reflection of water, see the way you could float on the surface, with your body this loose, and I will myself to be the ocean, to be the steady beat of waves on a roundly pebbled shore.

Trace your collarbones with trembling fingers, run my palms over the plane of your chest, the mound of your belly, the long smooth glide of your sides and across the curve of your breasts. Undone, I am undone and there is no restraint, now. I am beyond lingering, beyond savoring, and the time has come for abandon, for high winds and torrential downpour.

BUTCHES DON'T

D. Alexandria

Butches don't do this. Butches DO NOT do this. I kept repeating this in my head as my girl, Sonja, knocked on the door. She flashed me a wicked grin as she leaned back, pressing her ass into my crotch.

"You packed," she murmured, grinding against me.

"Of course," I replied, momentarily allowing myself to enjoy the feel of her.

"It feels different…" she began, but the door swung open and her friend, Lani, greeted us with her trademark Kool-Aid smile.

"Girl, you look great!" Lani cried as she and Sonja hugged. Then she turned to me, gave me the once-over, and smirked. "Sonja, you're lucky I got a woman of my own, 'cause you best believe I couldn't let a butch this fine go past me without trying something."

Sonja rolled her eyes in amusement as Lani showed us into the living room. "Better not let *your* woman hear you. You ready?"

"Almost, have a seat." Lani rushed out of the room as Sonja

and I sat on the sofa. I removed my jacket, since I was staying.

"You sure you're okay with this?" she asked me softly.

No. "Yeah, I'll be chill."

She kissed my cheek sweetly. "Thank you for doing this."

You are so not going to be thanking me later. "Of course, baby." I kissed her back.

I was full of shit. I wasn't chill and I certainly wasn't going to be okay. While Sonja and Lani were going to have dinner with some friends of theirs, Sonja thought it would be great for me to hang with Lani's girlfriend, Vicki. Lani, who relocated to California five years ago, had temporarily moved back for a couple of months for a job, and she and Sonja were enjoying getting reacquainted. But of course, as girls do, Sonja felt that since Vicki didn't know anyone, it made sense for the two of us to become friends; she and Lani felt we had a lot in common.

Little did they know.

"I'm ready." Lani finally walked out of her bedroom, sporting a very little black dress. She struck a model pose as she stepped into the center of the room.

"We're going out to dinner, *not* the club," Sonja commented as she got to her feet, but she whistled as she eyed the outfit.

"That's what I said."

I turned to see Vicki emerging from the bedroom, her arms crossed in front of her as she gave her girlfriend a half-disapproving look. "There's no reason for that. Look at your girl, *she's* covered." Which was true. Sonja was wearing black slacks and a semisheer blouse that still looked classy. But that was Sonja's style; always a bit conservative.

"Sonja's always been the sugar..." Lani began.

"...and Lani's always been the spice," Sonja finished, before they erupted in a fit of giggles, looking like teenagers again instead of the thirtysomethings they actually were.

"Baby, I told you, no worries." Lani gave Vicki a very deep kiss that forced Sonja and me to look away. "We'll be back around midnight and..." I turned in time to see her whisper the rest of her statement in Vicki's ear, making Vicki blush.

"C'mon, heifer, before we're late." Sonja gave me a gentler kiss, before giving me the "try to have fun" look. After a few more rushed comments and reminders, they were gone.

And then it was just me and Vicki.

She still hadn't moved away from the bedroom doorway and from my position on the sofa, I was giving her an uneasy look. *Why am I here?*

"Did you bring the beer?" she asked.

"Uh, yeah." I had completely forgotten the six-pack at my feet. "You want it in the fridge?"

"I'll do it." She picked up the beer and headed for the kitchen. "Lani made all this snack shit, you hungry?"

"What you got?" I asked, as I tried to calm myself.

"Come look, fool, this ain't no restaurant."

Dammit. Reluctantly, I got to my feet and went into their kitchen. It was entirely too small, barely room enough for the stove, fridge and sink, let alone the meager cabinet space and their tinyass table. On the table was a spread of rolls, sandwich meats, chips and potato salad. Vicki was making herself a sandwich, and for a moment I forgot myself and just watched her. Vicki was your stereotypical Californian: body conscious and into just about any kind of physical fitness you could imagine. Dressed in a tank and jeans, you could see how toned she was as she simply fixed herself some food, her muscles moving beneath the skin of her arms in a rhythm that made me bite my lip.

"You gonna just stand there or make something?"

My eyes rose. "Huh? Oh, yeah...sandwich."

She gave me a questioning look before finishing up and

squeezed by me on her way out. As soon as I was alone, I started mentally kicking my own ass. Why was I here? Why hadn't I just told Sonja that this wasn't a good idea? Well, because then she'd want to know why. And there was no explanation I could give that she'd be satisfied with, short of my claiming to be sick—which wouldn't fly since Sonja was a nurse. And, of course, telling her the truth would be suicide, so I had no choice but to come.

As I made a couple of sandwiches, I kept telling myself I'd have to be cool. But that was pointless, because deep in my gut I knew what was going to happen...and I still wasn't sure if I wanted it to happen or not. Butches didn't do shit like this. At least not any butch that I knew. But despite feeling like I couldn't do it, I also couldn't ignore what had been happening. The lingering looks, the nervousness in each other's presence, the accidental touches that always ignited sparks...and that fucking kissing episode.

Yes, yes, yes, you heard right. I couldn't replay it exactly; all I remembered was Vicki and me meeting before having to hook up with the girls for a late dinner, sharing some beer and before I knew it we were kissing. Never in my life had I even looked at another butch in a sexual way, but from the first moment I saw Vicki...something was there. Her look, the way she carried herself, damn even the fact that she shaved her head completely bald. And if that alone didn't freak me out, the revelation of her attraction to me sure did. But for the couple months we were around each other, despite the situation, we were able to deal.

"There's no game on, wanna watch a movie?" Vicki called from the other room.

"Depends on the movie," I answered as I finished up. I grabbed a beer from the fridge and walked back into the living room. It was also small, so there was only the sofa to sit on.

Vicki was on one end and I took the other, setting my bottle and plate on the coffee table before me. Vicki was flipping through TV channels, and of course there was nothing we found interesting. She started listing all the DVDs they had, but nothing caught my interest.

I occasionally glanced at Vicki, wondering if she was thinking what I was thinking. I knew all the searching for movies and the small talk was just a way to ease the tension. We both knew what could happen tonight. We had never acknowledged the attraction we had for each other, never talked about the kiss, but every time we saw each other, I could see that her eyes mirrored mine. We both wanted to know what could happen, given the chance.

We settled on watching some music videos as we ate, barely talking, only commenting on whatever video was on. But when 50 Cent's *P.I.M.P.* came on, Vicki grinned.

"I love this video," she announced. "That scene with the chick pimp and the two girls on the leash is hot."

"Hell, yeah," I agreed, watching the video with anticipation.

Even though I had seen the video countless times, that one scene was worth seeing any time. And as soon as it came on, we both whistled.

"That shit always turns me on," she said.

"Oh yeah?" I asked.

She nodded. "I got no shame in admitting I get freaky and shit. That's why I dig Lani. She's up for anything."

I turned in my seat to face her. "She be letting you tie her up and shit?"

Vicki grinned. "That and more. Believe me, man, much more."

"What else?" Even though Lani was my girl's friend and all,

I couldn't deny the fact that she was hot and her doing the shit Vicki was suggesting was something I definitely wanted to hear more about.

Vicki shrugged. "I've tied her up, blindfolded her, spanked her, flogged her—you know, shit like that."

Unconsciously, I was groping my dick through my jeans, feeling it press against my clit. "Damn. I can't believe Lani's into that shit. Sonja's open and all, but I don't think she's *that* open. Although it would be cool to find out."

Vicki was staring at me intensely, as if she was measuring me. "There's something I got you may want to see."

"What?"

"Hold up." She got up and disappeared into the bedroom. A few moments later, she was back with a DVD in hand, walking over to the entertainment system. I watched her load the movie and sit back on the sofa, remote ready.

I was finished with my food, and now held a second beer in my hand as I watched the screen. It was black and then the title, *The Black & the Bound,* appeared. My eyebrow rose as the title faded and the screen was lit up with a dark-skinned sista on a table. She was on her stomach, naked and spread-eagle, her ankles and wrists tied with rope. As soon as I took that shit in, my nipples tightened and I let out a measured breath.

Vicki had just played her hand.

At first, the girl on the screen was still, just lying on the table—and no lie, that alone was arousing to see. But then we could hear loud footsteps offscreen, causing the girl to writhe against her restraints. After a few seconds, we saw another sista approach the table. Sporting a PVC catsuit and extreme killer heels, she was holding a wooden paddle in one hand, while her other began caressing the naked girl's body.

"I'm not really into dominatrixes all dressed up like this,"

Vicki said suddenly. "But it's all good."

Apparently it was. Out the corner of my eye I could see her groping herself like I had been doing myself earlier. My eyes went back to the screen just in time to see the dominatrix swing the paddle and it landed a blow on the girl's ass with such a loud smack, the sound echoed throughout the room. The girl on the table cried out, but got no time to relax as the paddle quickly came down on her ass again. The dominatrix was pretty relentless, wielding the paddle with finesse as she decorated the girl's ass with hit after hit, and even through the dark skin, we could see the discoloration beginning to appear.

As much as I had some interest in that S&M shit, I had never seen an actual video, so I was watching in semishock. But that was nothing to the shock I felt when I turned to say something to Vicki and found her slumped beside me, her hand shoved down her unzipped jeans. Damn, I'd been so into the porn, I hadn't even heard her unzip.

She looked over at me and just smirked before turning back to the TV. My eyes went back to the screen, but I was thinking that not even two feet away, Vicki was getting herself off. I couldn't believe she was doing it with me in the room. I had never seen another butch get herself off. It was one of those things you just did on your own. But as I sat there, feeling the sofa jiggle with Vicki's movements, and now watching the dominatrix switch to a flogger, it was as if my dick was screaming at me to touch it. All I had to do was unzip and slide my hand inside. All I had to do was grab my shit and just stroke it, feeling the base of the dick press into my clit. I've mastered jacking off that way and could reach a climax within five minutes if necessary, and not touching myself was too much to bear with all the sexual energy in the room. But I was feeling rather embarrassed about it. I didn't know any other butch who masturbated using her dick that way. And I wasn't sure if I was strong enough to handle the possible ridicule.

"You gonna just sit there?"

My head turned. Vicki's hand was still shoved down her jeans, but she was looking dead into my eyes.

I just shrugged, the embarrassment spreading. Usually I was not the type to be shy about sex, but in this situation, I felt out of my element and couldn't find my footing.

"You can't fool me. I know you wanna do it."

I didn't say anything, but I could tell from her eyes that she understood how I was feeling.

"If you show me yours, I'll show you mine."

My eyes widened. "You're strapped?"

"Hell, yeah," she said. That's when I realized the exact movements her hand had been making within her jeans. She was stroking her dick.

I relaxed for a moment, enjoying the newfound knowledge. I took a deep breath and closed my eyes as my hands moved to my waist. I quickly unbuckled my belt, unbuttoned my pants, unzipped, and slipped my hand inside—but then I stopped.

"I'll go first," she said suddenly. My eyes opened and I watched as she lifted her hips and tugged her jeans down to midthigh. She reached inside the opening of her boxers and pulled out one of the most perfect dicks I've ever laid eyes on. It matched the color of her skin almost exactly. It looked to be about six inches, average width, not too veiny, and her hand fit around it as if it belonged there. She resumed stroking it and I sat there in amazement, watching someone else do what I thought I alone had done.

"Your turn." Her voice had grown softer with arousal.

I tugged my pants down like she had, revealing my own boxers. And just as she had done, I pulled my dick out through the flap. My own was jet black, completely smooth and seven inches—bigger than the one I usually packed. But, for some reason, deep down I had wanted to impress Vicki tonight.

And she indeed looked impressed. She winked at me as she reached behind a cushion, retrieving a bottle of lube. I watched her apply some to her hand and dick before tossing the bottle to me. I couldn't help but smile as I did the same, and then we just sat there together, watching each other as we jacked off, the porn completely forgotten. To say that it was arousing is a gross understatement. Just watching her slick hand move up and down the shaft, the way she would occasionally play with the head or slow her movements teasingly, was a sight that had me about ready to cum. My own stroking was more leisurely; I was just enjoying the moment I was in, wanting this to last for as long as it could despite every downstroke threatening to push me over the edge.

"Damn, look at that," Vicki said suddenly.

I looked back to the television and watched the dominatrix press a large dildo into the girl's ass. At some point, the dominatrix had placed a ball gag in the girl's mouth, so as the dick was sinking into her, her cries were muffled. Her limbs were taut, hands balled into fists, as the dominatrix kept telling her to be a good slut and take it. You could see the pain on the girl's face, but she was pressing her ass back, trying to take as much as the dominatrix was willing to give.

"You like anal?" I asked.

Vicki's eyes met mine again. "Yeah, I'm into that. Lani loves taking my dick in her ass. You?"

I nodded, but looked away. Only Sonja knew that I enjoyed getting fucked in the ass, and, surprisingly, she had obliged me a few times. It wasn't something I was entirely proud of, since just about all my butch friends refused to bottom for their girls.

So, the fact that I not only enjoyed bottoming, but also enjoyed receiving anal was something I kept on the down-low.

I heard a sudden movement beside me and before I knew it, Vicki had gotten to the floor and was kneeling before me. Our eyes met briefly before she moved my hand away and wrapped her strong hand around my dick. I let out a soft groan as I watched her stroke me. She pumped me for a few moments before lowering her head to take me in her mouth.

"Yo, that got lube on it," I protested, half wanting to shove her head down on my dick, half wondering if I could let her.

"It's flavored, don't worry." And with that, I watched her swallow my entire dick with skill. I watched in awe, not able to believe this was actually happening. Never in my life would I ever have thought that I'd see another butch suck my dick, let alone do it with such hunger. She bobbed her head with ferociousness, her sucking beyond audible, the sounds bouncing off the walls, and she stroked the remaining inches in perfect timing. My clit was rock hard, screaming from the pleasurable pressure, and I was afraid that I was going to cum too soon. I raised my hands to try to get her to back off, but I ended up grabbing her head, feeling the slickness of her scalp in my hands as I pressed down instead. She gagged for a slight moment, but didn't back away; then she gave a loud, muffled moan that I swear I felt through my clit and down to my very toes.

I held her head tightly and started fucking her mouth. Vicki's hands gripped my hips for balance as I just lunged at her, moving with an aggression I'd never felt before. I was intensely watching her lips stretched around my dick, the way her cheeks hollowed as she sucked me with urgency, how her saliva was coating my dick so perfectly that entry between her swollen lips was effortless.

My head fell back as I lost myself in the sensation, trying to ignore the words screaming in my mind that this was beyond gay. Hell, I've heard people say that butch-on-butch sex was Super Gay. Butches didn't do this. But feeling the strength in Vicki as she sucked my dick, I didn't care. This shit right here was purely animalistic, hedonism at its best—raw heat and desire, just the need to get off. I understood all this as I felt myself start to cum. I held her head firmly as I shoved my dick down her throat, feeling my thighs twitch and my clit swell. I came, holding Vicki's head to my crotch, feeling the heat of her on my pussy through the boxers, knowing that she probably couldn't breathe but not caring. I was loud and unashamed as I gave my cum to her, feeling my entire body just cave in on itself.

After a few moments I slumped back against the sofa, letting Vicki's head go. I was expecting her to give me an angry look for the roughness, but her eyes were filled with pure lust and delight. She sat back on her heels just smiling at me smugly, her lips puffy and red. Her dick was in her hand and she was stroking it slowly as she looked me over hungrily.

She was ready to get hers.

I forced my weary body to sit up. "Sit down."

Vicki shook her head, that wicked smile still on her face. "Naw, baby boy, I don't want it like that."

My eyebrow rose in confusion. "What do you mean?"

She reached in her pocket and pulled out a condom. "I want that ass."

"Hells, no."

"You can't say you don't want it," she said. "I saw that look in your eyes. Now get on your knees."

"I ain't going down like that with you. I'll suck you off, but that's it."

"Tell me you don't want to feel my dick in your ass." She held my gaze challengingly. "Tell me you don't want to bend over right now and feel me slide in that tight hole."

"I don't care, yo. That shit's too far."

"It's just me and you, son. No one else gotta know that you did it. I know you want it, you know you want it. So stop worrying about your fucking pride and get what you want."

My jaw was tense as I returned her gaze, but I couldn't deny her words. God I wanted it. I wanted to feel what it would be like to get fucked the way I fuck. Sonja was great, but it wasn't the same. And I knew, at this moment, I was being handed the chance.

My pride wouldn't let me answer her. So I just stood, slowly turned my back, and lay on the sofa, my ass facing her. I felt Vicki's hands on my boxers and as she pulled them down to my knees, my eyes closed in shame. I tried to pretend it was Sonja kneeling between my awkwardly spread legs, that her hands were caressing my ass, gently pinching and swatting each cheek. But as soon as I heard the snap of the condom, I couldn't pretend anymore. And the way my pussy was swelling again from that very sound, I knew I didn't want to. I felt Vicki reach for more lube, heard her apply some to her dick, and the cold shock of her applying some to my asshole made me tense up.

I felt her body over mine, her voice in my ear. "You're gonna want to relax that ass, baby boy, or it's gonna hurt."

I took a deep breath, trying to relax my entire body, telling myself it was just going to be like it was with Sonja: slow, measured, and as soon as I was ready, I'd be able to take it all. But I should have known better. I should have expected the same thing I'd have done if I'd been in Vicki's position at that moment. As soon as I felt her dick at my hole, she pushed in quickly, and I growled from the pain, pressing my face into the cushion. Vicki pressed all the way in, till I felt her boxers against my bare ass and she held herself still for a moment. Then I heard her groan as her hands found my waist, holding me to her, literally grinding her completely embedded dick into me. I was gasping at how full I felt; the dildos I had used before had never felt this big, despite my always secretly craving more. Well, I was getting more now, and on the other end of that dick was a butch who knew what she was doing.

Vicki pulled out halfway, then pushed in just as quickly, and as before, she held herself against me tightly, forcing me to feel all of her. The pain had already subsided and all I felt was pleasurably full, my body starting to relax in the blissful feeling. But as soon as I did, Vicki started up again. She pulled out, this time letting only the head of her dick remain, before she snapped her hips forward, driving it back into me. I gritted my teeth, my hands balling up in fists from the forcefulness. She pulled back again and repeated the quick thrusting, this time so hard that my head hit the back of the sofa. My hands reached out to brace myself as Vicki fucked me, each thrust powerful and unyielding. I knew that this was not the way she fucked Lani. This was the way you fucked someone who was as tough as you were. Someone who could handle it as rough, aggressive, and uncaring as you wanted to give it. Someone who understood that you just wanted to fuck.

She was methodical in her fucking, each stroke as measured as the one before, slamming into me so hard she might as well have been swinging a hammer. But hell, I was enjoying it. I loved being opened this way, impaled. Her grip on my waist was tight, and she began pulling me back to meet her thrusts. Instinctively I moved with her and in no time, she didn't have to guide me, because I was throwing my ass back, trying to get as much as I could. Our grunts and groans echoed through the apartment, and maybe even through the building. It felt beyond incredible. She was giving it to me just the way I've always wanted it done.

And when I felt her lie on top of me, her dick in deep again, and hold herself still, I was gasping. She rotated her hips and it felt as if she was stirring my insides, my body flinching from the sensations.

One of Vicki's arms moved up to encircle my shoulders, and when she started fucking me again, she kept her dick in deep, only withdrawing a couple of inches for her thrusts. Her body molded to mine as she fucked me slowly, and I let my head fall forward, unsure of what to do with all that I was feeling. I felt her other hand reach round my body and grab my dick, making me moan. She was stroking me as she fucked me; every time she pushed in, I'd feel the base of my dick hit my clit and my eyes rolled in my head. She pumped me deeply, her teeth nipping the back of my neck, her growls signaling that she was about to cum. In response, I pressed my ass back to meet her thrusts, in turn helping her jack me off. Her arm around my body was tightening, and I reached back and grabbed her thigh, pulling her closer as I worked my ass on her dick.

"Oh shit..." she whispered in my ear.

She was riding my ass faster, groaning louder and louder, yanking hard on my dick now, while I bucked even faster. Vicki suddenly grabbed both my wrists and pulled them behind me. With one hand, she pinned my wrists to my back then started to ram me. If I hadn't turned my face in time, I wouldn't have been able to breathe, because now she was completely gone. She stroked me harder and harder, and before I knew it, my second orgasm of the night peaked and I yelled from the pleasure, clenching my thighs and asscheeks together, which triggered Vicki. She pressed me down into the sofa, pounding me harder and harder as she came, calling me every nasty name in the book, her voice laced with unbridled lust, and I just took it...gladly. She kept humping me until her body finally gave up, and then she slowly pulled out of me.

We didn't speak for a few moments, then she playfully swatted my ass and said, "You a'ight?"

"Yeah," I answered, glancing at the clock on the wall. We still had a couple of hours before the girls were supposed to come back. I felt Vicki move, and I gingerly got to my feet, pulling my boxers and pants up. "I'll be right back," I said, heading to the bathroom to clean up.

When I finally came back to the living room, Vicki was on the sofa, eating a sandwich and watching the news. My stomach growled. I attempted to walk as steadily as I could but sensed her smirking as I passed her on my way to the kitchen. I fixed myself something to eat and grabbed another beer before joining her.

We didn't talk about it. We just ate, watched television and talked shit about everything else under the sun until Lani and Sonja came back a little after midnight. The girls were all teary as they said their good-byes; Lani and Vicki would be leaving in a couple of days. Vicki and I gave each other daps and the mandatory butch nod before Sonja and I left.

"Did you have a good time?" Sonja asked, as she laced her arm through mine.

"It was a'ight," I replied.

"It better have been more than *a'ight* since you're walking all funny," she said, winking at me.

THE ROCK WALL

Peggy Munson

Stone

We are leaning against the rock wall by the high school where I have taken him because it's deserted. He has that board-splitting butch gaze. He's worn his letter jacket, the one he earned back in high school, and today he delicately wraps it around my shoulders and says, "Do you want to be my girl? Do you want me to be your Daddy boyfriend?" And I nod shyly and say, "Yeah, okay." He holds my hand and we walk.

This is how it begins. It begins with something made from stone.

The bed he has me in is firm. Daddy's calloused hands are hard. Daddy's face looks like it was chiseled off Mount Rushmore. The wind is parting the curtains the way he brushes my hair back from my eyes. He gets serious. "Do you want to play a game, little girl?" he asks me. I know Daddy's games: rock beats scissors, scissors beat paper, paper beats rock. Hands equal power. Sometimes I am a paper doll and my clothes fold on with paper tabs, and Daddy undresses me absently, like he's opening mail. Sometimes I am a stone tablet, the stone on which commandments are carved. Sometimes, my legs are safety scissors, lying like dull blades, waiting to be crushed by rock. And Daddy spreads them open and they pull reflexively shut. He kisses to relax me. He curls his hand into a fist, into a stone. He slides that power into me. This simple game of hands.

But this is not just a game, Daddy-Girl. This is not just a game, Paper-Scissors-Rock. These are the scissors that cut up paper guises. This is the crane that breaks buildings. This is the fist that destroys orderly origami. This is the red paper of my cunt unfolding. This is me coming. This is how real. "Take it, bitch," says Daddy's voice into my ear. "Be a good girl. Take my fist." This is me pressed against surfaces. This is the stone that does not acquiesce. This is the statue becoming a Girl.

Quarry

Some days, I hate everything about Daddy. I hate how orphaned I feel when Daddy goes to work. I hate how Daddy can choose the simplest onomatopoeia and roll it off the tongue, so that *cock* sounds as hard as it is. How I sit all day with that word jammed in my head, cock, Daddy's cock, Daddy's hard cock, spreading out with acres of modifiers, until it becomes Daddy's hard cock that isn't fucking me. I hate it that I am so Electra. I hate it that Freud is on my shoulder and that he told me so. I hate it that I need a Daddy. I hate it that words never add up to cocks.

I lie on my back all day waiting and watching TV. I like watching teenage rock stars almost as much as anorexic figure skaters. I used to read about anorexia and about gymnasts and I would think about their discipline when the dentist was drilling pain into my smile. And I would read about how the girls didn't want to grow up and I would walk around for days with the pain in my smile and it was such good pain. And with my fading numb lip I thought of how benevolent the dentist was when he told me I was brave, and such a good girl. I hate Daddy for not being a dentist. I watch the Britney Spears video where she sings "Hit me baby, one more time" and dances around in a Catholic-schoolgirl outfit. I want to pull up my pleated skirt and show Daddy that we can end biblical racism right here, because the devil is made of white cotton. That's what little girls are made of. This exquisite, pretty rage.

I go to therapy and I want to talk about Daddy but I don't even want to get into it with my shrink. I can't explain how my girlfriend is a boyfriend who makes me call him Daddy. Sometimes when my shrink listens to me talk he thinks about other things. I can see the Viewmaster clicking in front of his eyes. Sometimes he thinks about what I would look like naked, and how he finds the professional boundary titillating. I sit in the waiting room and think about Daddy's cock and my pussy is all wet and I decide to go wipe myself before going into therapy but the bathroom lock has been ripped off the wall. My shrink might walk in on me, or smell me. He might see what a bad girl I really am. I return to the waiting room, still wet.

I don't talk about Daddy's cock but every word I say in therapy sounds like cock and I know my shrink can see right through me. I know he has linguistic X-ray vision and that he knows I am really saying cock, cock, cock and he wants me to sit on his lap but I am thinking about Daddy. How I want the day to go faster so that Daddy will get home from work. My shrink tells me to have a good week but he is really saying cock. The double doors shut behind me, cock, cock. And far away somewhere, in San Francisco, lesbians are pouring silicone into dildo molds and not thinking cock at all. Happily distracted, they are chattering and squeezing cock after cock out of molds and thinking business. I hate Daddy for thinking business. I wish he would think about my pleasure.

I hate how without Daddy I am a book with one bookend, so I just fall and my words get crushed. I hate it how Daddy is a petty thief. Because if he steals what's petty, then what am I when he takes me? I hate how Daddy makes me sputter inarticulate phrases, so that I choke out sounds that have nothing to do with theory. I hate how Daddy makes me write him stories, because I cannot sculpt a sentence out of cock. I hate it how that word becomes so eloquent inside of me, pushing through me and out of my mouth.

I hate how Daddy's cock knows the way to hidden quarries, the watery places that were mined. How Daddy sees the drunken dives that kill sixteen, euphoric girls kissed to epiphanies on their mossy knees. Sophomoric girls getting their nipples touched on their mossy knees. And the skin scraped against sharp things, and the rustle of cops approaching, and the second before the kids run, and the hastily abandoned trunks. How he knows what to do about each truncated fuck. Of each lifetime. Daddy takes care of things.

I hate it how Daddy makes me need his cock. Because then I am a place that once held diamonds, sitting home yearning for him, waiting for a girl's new best friend. Because then I am always too ready for him. So hungry every time his key turns in the lock. So hungry for that handcuff sound of his key in the lock. So hungry for that four o'clock, drowsy, sharp sound. I hate it how Daddy walks in and feels me to see if I'm wet, and wonders what I anticipate, and then ignores me while removing his jacket. I hate it how those fingers on my pussy make me whimper like a little dog.

I hate how seconds turn to hours before Daddy leads me into

the bedroom, and his belt buckle glints like it's submerged. How sweetly Daddy takes my hand and says, "Baby girl," and then pulls me to his denim lap. And how the things to be filled must be emptied, must be stripped. Daddy grips me and undoes me and lowers me to the bed. And I shiver because I need it. I give when Daddy pushes. Daddy pulls on my hair.

I hate how good and raw he strips me. How good it feels to be this bare.

The Rock Wall

Every night I go back to the rock wall. It is covered in moss and the rain is drizzling and I search for grips. I am ripped and mud-covered and hungry. My grasp is tenuous and my fingers are slipping. I'm tired of being a wide-eyed waif always scrambling over walls where there are more walls and more slippery rocks and more places to bruise and nowhere good to land. The rain is so irritating, the noise, the noise that's always a soft fuck when you need it hard, that's always a drizzle when you need a thunderstorm to break the air and shock the animals so they run frenzied—wild—crazed—scattershot—into spaces they never dared to go. The wall is unforgiving and I begin to slide. I land on my knees in a muddy pool and my dress is ripped and I'm old and there is no Daddy. The landing is soft. Nothing impaling me. Nothing tearing me and ripping me. No fairy-tale wolves, though I always thought they would be there, their dripping incisors and hunger, waiting for me to fall. There is nothing to wound me, no imaginary battles to reenact. No hole in the earth to open up and swallow me there.

Maybe I am already in the hole. Maybe I am the hole. This dark and damp place that feels like the inside and not the outside and my dress is ripped and I start crying. I hold my face in my muddy hands and my tears clean my hands and my hands smear the mud into my tears. Everything undoes everything. Nothing undoes me. Nothing does me.

Then suddenly, so dark and quick and I can't even scream, something reaches from behind and grabs me with its arm under my throat and drags me backward, and drags me while whispering things. "Daddy's here now, little girl. Daddy's got you." He's not comforting and not scary, just unsettling, just the kind of thing that makes me all animal, all animal splitting from the pack the way the wolves want it to be, all animal confused and asking for it. I try to flail around and pull away. I try to break the grip, the wall is waiting. Doesn't Daddy understand the wall? How I need to climb it always, climb and climb and climb it? Daddy pulls my muddy body so that I'm sitting on his lap and I still can't see him but I feel his hard cock. "Daddy's got you," he says again.

I want not to want it. I want not to feel how my thighs are smeared with mud and my pussy feels smeared, but it's not, it's just mine. There is nothing between my pussy and his cock but a thin layer of fabric. And he is rubbing his cock against my panties and I squirm. I want to squirm away but he rubs me so hard and I start to want to push down onto him. I start to push down as if the fabric will just dissolve. He pushes the tip of his cock against the fabric and the fabric goes into me. And the elastic of my panties follows the fabric and pulls me, pulls my legs, into me. I'm going to fall into me. I have to fight. I try to struggle but Daddy holds me against his moving pushing cock. "Daddy, wait," I say, but I keep pushing to make the fabric go away, and I want him. "Daddy, stop!" Daddy grabs under my arms and pushes me slowly forward so that my face is down but he pulls my hips back. "Daddy wants you to take his cock," he says. "All of it. Can you be a good girl and do that?"

I want to taste the mud. The mud smells oddly like Daddy.

Daddy slides my panties down my legs so I'm just there in the night air and my pussy and my ass are high up behind me. "Daddy, no," I say, but this time weakly. This time it's all reverse psychology. This time I'm not sure at all.

"Daddy can just leave you here in the mud if you want, little girl. Is that what you want?" He snarls this.

"Daddy...no," I say. "No, please, no."

"Beg for what you want."

"I want you, Daddy."

"Beg me."

"I want Daddy. I want Daddy to fill me up."

"Daddy's very hard for you. Is this what you want?" He slides the tip of his cock into me. "Is this what you want?"

"Yes, Daddy. Please."

"Beg me."

"I want you inside of me. Please."

"What?"

"I want you, Daddy, please." I say it with the urgency I use to climb the walls.

Daddy starts sliding his cock into my pussy and I push back onto him but he holds my hips and makes me wait for him. And the rain gets harder, the drops batter my cheeks, the rain turns everything to mud while Daddy fills me up and my hands slide in front of me for something to hang on to but there is nothing, nothing there, nothing but my hips pushing back and Daddy's hard cock and my need. And I need to hold something. I need to hold on because I am used to holding and I need the wall and Daddy pushes in so hard and I want to scream, it feels so good. My hands are fumbling forward for any handhold but there is nothing there....

"Daddy's got you, baby," he says soothingly. "Fall back into me."

Gravel

The gravel reminds me of old roads cutting between fields to deserted places, the way it clatters and then hums, keeps me unsteady. Once I cut my chin on the gravel in the Dairy Queen parking lot, holding onto my Dilly Bar all the way to the ground. I remember losing my footing, bleeding on the car upholstery, wondering if kids found reddened chunks of rock where I landed. I think about all of these things now, now that I'm old being young, riding next to Daddy in the truck. The big wheels slide over the gravel. The dark moves from beneath trees to the sides of buildings. We are near a warehouse with broken windows. And the gravel is not the kind you buy in bags at Home Depot, but stained. I get out and stumble like a tipsy slut. I straighten my skirt and start to walk but Daddy is there already, and he grabs my arm. "No," he says, pointing. "You little whore. Right here."

I look down distastefully, then up at Daddy. "Here?" I sneer. I can't believe he means it. The rock is soaked dark with things dying, bled oil and shoe rubber. I look at him again, his stern expression, then kneel down. The rocks are sharp against my knees. Daddy gives a little push on my back so I fall forward and my palms slide through the rocks. Then, when I'm on all fours, he pulls up my skirt from behind, just flips the material so that it lands on my back and I feel the breeze trying to go into me. I've got no panties on.

"Such a pretty little ass," he says. "Untainted lily-white ass. Not dirty like the rest of you." The breeze seems to follow the current of his voice and rubs the goose bumps on my ass. "Are you afraid to have Daddy's big cock in your pretty ass?"

"Maybe," I say. I feel defiant. I feel the way the rocks are cutting me and I don't move my hands.

Daddy's hands fondle my asscheeks, spread them open, press

against them so I slide forward more. He's so much stronger than I am. I let myself fall and feel the rocks against my cheek. I think of how I fell that time, when I was young, and tried to taste my blood. And how I always tried to taste my blood when I got cut. But what I liked to taste was not just mine, but also that which made me bleed. It was the thing that made the cut, the flavor mixed into the blood. It was the combination of the two, the grit that touched the cutter and the flesh. It was the generosity of both, and how my bleeding made the two combine. I think of all of this while Daddy moves his cock against the hole, and pushes hard because it's tight.

He pushes hard because it's tight, and pulls my hips against him. My face gets scraped against the gravel. My lip begins to bleed. I taste the blood and salt and earth and pain and fear and trampling. I taste the blood and all that has been done to it and lick and give it back to me. I give me back to me. And Daddy gives me, too.

"Who gives you what you need?" he asks. The natural light has fled. A streetlight shines behind his hair. I smell the tires. I smell the dew. I feel the walls that crumble into gravel. I feel the girls who must undo.

"Daddy," I say. He looks like a monument. "You do."

BECOMING STONE

Sandra Lee Golvin

Summer is becoming. Gone to Africa says A. Now you on the blue couch becoming my fist. My arm becoming the cradle. Your hair becoming the yellow dream.

I did dream you another summer. I was trying to decide about my life. I was believing in the *I* of decision making. I was believing in the *I* of dreaming. Now that *I* does not know so much and would say you dreamed me or perhaps the dream dreamed us both. An old lady's corpse was being kissed. In the kissing she became you, the fairy tale princess. Someday my prince(ss) will becoming. I will becoming her. Or him. We had not yet met, my *I* and yours. Not then. Not that summer.

You were wearing chocolate panties. Even now, with my fist inside, the wet silk wraps my wrist at the place where it wants cutting open. You let me be the one who knows. I so wanted that. I have a chocolate dick, the one A never liked because it looked too real. You don't mind though. You're such a girl. Until you, being the girl was *my* job.

When you first approached I had no way to understand. You, all Midwest blonde, the wife and mother, legs long as prairie sky. Can you hear the longing for what I thought could never be mine? Me, the frog, my lipstick androgyny a cover for what only you saw living in stone.

You would chip away my protection bit by bit until I knelt naked before you in an attitude of wanting. I did not make your job easy any more than the stone yields to the chisel with the first blow. No, persistence was required, and more than that, desire. Inexorably you made me, a me who I did not know was there. Is the figure the creation of the artist or is it hidden there in rock, only waiting to be revealed? Am I now what you imagined, or was I always so?

It's not only the change in clothes, the end of dresses and wide-brimmed hats. My hips have narrowed, my jaw grown more square, suddenly I know how to let my gaze linger on the pretty girl as if I might presume to know her. And my friends, those few who remain, do not recognize me. All of this I want to say you wrought. Lady of alchemy, Aphrodite of dreams.

Another one last night, another not able to reach you. You were in a Presbyterian hospital by the sea. You had given birth to our daughter. Things are breaking all around me. Things made of glass like the nautilus you brought me from Paris after you already knew you were done with me. (That week with your mother rendered me an impossibility.) Still months later I dream of you and my hand awakens hot, curled in on itself, bereft of you.

Jealous of my own fist. It knows something I never will. Your wet heat imprinted in traces at the grooves that mark the knuckles. My palm forever empty of the sweet, flat place at the base of your spine. My thighs that held the curve of your ass, lonely. I never held a woman that way before. Don't you see?

I was your mother, your boylover, and you my midwife, my child.

There was A, for many years my man. I'd been faithful to her. You had your husband and two sons, your woman lovers on the side (you'd brought them out). For nine months I refused to be one of them. You always got what you wanted, on your terms. This time you wanted a real dyke. I needed terms of my own.

Then A went to Africa.

When the sculptor works with stone, a long time passes where nothing shows. There is a circling and a tapping, and it is all an act of faith. Then comes a moment, seemingly out of nowhere, in which what has been only surface and raw edges suddenly becomes the thing that was always there. The soul in the stone unfolds.

I don't want to tell this story. Once it is written it is over. I can't bear that. When the phone rings I still imagine it might be you. When it is silent I wonder why you do not call. How ridiculous I am.

The moment.

You didn't come to class, and we exchanged angry messages. I remember I called you chickenshit. You gave it right back. Your temper opened up the place in me where violence fuels my sex. It felt good, the lust and the killing rage. Made it possible for me to say I humble myself and demand your presence at the same time. You liked that and came to find me at the beach. As I told you to do. In the parking lot I didn't say hello, just pulled your head down to mine and gave you the kiss you'd been wanting. What I wanted was to fuck you there in public. I didn't. I made you demonstrate your desire though, all the way back to my house, and a man on a bicycle rode by calling, "Lovers, yoo-hoo, lovers" like an enchanted bird.

I made you wait on the blue couch while I searched for the

poem. The one by Judy Grahn where Ereshkegal Butch Queen of the Underworld dares Inanna Queen of Beauty to face her secret want. This is you, I said, Queen of Beauty. And you were, too, so lovely in the shock of what you had provoked in me. I grabbed your hair, that blonde mane, tight and read to you. Do you remember the words?

Strange to everyone but me that you would leave the great green rangy heaven of the american dream, your husband and your beloved children, the convenient machines, the lucky lawn and the possible picture window—to come down here below. You left your ladyhood, your queenship, risking everything, even a custody suit, even your sanity, even your life. It is this that tells me you have a warrior living inside you. It is for this I could adore you.

My fist is remembering the rough of your hair.

You cried as I forced your face down into my lap. Being a dyke isn't fun and games, baby. It's serious business. It's warrior business. Like the poem says. I think you complained then, that I was being hard on you. You should thank me for that, I shook you, thank me for caring enough not to play your little secret on the side. For caring enough to try to bring you down here, to my world. To where you want to be. You cried some more. And then you thanked me. You did.

You were the most beautiful to me then, all your perfect passing prettiness stripped away by real grief.

Was that when you bared your belly, so that I could witness the site of your devastation? Not only the scars of childbirth, but the ravages of bulimia, the muscles destroyed by years of laxatives and vomit. I thought of napalm, dead places too poisoned for anything to live, and I believed I understood something about the price of your fortune.

You were a connoisseur, bred for private jets and crystal. I was proud you'd picked me. Cocky. At one point—not that first night, but soon—I put Mick Jagger on and danced for you to "Gimme Shelter." *We all need someone we can cream on,* he sang. Baby, you squirmed with so much delight I thought I was king of the world. You had the power to put me there. And to take me down. You were the Queen of Beauty, after all.

I wouldn't let you touch me. I don't know how I knew to do that.

Not much happened that first night. You remembered your boys whom you'd dumped at a neighbor's for a minute, not knowing I had other plans. I didn't like it, you leaving in the middle of a scene. You begged for a return engagement the next night, and I said I'd think about it. In the morning you called, and I told you what to wear. A dress with a full skirt. No underwear. A more interesting bra. You confessed you'd thrown out all your sexy bras and bought plain ones because you thought that's what lesbians like. Since you were trying to please me I forgave you. But I was clear. I wanted you in lace.

So cool and yet out of my mind. What was happening to me? My hands, my hands, my hands do all the remembering.

I put on my man's suit. You swooned at the door. Trousers, you whispered, eyeing me in a way no girl ever had before. I said we're going out in public. Your assignment is to let everyone know you are with me. That you're mine. We went to the Pleasure Chest. We looked at dildos and porn. I said I need to know what you like. You fumbled, dropped your keys, acted silly. Then I took you to an upscale industry panel on gay parenting. The kind of thing I hate. But I endured it because I wanted you to see there were people like you with children and money. I wanted you to be able to imagine a life with me.

I think that was the night I danced for you. Yes, I'm sure of it now. You got on your knees in front of me, undid my slacks.

It was a mistake to let you touch me. I knew it right away but didn't know how to stop. You went home to your husband, and I raged all night, feverish to find my way back to that place of power I'd let slip away under the stroke of your fingers.

At 6:00 a.m. I telephoned, woke you. I knew he'd be gone already. Come to me now, I demanded. I'm not through with you. Of course you couldn't comply, couldn't leave your boys. What can I do for you, you asked. I said I need you to touch yourself. As if you were me. Now. And you did. Are you touching yourself? Yes, yes I am. Are you thinking of me? Yes, yes I am. Does it feel good. Oh yes. Do you want me to fuck you? Yes. Say it. Yes. Please fuck me. Now say this: I'm a dyke. I'm a dyke. I've always been a dyke. I've always been a dyke. I love women. I love women. I want to be fucked by women. I want to be fucked by women. I want to be fucked by you. I want to be fucked by you.

That afternoon you told me you'd decided. No more lies. You wouldn't come to me again until you told him. It was not what I expected. I didn't believe you. That you would risk everything. *Even a custody suit, even your sanity, even your life.* To come to me. To come to yourself. But you had already made the plan to speak with him that night. I was in awe.

Walking the long stretch of beach miles beyond home I thought only of you and your courage. How I could hold you while you did this warrior thing you could only do alone. For three days and three nights I hadn't taken in food or been able to sleep. Running on some other source, my body feeding on a part of itself I no longer needed. The detritus of my own passing. A fire burned. What becoming was happening to me? Then I remembered the poem, the invocation between us. How for three days and three nights Inanna hung on the peg of the underworld stripped to nothing. And when they stole into Hell to find the

Queen of Beauty, they found Ereshkegal writhing on the ground beside her, out of her mind. Giving birth to Inanna.

Yes, I am the Butch of the Realm, the Lady of the great Below. It is hard for me to let you go. When next you say "you bitch"— "wild cherry"—and "it just happens"—you will think of me as she who bore you to your new and lawful place of rising, took the time and effort just to get you there so you could moan Inanna you could cry and everyone you ever were could die.

You told him you were a lover of women. He said that's okay, just tell me the truth. I slept then. We had one more night before A returned from Africa. You were waiting for me when I got home. I had on trousers. You wore a red dress. Tight so I could know you had nothing underneath. You had made me dinner. Up against the kitchen counter, I wrapped my hands strong around your rib cage. You said, You make me feel so female. You said, You're my man. I think I died then. In that moment. Everything I'd ever pretended to be. Gone. With you in my hands.

I must have taken you on my lap then, on the blue couch, the sweet of you all over me, and I think I called you baby, baby. You must have moaned or I did and then my hand went looking for you. I remember my hand and the weight of you and my face in your hair. Jesus how you opened to me. Let me reach up into the wound, curl inside and fill your empty places. Did I do it? Did I ease the rawness for a moment? Is it sacrilege to try to speak of this? To describe the unnameable? Something eased in me, a coming home, a landing. Into a hot pink hyperactive stillness.

Who is screaming? My hand has not forgiven me for leaving. If I'd believed I could not return I would never have left. But I thought it was only the beginning, and that night I wanted you to have it all. So I strapped on the chocolate dick, lay you down on the carpet among the pillows, and knelt over your belly.

I traced the folds and pocks of that tender place with my fingers, a sureness in my hands that meant something about arriving into a knowing that was mine and more than mine— a birthright, an ancient lineage. I guess I was praying for a healing when I saw them. Judy Grahn and Pat Parker and other butch elders there in the room. I didn't say anything at the time because I didn't know if I was going crazy. You had taken me so far from all I'd been, I could easily have been out of my mind. They gathered around us to watch. And then I knew they were there to welcome me into a secret circle. Into the same sacred holy office they'd held for me two decades before in Berkeley, when I was trying to find a way into my life and their poetry was all I had to go by. I've never had a vision before, actually seen people not in the flesh. Even now talking about it I know it sounds like fiction. But those poet butches were there with us, and they were telling me what I needed to know. That I had descended to the underworld and now had to learn to live there. That it was not at all clear between you and me who had taken whom down. That this was not only your initiation, baby, but mine. That they would watch over me on the long rock road ahead.

That was the moment, really. You know the rest. How I left A to wait for you, how school ended, how you said you needed to not see me while you went through the process of divorce. I didn't tell you how stupid I felt that last time you came by. Me in my new trousers I'd bought with you in mind. You asked me about them, as if you knew I was trying to look sexy for you. As if you knew how I needed you to find my way home. I knew better than to let you kiss me on your way out the door, but I couldn't stop myself. If only I'd really done it, gotten on my knees and pleaded, in the attitude of the beggar you'd revealed in me. Chipped away, bit by bit, with your wild beauty.

Stone is a living thing. Only more slow moving than most. There are processes. Once in a great while eruptions come, fire, ice. It is in these moments that the stone comes to know itself as stone. Its limitations. Its capacity. Its longing.

THE DINER ON THE CORNER

Sinclair Sexsmith

As soon as we walk into the diner on the corner, I visualize fucking Shanna on the counter. Or behind the counter, or against the counter, hell, I don't care—but I am certain the curve of the metal edge, the bar stools and that old-fashioned silver milkshake machine would go perfectly with her rockabilly-femme style.

This is our first date. She picked me up at the dyke bar last weekend while letting me think I was picking her up, and me being enamored with her immaculate femininity—the tattoos on her shoulders, the shade of pink her nails were painted, the faint flowery scent I wanted to lean into her neck to inhale, the low-cut dress and perfectly curved cleavage, the vibrant hair with streaks of dark purple and red—I didn't notice until halfway through the evening that, though I thought I was warming her up to ask for her number, she was secretly rolling her eyes, thinking, *Get on with it already*. She had control of every detail, but let me think I did.

Tonight, I've picked everything out precisely: black button-down shirt, my favorite sleek red tie, black slacks; solid black freshly polished shiny wingtips; plain, simple black fedora on top, because it may rain tonight.

And because she likes them.

We meet at the movie theater. She looks incredible: four-inch heels with small straps over the arch of her foot, a little buckle on the side; dark hair down over her shoulders and touching her neck; stockings and a fifties dress that comes just above her knees, with a slightly flared and layered skirt, and low-cut, again, showing off the lovely curves of her breasts. I don't stare. *Don't stare*, I tell myself. *You're being an asshole.* I try not to stare. Talk to her face, not her tits.

"I like your...hat," she giggles, dark eyes lowered, looking up at me through those lashes, slyly, shyly, from the side, that glance of submission.

I don't blush, but my cheeks get a little warm. "Thanks." I rarely wear hats. I love the way they look, love the tough butchness they play into, but I get self-conscious about what it's doing to my perfectly messy hair—my singular vanity. As soon as we get to our seats, I balance the fedora on my knee and run my fingers through my hair to see how it's holding up. (A little smashed. I try not to care.)

I don't remember the film. Something about music, Dublin, and falling in love. I remember thinking that there should be more sex in it. And that I forget how crowded and bright movie theaters are here in New York City—I miss being able to mess around in the darkest back row.

I do remember the way she laughed, the way she got teary once or twice, the way she kept stealing glances at me. Her hand on my thigh and the—oops—accidental brush against the bulge in my pants. The way her lips circled and sucked the straw in her soda, slow.

After the film, we walk to the corner twenty-four-hour diner. I slide into the booth and she slides in next to me, stockings on vinyl. Her left thigh touches my right, and I feel the brush of her leg against my slacks.

There are a few other diners scattered at tables, but it's late. There's one old man gumming through chicken fingers and reading the newspaper, and one table of teenagers blowing straw wrappers and eating fries off each other's plates. The waitress comes over, and I order a vanilla milkshake and a slice of apple pie, heated. "We'll share," I tell them both.

We chitchat. I toy with the sugar packets and crunch ice cubes from my water glass. She eases her leg over my thigh, which catches my breath, stirs my cock. I gently put my hand on her knee and let myself finger the thin, silky fabric of her stockings. She's still chatting as if nothing is happening. She liked the film, she's saying. The male lead was cute and sweet in a butch sort of way. "Do you think men can be butch?" she asks me.

My fingers are crushed against her thigh, seeking her creamy skin. I try to pull my consciousness from between her legs to say something intelligent.

"Well, I think that's complicated," I start, "because...while I think the gender identities of butch—and femme, too—are inherently queer by definition, I also notice some men with a particularly *female* flavor of masculinity that is closer to butch than any other word or description...."

"Yeah!" She has an eager and excited edge to her voice and presses her leg farther into my lap, twisting her torso a little to look more directly at me, opening her thighs. "I know what you mean—but if men begin to have a butch identity, does that invalidate it for the women who have to fight so hard to claim it?"

The layers of her dress are pushing up her thighs and I can

feel the edge of her stocking under my fingers, lace and elastic, the line of ribbon up her thigh to her hip: a garter belt. I brush my fingers against the rough edge and press them into her inner thigh, just a little. I wonder how far she'll let me go.

I want to find out how far she'll let me go.

The teenagers clear out and the diner quiets. She leaves her hands on the table but parts her lips. She's looking at me, gazing at my mouth; I bite my tongue and feel it swollen.

Shanna leans in slightly, slowly, ever so subtly, tilting her head without realizing it as my grip on her thigh strengthens. Neither of us notices as we do this, we only notice the space between our bodies crackling electrically.

I find the crease of her hip with my fingers, that line where her thighs meet her pelvis.

Her mouth gets closer to mine, inches away. I can feel her breath. She doesn't move any closer but is begging me with her whole body to make a move. To kiss her. To keep moving my fingers up her skirt. She lets me think it's all my idea. She is shifting, something is happening in her body and mind, an intentional submission, an offering up of her mouth and cunt and hungry body. We can both feel it, but it is nearly imperceptible.

"You want...this, okay?" I whisper, fingers getting bolder, brushing against her cunt, the swollen outer labia. I can feel the air between our mouths stirring. The movement of my lips makes them touch hers, briefly, softly. I can nearly see the swirls of her breath, hot and heavy.

She bites her lip at the touch, nods, without moving her head; submits a little deeper with explicit permission.

"One vanilla milkshake—" The waitress clears her throat and sets it down in front of Shanna, who jumps, but I stay exactly where I am, smiling, amused, then turn my head slowly without moving my hand.

"One apple pie." The waitress sets the small white plate in front of me.

"Thanks," I say, taking a fork with my left hand, my right still between Shanna's thighs.

The waitress raises her eyebrows. "You two okay here?"

"Yep." I say. Shanna's cheeks are hot and flushed. She examines the milkshake, stealing a glance at me. My fingers are quiet but persistent, still on the softness of her cunt.

The waitress raises her eyebrows at me again and I can't quite tell, but I think she winks. She's cute, the waitress. Dyed black hair, thick tattoo of a faery on her left bicep, those chunky black glasses. She's the only one working, but it's dead in here, so after a round she goes back to reading her book at the counter. She's not paying us any attention.

I twist and shift in the booth and adjust so I can flatten the palm of my hand against her cunt, slowly, cupping it. She's not wearing panties. She knew she could have me. She's controlling every detail.

She inhales and can't look at me, tongues her lip gently. "Are you...will you...?" she begins, but can't finish. She wants me to kiss her. I want to ravage her, thrust her up against the vinyl. Want her hands gripping at the sides of the booth as she comes against my hand.

I grin, that sly cocky grin that says I know what she's asking, I know what she wants, and I'm taking my own damn time giving it to her. She knows she'll get it from me, so my only power here is how and when she'll get it. She offers me her neck and I take it, leaning in, kissing her shoulder, her collarbone, exposed in her low-cut dress. "You have to be quiet," I say. "We're not alone."

"We almost are," she breathes, closing her eyes and tilting her head so I can get to her neck. My fingers run lazy circles around her clit and inner lips, slick already. I dip two fingers inside and feel her muscles pulsing, slide them in and out while she begins to pant. I circle her clit again, flick it gently and feel her body contract and respond.

"Anybody could walk in at any second," I say. "Anybody could see my hand under your skirt, if they looked for just a second." She shivers and presses her thighs open, presses her cunt against my hand, grips my forearm in one hand. I'm working her clit a little harder, a little faster, and her breathing is coming heavier, her body is tense. She's trying to keep her face still.

"You haven't even touched that shake," I say, nodding toward it. She shoots me a look like she wants to tear me apart with her eyes and attempts to move the tall milkshake glass toward her with one hand. She still wants me to kiss her and I am not letting up with my fingers on her cunt, on her clit, swirling, flicking against the hood, finding that sweet spot where her pelvis tenses and her limbs go limp.

Shanna's eyes don't leave my face as she opens her mouth for the straw and sucks the milkshake into her mouth. Cold. I can see it hit her tongue and explode in creamy sweetness; her eyes roll a little and her pussy responds, presses harder into my hand. She takes another sip, and I work two fingers against her clit.

She bends her head back—just a little, just the slightest bit, she wants to be able to throw it back and scream but she can't, she's in a diner, my hand against her, fingers circling, working, flicking, pressing, and her whole body shudders, and she grips my forearm in her fist, gasps a little, just a little, and her thighs contract to grip my wrist and she comes, with no sound at all, her body absorbing the noise she wants to make, and I don't let up, don't let up at all, until—she gasps, inhales deeply, and pulls on my hand to back off.

I grin and watch her face. She's trying to keep her features together and make it not look like she's just come. Trying to regain her composure. She looks at me a little shyly and embarrassed, unsure how loud she was, how obvious, and she glances around quickly but there's no one in the diner anymore, the few patrons have all left. It's just us, and the waitress at the counter.

"Holy. Shit," Shanna says softly, still breathing hard. I still have that stupid grin on my face, that power-top grin.

I lean in and kiss her, gently, soft, on the lips. Her mouth is cold and creamy, tastes of vanilla. Sweet. She's a fantastic kisser, all supple and slow. We kiss for a moment and I pull away, still smiling, and she tilts her chin down and looks up at me through her lashes.

"Want some pie?" I ask. I gather a bite on my fork, she nods, and I slip it between her lips.

"Oh," she says, chewing, warm apples and cinnamon on her tongue. "It's good. Want some shake?" I take a few sips. It's partly melted now.

The waitress comes over as we are giggling. "Would you two mind—?" she starts. "I'm out of smokes. I'm just gonna run to the corner, be right back."

"Sure," I say. The waitress nods, gives us another quick once-over glance, and spins on her heel. The diner is deserted. It's just me and Shanna. I watch the waitress walk out, the bell on the glass door ringing softly, and turn to look at this gorgeous femme. She's smoothing her hair, already watching me, watching my face, and she slides out of the booth and holds out her hand. I take it and slide out behind her.

"Your turn," she says. Crossing the diner floor, her heels click against the hard linoleum, and I watch her ankles as she walks, her calves, her knees. She keeps her legs tight together, crisscrossing like a model. My mouth waters.

She stops at the counter and raises her arm, guiding me back behind the bar as if we're on the dance floor. I grin and nearly flush, a little embarrassed, flustered to be somewhere I'm not supposed to be, seeing the clutter of dishes, rags, coffee mugs, silverware, napkins, salt and pepper shakers, ketchup and Tabasco bottles. And, of course, the gleaming, polished silver milkshake machine.

I slide behind the counter and she spins on a stool, crossing her legs at the ankle. She leans over, spilling out of her dress. I lick my lips, run my thumb over them, position myself behind the bar. I grip the handle of the milkshake machine and run my hand over it, stroking.

"So," I say. "Can I get you something?" I'm having trouble keeping my face straight. It feels a little silly, but it's also hot. What will she do? Let me fuck her, here, really?

Shanna purses her lips. "What do you have back there?" She leans over the counter and shifts her hips, then reaches for my belt.

I grab her wrist and hold it for a moment, surprising her. I bring her hand to the package behind my fly and make her feel my hard-on. She *oohs* a little, still in character, and lifts her ass onto the counter, swings her legs over it, opens her knees. She grabs my tie and pulls me to her, kissing me hard, running her fingers along the short hairs on the back of my head, wrapping her legs around my waist.

"I want..." I say between kisses, "I want you, I want you to...suck me. Would you do that?"

She nods yes and closes her eyes, just for a second, tips her chin down, and slides off the counter. She kisses me again and, palm flat against my cock, fingers on my fly, she unbuckles my belt, unzips, and pulls out my packing strap-on. Swiftly. Expertly.

She kisses me while she does this, hard; kisses the corner of my mouth, my cheek, my jawline; my neck, next to my collar; and she sinks to her knees.

The tip of my cock touches her lips and it feels tender, sensitive. As though I can feel her, sucking it into her mouth, working her tongue down the shaft. This is the thrill of the borrowed cock, the filling of it, the way it becomes mine. It is hitting my clit perfectly and her mouth, oh, god, her mouth feels exquisite. I want to release into her—want to grab her hair and work her against me, push down her throat.

I hold on to the counter instead. The metal edge cuts into my palm. She works her tongue on the underside of the head of my cock and my hips buck, pelvis tightens. I tip my head back, hips forward.

"God," I groan, aware that it is what would give this whole thing away, should someone walk in the door. My expressions. I keep one eye toward the door but my eyelids keep closing. God, her mouth feels fantastic.

Shanna looks up at me, eyes wide and shining, cheeks taut, hands on the thighs of my black slacks. I want her, want to fuck her. I look around—where? We can't have much time, but I already feel close to coming. She sees me glancing around, my stance has changed.

I groan as she sucks me hard, particularly deep, and pull my cock from her mouth. "Wait," I say, "somewhere...else." I offer my hand and she takes it, rises off her knees back onto her feet.

I have a perfect sightline into the kitchen, and notice the huge walk-in freezer right behind the doorway. There may be people back there, a line cook, a busser, but they wouldn't notice us. We could sneak right in. Shanna sees where I'm looking and waits for me to take a step.

Tiptoeing, almost, once I move she follows and we reach the door in a few quick strides. My cock bobs from my fly. I pull on the industrial handle, somewhat thick in my hand and satisfying to grip. I let her go in first.

She turns to face me and brings her shoulders up. "Brr." The air is cloudy and it burns my throat a little to inhale.

I survey the situation. A few boxes, milk crates, stacked up in the corner, filled with some heavy containers, jars, lidded plastic. Some of the boxes have been peeled open, others are still wrapped and sealed. Shanna's face reads skepticism.

I sit perched on the edge of the crates and boxes and say, "Come here."

She frowns a little. "What, here? I'm not sure—"

"Oh, hell yes." I stand, take a step toward her, reach out and wrap my arm around her waist. She fits well against me this way. Her arms go up around my neck somewhat instinctively.

"But—" she says, a little too sweetly, batting her lashes at me. She has control of every detail.

"Mmmhmm." I lift her skirt and she gasps at the cold air, it contracts her thighs a little. I take her left knee to the crook of my elbow, and bend my legs to get underneath her, gripping my cock in my fist, sliding inside her slowly but easily. She moans and it is a lovely sound. She's not holding back, begins working her hips against mine, thrusting and circling in S-curves, figure eights. She hooks her foot behind my back and I bend, balancing the weight of our bodies, taking a few steps backward again to lean against the boxes for support. Perfect. Perfect—my shoulders lean and my hips thrust freely, deeper and a little harder, my cock already so hard and her lips on me, on my neck again; I can see my breath hanging in the air as I exhale, hard, groaning every time she presses against me, and she kisses me, lips full on mine, tongue softly fierce, mouth open, open.

My hands are on her hips, pressing against her hard. I can feel every place our bodies collide, the heat in such stark contrast to the frigid air. She arches her back and presses me deep; I thrust harder and lose myself in the rhythm, hard, and again, again, against her as my muscles contract, face tenses, pelvis thighs ass tense, hard, harder...and then shuddering release, still thrusting and vibrating against her, getting softer, slower, coming down.

I hold on to her and breathe into her neck, her hair, for a moment. We kiss, giggle, weave that sex haze, gather ourselves.

Shanna exits the freezer first and returns to our table, and I follow. I pull my wallet out of my back pocket and the bell on the door jingles, the waitress tosses her cigarette into the street after she's opened the door, and then turns to see me tossing a few bills onto the table.

I pick my fedora up from the table and set it on my head, run my fingertip over the rim, and slide my wallet back into my pocket. Shanna has one knee on the vinyl booth and takes another mouthful of vanilla milkshake.

"C'mon, doll," I say, offering my hand. She takes it and the sound of the milkshake glass on the table echoes. "Let's blow this joint."

She laughs. I'm being a bit ridiculous. Ah, well, why not? I circle my arm around her waist, wink over my shoulder at the waitress, and we walk out of the diner on the corner.

For more information about the authors, visit them online or email them.

D. Alexandria: dalexandria@yahoo.com
Toni Amato: writeherewritenow.org
A. Lizbeth Babcock: pie.73@hotmail.com
Samiya A. Bashir: samiyabashir.com
S. Bear Bergman: sbearbergman.com
Isa Coffey: isacoffey@gmail.com
Shannon Cummings: shywetstone@yahoo.com
Amie M. Evans: amiemevans.com
Lynne Jamneck: lynnejamneckdiaries.blogspot.com
Rosalind Christine Lloyd: rosalindchristinelloyd.blogspot.com
Elaine Miller: elainemiller.com
Peggy Munson: peggymunson.com
Joy Parks: facebook.com/parksjoy
Kristen Porter: dykenight.com
Sinclair Sexsmith: Sugarbutch.net
Alison L. Smith: namealltheanimals.com
Sparky: sparklesworth@gmail.com
Jera Star: spinsbw@yahoo.ca
Anna Watson: bostonbooklady@gmail.com

ABOUT THE EDITOR

TRISTAN TAORMINO (puckerup.com and openingup.net) is an author, columnist, editor and sex educator. She is the author of six books: *The Big Book of Sex Toys; The Anal Sex Position Guide; Opening Up: Creating and Sustaining Open Relationships; True Lust: Adventures in Sex, Porn and Perversion; Down and Dirty Sex Secrets* and *The Ultimate Guide to Anal Sex for Women.* She is the creator and original series editor of *Best Lesbian Erotica,* which has won three Lambda Literary Awards. She runs her own adult film production company, Smart Ass Productions, and is currently an exclusive director for Vivid Entertainment. She lectures at top colleges and universities on gay and lesbian issues, sexuality and gender, and feminism and she teaches sex and relationship workshops around the world.